BY RAY BRADBURY

When Elephants Last in the Dooryard
    Bloomed (poetry)
The Halloween Tree
I Sing the Body Electric!
The Machineries of Joy
The Anthem Sprinters
Something Wicked This Way Comes
A Medicine for Melancholy
Dandelion Wine
Switch on the Night
The October Country
Moby Dick (screenplay)
Fahrenheit 451
The Golden Apples of the Sun
The Illustrated Man
The Martian Chronicles
Dark Carnival

Long
After
Midnight

Long
After
Midnight

Ray
Bradbury

Alfred A. Knopf New York 1976

THIS IS A BORZOI BOOK
PUBLISHED BY ALFRED A. KNOPF, INC.

LIBRARY OF CONGRESS CATALOGING IN PUBLICATION DATA
Bradbury, Ray [date]   Long after midnight.
    I. Title.
PZ3.B72453LO   [PS3503.R167]   813'.5'4   76–13689
ISBN 0–394–47942–4

MANUFACTURED IN THE UNITED STATES OF AMERICA
FIRST EDITION

*This book, with love,
is dedicated to William F. Nolan,
amazing collector, fantastic
researcher, dear friend.*

Contents

Long
After
Midnight

The Blue Bottle

The sundials were tumbled into white pebbles. The birds of the air now flew in ancient skies of rock and sand, buried, their songs stopped. The dead sea bottoms were currented with dust which flooded the land when the wind bade it reenact an old tale of engulfment. The cities were deep laid with granaries of silence, time stored and kept, pools and fountains of quietude and memory.

Mars was dead.

Then, out of the large stillness, from a great distance, there was an insect sound which grew large among the cinnamon hills and moved in the sun-blazed air until the highway trembled and dust was shook whispering down in the old cities.

The sound ceased.

In the shimmering silence of midday, Albert Beck and Leonard Craig sat in an ancient landcar, eyeing a dead city which did not move under their gaze but waited for their shout:

"Hello!"

A crystal tower dropped into soft dusting rain.

"You there!"

And another tumbled down.

And another and another fell as Beck called, summoning them to death. In shattering flights, stone animals with vast granite wings dived to strike the courtyards and fountains. His cry summoned them like living beasts and the beasts gave answer, groaned, cracked, leaned up, tilted over, trembling, hesitant, then split the air and swept down with grimaced mouths and empty eyes, with sharp, eternally hungry teeth suddenly seized out and strewn like shrapnel on the tiles.

Beck waited. No more towers fell.

"It's safe to go in now."

Craig didn't move. "For the same reason?"

Beck nodded.

"For a damned *bottle!* I don't understand. Why does everyone want it?"

Beck got out of the car. "Those that found it, they never told, they never explained. But—it's old. Old as the desert, as the dead seas—and it might contain anything. That's what the legend says. And because it *could* hold anything—well, that stirs a man's hunger."

"Yours, not mine," said Craig. His mouth barely moved; his eyes were half-shut, faintly amused. He stretched lazily. "I'm just along for the ride. Better watching you than sitting in the heat."

Beck had stumbled upon the old landcar a month back, before Craig had joined him. It was part of the flotsam of the First Industrial Invasion of Mars that had ended when the race moved on toward the stars. He had worked on the motor and run it from city to dead city, through the lands of the idlers and roustabouts, the dreamers and lazers, men caught in the backwash of space, men like himself and Craig who had never wanted to do much of anything and had found Mars a fine place to do it in.

"Five thousand, ten thousand years back the Martians made the Blue Bottle," said Beck. "Blown from Martian glass—and lost and found and lost and found again and again."

He stared into the wavering heat shimmer of the dead city. All my life, thought Beck, I've done nothing and nothing inside the nothing. Others, better men, have done big things, gone off to Mercury, or Venus, or out beyond the System. Except me. Not me. But the Blue Bottle can *change* all that.

He turned and walked away from the silent car.

Craig was out and after him, moving easily along. "What is it now, ten years you've hunted? You twitch when you sleep, wake up in fits, sweat through the days. You want the damn bottle *that* bad, and don't know what's in it. You're a fool, Beck."

"Shut up, shut up," said Beck, kicking a slide of pebbles out of his way.

They walked together into the ruined city, over a mosaic of cracked tiles shaped into a stone tapestry of fragile Martian creatures, long-dead beasts which appeared and disappeared as a slight breath of wind stirred the silent dust.

"Wait," said Beck. He cupped his hands to his mouth and gave a great shout. "You there!"

". . . there," said an echo, and towers fell. Fountains and stone pillars folded into themselves. That was the way of these cities. Sometimes towers as beautiful as a symphony would fall at a spoken word. It was like watching a Bach cantata disintegrate before your eyes.

A moment later: bones buried in bones. The dust settled. Two structures remained intact.

Beck stepped forward, nodding to his friend.

They moved in search.

And, searching, Craig paused, a faint smile on his lips. "In that bottle," he said, "is there a little accordion woman, all folded up like one of those tin cups, or like one of those Japanese flowers you put in water and it opens out?"

"I don't need a woman."

"Maybe you do. Maybe you never had a *real* woman, a woman who loved you, so, secretly, that's what you hope is in it." Craig pursed his mouth. "Or maybe, in that bottle, something from your childhood. All in a tiny bundle—a lake, a tree you climbed, green grass, some crayfish. How's *that* sound?"

Beck's eyes focused on a distant point. "Sometimes—that's almost it. The past—Earth. I don't know."

Craig nodded. "What's in the bottle would depend, maybe, on who's looking. Now, if there was a shot of *whiskey* in it . . ."

"Keep looking," said Beck.

There were seven rooms filled with glitter and shine; from floor to tiered ceiling there were casks, crocks, magnums, urns, vases— fashioned of red, pink, yellow, violet, and black glass. Beck shattered them, one by one, to eliminate them, to get them out of the way so he would never have to go through them again.

Beck finished his room, stood ready to invade the next. He was almost afraid to go on. Afraid that *this* time he would find it; that the search would be over and the meaning would go out of his life. Only after he had heard of the Blue Bottle from fire-travelers all the way from Venus to Jupiter, ten years ago, had life begun to take on a purpose. The fever had lit him and he had burned steadily ever since. If he worked it properly, the prospect of finding the bottle might fill his entire life to the brim. Another thirty years, if he was careful and not *too* diligent, of search, never admitting aloud that it wasn't the bottle that counted at all, but the search, the running and the hunting, the dust and the cities and the going-on.

Beck heard a muffled sound. He turned and walked to a

window looking out into the courtyard. A small gray sand cycle had purred up almost noiselessly at the end of the street. A plump man with blond hair eased himself off the spring seat and stood looking into the city. Another searcher. Beck sighed. Thousands of them, searching and searching. But there were thousands of brittle cities and towns and villages and it would take a millennium to sift them all.

"How you doing?" Craig appeared in a doorway.

"No luck." Beck sniffed the air. "Do you smell anything?"

"What?" Craig looked about.

"Smells like—bourbon."

"Ho!" Craig laughed. "That's *me!*"

"You?"

"I just took a drink. Found it in the other room. Shoved some stuff around, a mess of bottles, like always, and one of them had some bourbon in it, so I had myself a drink."

Beck was staring at him, beginning to tremble. "What— what would bourbon be doing *here*, in a Martian bottle?" His hands were cold. He took a slow step forward. "Show me!"

"I'm sure that . . ."

"*Show* me, damn you!"

It was there, in one corner of the room, a container of Martian glass as blue as the sky, the size of a small fruit, light and airy in Beck's hand as he set it down upon a table.

"It's half-full of bourbon," said Craig.

"I don't see anything inside," said Beck.

"Then shake it."

Beck picked it up, gingerly shook it.

"Hear it gurgle?"

"No."

"I can hear it plain."

Beck replaced it on the table. Sunlight spearing through a side window struck blue flashes off the slender container. It was the blue of a star held in the hand. It was the blue of a shallow ocean bay at noon. It was the blue of a diamond at morning.

"This *is* it," said Beck quietly. "I know it is. We don't have to look anymore. We've found the Blue Bottle."

Craig looked skeptical. "Sure you don't *see* anything in it?"

"Nothing . . . But—" Beck bent close and peered deeply into the blue universe of glass. "Maybe if I open it up and let it out, whatever it is, I'll know."

"I put the stopper in tight. Here." Craig reached out.

"If you gentlemen will excuse me," said a voice in the door behind them.

The plump man with blond hair walked into their line of vision with a gun. He did not look at their faces, he looked only at the blue glass bottle. He began to smile. "I hate very much to handle guns," he said, "but it is a matter of necessity, as I simply *must* have that work of art. I suggest that you allow me to take it without trouble."

Beck was almost pleased. It had a certain beauty of timing, this incident; it was the sort of thing he might have wished for, to have the treasure stolen before it was opened. Now there was the good prospect of a chase, a fight, a series of gains and losses, and, before they were done, perhaps another four or five years spent upon a new search.

"Come along now," said the stranger. "Give it up." He raised the gun warningly.

Beck handed him the bottle.

"Amazing. Really amazing," said the plump man. "I can't believe it was as simple as this, to walk in, hear two men talking, and to have the Blue Bottle simply *handed* to me. Amazing!" And he wandered off down the hall, out into the daylight, chuckling to himself.

Under the cool double moons of Mars the midnight cities were bone and dust. Along the scattered highway the landcar bumped and rattled, past cities where the fountains, the gyrostats, the furniture, the metal-singing books, the paintings lay powdered over with mortar and insect wings. Past cities that were cities no longer, but only things rubbed to a fine silt that flowered senselessly back and forth on the wine winds between one land and another, like the sand in a gigantic hourglass, endlessly pyramiding and repyramiding. Silence opened to let the car pass, and closed swiftly in behind.

Craig said, "We'll never find him. These damned roads. So old. Potholes, lumps, everything wrong. He's got the advantage with the cycle; he can dodge and weave. Damn!"

They swerved abruptly, avoiding a bad stretch. The car moved over the old highway like an eraser, coming upon blind soil, passing over it, dusting it away to reveal the emerald and gold colors of ancient Martian mosaics worked into the road surface.

"Wait," cried Beck. He throttled the car down. "I saw something back there."

"Where?"

They drove back a hundred yards.

"There. You see. It's *him*."

In a ditch by the side of the road the plump man lay folded over his cycle. He did not move. His eyes were wide, and when Beck flashed a torch down, the eyes burned dully.

"Where's the bottle?" asked Craig.

Beck jumped into the ditch and picked up the man's gun. "I don't know. Gone."

"What killed him?"

" I don't know that either."

"The cycle looks okay. Not an accident."

Beck rolled the body over. "No wounds. Looks like he just— stopped, of his own accord."

"Heart attack, maybe," said Craig. "Excited over the bottle. He gets down here to hide. Thought he'd be all right, but the attack finished him."

"That doesn't account for the Blue Bottle."

"Someone came along. Lord, you know how many searchers there are. . . ."

9

They scanned the darkness around them. Far off, in the starred blackness, on the blue hills, they saw a dim movement.

"Up there." Beck pointed. "Three men on foot."

"They must have . . ."

"My God, look!"

Below them, in the ditch, the figure of the plump man glowed, began to melt. The eyes took on the aspect of moonstones under a sudden rush of water. The face began to dissolve away into fire. The hair resembled small firecracker strings, lit and sputtering. The body fumed as they watched. The fingers jerked with flame. Then, as if a gigantic hammer had struck a glass statue, the body cracked upward and was gone in a blaze of pink shards, becoming mist as the night breeze carried it across the highway.

"They must have—*done* something to him," said Craig. "Those three, with a new kind of weapon."

"But it's happened before," said Beck. "Men I knew about who had the Blue Bottle. They vanished. And the bottle passed on to others who vanished." He shook his head. "Looked like a million fireflies when he broke apart. . . ."

"You going after them?"

Beck returned to the car. He judged the desert mounds, the hills of bone-silt and silence. "It'll be a tough job, but I think I can poke the car through after them. I *have* to, now." He paused, not speaking to Craig. "I think I know what's in the Blue Bottle. . . . Finally, I realize that what I want most of all is in there. Waiting for me."

"I'm not going," said Craig, coming up to the car where Beck sat in the dark, his hands on his knees. "I'm not going out there with you, chasing three armed men. I just want to live, Beck. That bottle means nothing to me. I won't risk my skin for it. But I'll wish you luck."

"Thanks," said Beck. And he drove away, into the dunes.

The night was as cool as water coming over the glass hood of the landcar.

Beck throttled hard over dead river washes and spills of chalked pebble, driving between great cliffs. Ribbons of double moonlight painted the bas-reliefs of gods and animals on the cliff sides all yellow gold: mile-high faces upon which Martian histories were etched and stamped in symbols, incredible faces with open cave eyes and gaping cave mouths.

The motor's roar dislodged rocks, boulders. In a whole rushing downpour of stone, golden segments of ancient cliff sculpture slid out of the moons' rays at the top of the cliff and vanished into blue cool-well darkness.

In the roar, as he drove, Beck cast his mind back—to all the nights in the last ten years, nights when he had built red fires on the sea bottoms, and cooked slow, thoughtful meals. And dreamed. Always those dreams of *wanting*. And not knowing what. Ever since he was a young man, the hard life on Earth, the great panic of 2130, the starvation, chaos, riot, want. Then bucking through the planets, the womanless, loveless years, the alone years. You come out of the dark into the light, out of the womb into the world, and what do you find that you really want?

What about that dead man back there in the ditch? Wasn't he always looking for something extra? Something he didn't have. What *was* there for men like himself? Or for anyone? Was there anything at all to look forward to?

The Blue Bottle.

He quickly braked the car, leaped out, gun ready. He ran, crouching, into the dunes. Ahead of him, the three men lay on the cold sand, neatly. They were Earthmen, with tan faces and rough clothes and gnarled hands. Starlight shone on the Blue Bottle, which lay among them.

As Beck watched, the bodies began to melt. They vanished away into rises of steam, into dewdrops and crystals. In a moment they were gone.

Beck felt the coldness in his body as the flakes rained across his eyes, flicking his lips and his cheeks.

He did not move.

The plump man. Dead and vanishing. Craig's voice: "Some new weapon . . ."

No. Not a weapon at all.

The Blue Bottle.

They had opened it to find what they most desired. All of the unhappy, desiring men down the long and lonely years had opened it to find what they most wanted in the planets of the universe. And all had found it, even as had these three. Now it could be understood, why the bottle passed on so swiftly, from one to another, and the men vanishing behind it. Harvest chaff fluttering on the sand, along the dead sea rims. Turning to flame and fireflies. To mist.

Beck picked up the bottle and held it away from himself for a long moment. His eyes shone clearly. His hands trembled.

So this is what I've been looking for, he thought. He turned the bottle and it flashed blue starlight.

So this is what all men *really* want? The secret desire, deep inside, hidden all away where we never guess? The subliminal urge? So this is what each man seeks, through some private guilt, to find?

Death.

An end to doubt, to torture, to monotony, to want, to loneliness, to fear, an end to everything.

All men?

No. Not Craig. Craig was, perhaps, far luckier. A few men were like animals in the universe, not questioning, drinking at pools and breeding and raising their young and not doubting for a moment that life was anything but good. That was Craig. There were a handful like him. Happy animals on a great reservation, in the hand of God, with a religion and a faith that grew like a set of special nerves in them. The unneurotic men in the midst of the billionfold neurotics. They would only want death, later, in a natural manner. Not now. Later.

Beck raised the bottle. How simple, he thought, and how right. This *is* what I've always wanted. And nothing else.

Nothing.

The bottle was open and blue in the starlight. Beck took an immense draught of the air coming from the Blue Bottle, deep into his lungs.

I have it at last, he thought.

He relaxed. He felt his body become wonderfully cool and then wonderfully warm. He knew he was dropping down a long slide of stars into a darkness as delightful as wine. He was swimming in blue wine and white wine and red wine. There were candles in his chest, and fire wheels spinning. He felt his hands leave him. He felt his legs fly away, amusingly. He laughed. He shut his eyes and laughed.

He was very happy for the first time in his life.

The Blue Bottle dropped onto the cool sand.

At dawn, Craig walked along, whistling. He saw the bottle lying in the first pink light of the sun on the empty white sand. As he picked it up, there was a fiery whisper. A number of orange and red-purple fireflies blinked on the air, and passed on away.

The place was very still.

"I'll be damned." He glanced toward the dead windows of a nearby city. "Hey, Beck!"

A slender tower collapsed into powder.

"Beck, here's your treasure! I don't want it. Come and get it!"

". . . and get it," said an echo, and the last tower fell.

Craig waited.

"That's rich," he said. "The bottle right here, and old Beck not even around to take it." He shook the blue container.

It gurgled.

"Yes, sir! Just the way it was before. Full of bourbon, by God!" He opened it, drank, wiped his mouth.

He held the bottle carelessly.

"All that trouble for a little bourbon. I'll wait right here for old Beck and give him his damn bottle. Meanwhile—have another drink, Mr. Craig. Don't mind if I do."

The only sound in the dead land was the sound of liquid running into a parched throat. The Blue Bottle flashed in the sun.

Craig smiled happily and drank again.

One Timeless Spring

That week, so many years ago, I thought my mother and father were poisoning me. And now, twenty years later, I'm not so sure they didn't. There's no way of telling.

It all comes back to me through the simple expedient of an examined trunk in the attic. This morning I pulled back the brass hasps and lifted the lid, and the immemorial odor of mothballs shrouded the unstrung tennis rackets, the worn sneakers, the shattered toys, the rusty roller skates. These implements of play, seen again through older eyes, make it seem only an hour ago that I rushed in from the shady streets, all asweat, the cry of "Ollie, Ollie, Oxen Free!" still excitedly trembling on my lips.

I was a weird and ridiculous boy then with brooding and uncommon ideas; the poison and the fear were only part of me in those years. I began making notes in a lined nickel tablet when I was only twelve. I can feel the stubby pencil in my fingers now, writing in those timeless spring mornings.

I paused to lick my pencil, thoughtfully. I sat in my upstairs room at the beginning of a clear endless day, blinking at the rose-stamped wallpaper, my feet bare, my hair shorn to a hair-brush stubble, thinking.

"I didn't know I was sick until this week," I wrote. "I've been sick for a long time. Since I was ten. I'm twelve now."

I scrouged up my face, bit my lips hard, focused blurrily on the tablet. "Mom and Dad have *made* me sick. Teachers at school also gave this—" I hesitated. Then I wrote: "*Disease* to me! The only ones who don't scare me are the other kids. Isabel Skelton and Willard Bowers and Clarisse Mellin; they aren't very sick yet. But I'm *really* bad off. . . ."

I laid the pencil down. I went to the bathroom mirror to see myself. My mother called me from downstairs to come to break-fast. I pressed close to the mirror, breathing so fast I made a big damp fog on the glass. I saw how my face was—changing.

The bones of it. Even the eyes. The pores of my nose. My ears. My forehead. My hair. All the things that'd been me for such a long time, starting to become something else. ("Douglas, come to breakfast, you'll be late for school!") As I took a quick wash I saw my body floating under me. I was inside it. There was no escape. And the bones of it were doing things, shifting, mixing around!

Then I began singing and whistling loud, so I wouldn't think about it; until Father, rapping on the door, told me to quiet down and come eat.

I sat at the breakfast table. There was a yellow box of cereal and milk, white-cold in a pitcher, and shining spoons and knives, and eggs planked with bacon, Dad reading his paper, Mom moving around the kitchen. I sniffed. I felt my stomach lie down like a whipped dog.

"What's wrong, son?" Dad looked at me casually. "Not hungry?"

"No, sir."

"A boy should be hungry in the morning," said Father.

"You go ahead and eat," said Mother at me. "Go on now. Hurry."

I looked at the eggs. They were poison. I looked at the butter. It was poison. The milk was so white and creamy and poisonous in its pitcher, and the cereal was brown and crisp and tasty in a green dish with pink flowers on it.

Poison, all of them, poison! The thought ran in my head like ants at a picnic. I caught my lip in my teeth.

"Unh?" said Dad, blinking at me. You *said?*"

"Nothing," I said. "Except I'm not hungry."

I couldn't say I was ill and that food made me ill. I couldn't say that cookies, cakes, cereals and soups and vegetables had done *this* to me, could I? No, I had to sit, swallowing nothing, my heart beginning to pound.

"Well, drink your milk at least, and go on," said Mother. "Dad, give him money for a good lunch at school. Orange juice, meat, and milk. No candy."

She didn't have to warn me on candy. It was worst of all the poisons. I wouldn't touch it again, ever!

I strapped my books and went to the door.

"Douglas, you didn't kiss me," said Mom.

"Oh," I said, and shuffled to kiss her.

"What's wrong with you?" she asked.

"Nothing," I said. "'Bye. So long, Dad."

Everybody said good-bye. I walked to school, thinking deep inside, like shouting down a long, cold well.

I ran down through the ravine and swung on a vine, way out; the ground dropped away, I smelled the cool morning air, sweet and high, and I screamed with laughter, and the wind threw away my thoughts. I tossed myself in a flip against the embankment and rolled down as birds whistled at me and a squirrel hopped like brown fuzz blown by the wind up around a tree trunk. Down the path the other kids fell like a small avalanche, yelling. "Ahh—eee—yah!" Pounding their chests, skipping rocks on the water, jumping their hands down to catch at crayfish. The crayfish jetted away in dusty spurts. We all laughed and joked.

A girl passed by on the green wooden bridge above us. Her name was Clarisse Mellin. We all hee-hawed at her, told her to go on, go on, we didn't want her with us, go on, go on! But my voice caught and trailed off, and I watched her going, slowly. I didn't look away.

From way off in the morning we heard the school bell ring.

We scrambled up trails we'd made during many summers over the years. The grass was worn; we knew each snake hole and bump, each tree, every vine, every weed of it. After school we'd made tree huts here, high up over the shining creek, jumped in the water naked, gone on long hikes down the ravine to where it emptied lonely and abandoned into the big blue of Lake Michigan, near the tannery and the asbestos works and the docks.

Now, as we panted up to school, I stopped, afraid again. "You go on ahead," I said.

The last bell tolled. The kids ran. I looked at the school with vines growing on it. I heard the voices inside, making a high, all-the-time noise. I heard little desk bells tinkle and sharp teacher voices reaching out.

Poison, I thought. The teachers, too! They want me sick! They teach you how to be sicker and sicker! And—and how to *enjoy* being sick!

"Good morning, Douglas."

I heard high-heeled shoes on the cement walk. Miss Adams, the principal, with her pince-nez and wide, pale face and close-cropped dark hair, stood behind me.

"Come along in," she said, holding my shoulder firmly. "You're late. Come along."

She guided me, one two, one two, one two, upstairs, up the stairs to my fate. . . .

Mr. Jordan was a plump man with thinning hair and serious green eyes and a way of rocking on his heels before his charts. Today he had a large illustration of a body with all its skin off. Exposed were green, blue, pink, and yellow veins, capillaries, muscles, tendons, organs, lungs, bones, and fatty tissues.

Mr. Jordan nodded before the chart. "There's a great similarity between cancer and normal cell reproduction. Cancer is simply a normal function gone wild. Overproduction of cellular material—"

I raised my hand. "How does food—I mean—what makes the body grow?"

"A good question, Douglas." He tapped the chart. "Food, taken into the body, is broken down, assimilated, and—"

I listened and I knew what Mr. Jordan was trying to do to me. My childhood was in my mind like a fossil imprint on soft shale rock. Mr. Jordan was trying to polish and smooth it away. Eventually it would all be gone, all my beliefs and imaginings. My mother changed my body with food, Mr. Jordan worked on my mind with words.

So I began to draw pictures on paper, not listening. I hummed little songs, made up a language all my own. The rest of the day I heard nothing. I resisted the attack, I counteracted the poison.

But then after school I passed Mrs. Singer's store and I bought candy. I couldn't help it. And after I ate it I wrote on the back of the wrapper: "This is the last candy I'm going to eat. Even at the Saturday matinee, when Tom Mix comes on the screen with Tony, I won't eat candy again."

I looked at the candy bars stacked like a harvest on the shelves. Orange wrappers with sky-blue words saying "Chocolate." Yellow and violet wrappers with little blue words on them. I felt the candy in my body, making my cells grow. Mrs. Singer sold hundreds of candy bars each day. Was she in conspiracy? Did she know what she was doing to children with them? Was she jealous of them being so young? Did she want them to grow old? I wanted to kill her!

"What you doing?"

Bill Arno had come up behind me while I was writing on the candy wrapper. Clarisse Mellin was with him. She looked at me with her blue eyes and said nothing.

I hid the paper. "Nothing," I said.

We all walked along. We saw kids playing hopscotch and kick the can and playing mibs on the hard ground, and I turned to Bill and I said, "We won't be allowed to do that next year, or maybe the year after."

Bill only laughed and said, "Sure, we will. Who'll stop us?"

"*They* will," I said.

"Who's they?" asked Bill.

"Never mind," I said. "Just wait and see."

"Aw," said Bill. "You're crazy."

"You don't understand!" I cried. "You play and run around and eat, and all the time they're tricking you and making you think different and act different and walk different. And all of a sudden one day you'll stop playing and have to worry!" My face was hot and my hands were clenched. I was blind with rage. Bill turned, laughing, and walked away. "Over Annie Over!" someone sang, tossing a ball over a housetop.

You might go all day without breakfast or lunch, but what about supper? My stomach shouted as I slid into my chair at the supper table. I held on to my knees, looking down at them. I won't eat, I told myself. I'll show them. I'll fight them.

Dad pretended to be considerate. "Let him go without supper," he said to my mother, when he saw me neglect my food. He winked at her. "He'll eat later."

All evening long I played on the warm brick streets of town, rattling the tin cans and climbing the trees in the growing dark.

Coming into the kitchen at ten o'clock, I realized it was no use. There was a note on top of the icebox which said, "Help yourself. Dad."

I opened the refrigerator, and a little cool breath breathed out against me, cold, with the smell of rimed foods on it. Inside was the wondrous half-ruin of a chicken. Members of celery were piled like cords of wood. Strawberries grew in a thicket of parsley.

My hands blurred. They made motions that caused an illusion of a dozen hands. Like those pictures of Eastern goddesses they worship in temples. One hand with a tomato in it. One hand grasping a banana. A third hand seizing strawberries! A fourth, fifth, sixth hand caught in midmotion, each with a bit of cheese, olive, or radish!

Half an hour later I knelt by the toilet bowl and swiftly raised the seat. Then, rapidly, I opened my mouth, and shoved a spoon back, back along my tongue, down, down along my gagging throat. . . .

Lying in bed, I shuddered and tasted the acrid memory in my mouth, glad to be rid of the food I had so eagerly swallowed. I hated myself for my weakness. I lay trembling, empty, hungry again, but too sick, now, to eat. . . .

I was very weak in the morning, and noticeably pale, for my mother made a comment on it. "If you're not better by Monday," she said, "to the doctor's with you!"

It was Saturday. The day of shouting, and no tiny little silver bells for teachers to silence it; the day when the colorless giants moved on the pale screen at the Elite movie house in the long theater dark, and children were only children, and not things growing.

I saw no one. In the morning when I should have been hiking out along the North Shore Rail Line, where the hot sun simmered up from the long parallels of metal, I lolled about in terrific indecision. And by the time I got to the ravine it was already midafternoon and it was deserted; all of the kids had run downtown to see the matinee and suck lemon drops.

The ravine was very alone, it looked so undisturbed and old and green, I was a little afraid of it. I had never seen it so quiet. The vines hung quietly upon the trees and the water went over the rocks and the birds sang high up.

I went down the secret trail, hiding behind bushes, pausing, going on.

Clarisse Mellin was crossing the bridge as I reached it. She was coming home from town with some little packages under her arm. We said hello, self-consciously.

"What are you doing?" she asked.

"Oh, walking around," I said.

"All alone?"

"Yeah. All the other guys are downtown."

She hesitated, then said, "Can I walk with you?"

"I guess so," I said. "Come on."

We walked down through the ravine. It was humming like a big dynamo. Nothing seemed to want to move, everything was very quiet. Pink darning needles flew and bumped on air pockets, and hovered over the sparkling creek water.

Clarisse's hand bumped mine as we walked along the trail. I smelled the moist dank smell of the ravine and the soft new smell of Clarisse beside me.

We came to a place where there was a cross trail.

"We built a tree hut up there last year," I said, pointing.

"Where?" Clarisse stepped close to me to see where my finger was pointing. "I don't see."

"There," I said, my voice breaking, and pointed again.

Very quietly, she put her arm around me. I was so surprised and bewildered I almost cried out. Then, trembling, her lips kissed me, and my own hands were moving to hold her and I was shaking and shouting inside myself.

The silence was like a green explosion. The water bubbled on in the creek bed. I couldn't breathe.

I knew it was all over. I was lost. From this moment on, it would be a touching, an eating of foods, a learning of language and algebra and logic, a movement and an emotion, a kissing and a holding, a whirl of feeling that caught and sucked me drowning under. I knew I was lost forever now, and I didn't care. But I *did* care, and I was laughing and crying all in one, and there was nothing to do about it, but hold her and love her with all my decided and rioting body and mind.

I could have gone on fighting my war against Mother and Dad and school and food and things in books, but I couldn't fight this sweetness on my lips and this warmness in my hands, and the new odor in my nostrils.

"Clarisse, Clarisse," I cried, holding her, looking over her shoulder blindly, whispering to her. "Clarisse!"

The Parrot Who Met Papa

The kidnaping was reported all around the world, of course.

It took a few days for the full significance of the news to spread from Cuba to the United States, to the Left Bank in Paris and then finally to some small good café in Pamplona where the drinks were fine and the weather, somehow, was always just right.

But once the meaning of the news really hit, people were on the phone, Madrid was calling New York, New York was shouting south at Havana to verify, please verify this crazy thing.

And then some woman in Venice, Italy, with a blurred voice called through, saying she was at Harry's Bar that very instant and was destroyed, this thing that had happened was terrible, a cultural heritage was placed in immense and irrevocable danger. . . .

Not an hour later, I got a call from a baseball pitcher–*cum*-novelist who had been a great friend of Papa's and who now lived in Madrid half the year and Nairobi the rest. He was in tears, or sounded close to it.

"Tell me," he said, from halfway around the world, "what happened? What are the facts?"

Well, the facts were these: Down in Havana, Cuba, about fourteen kilometers from Papa's Finca Vigía home, there is a bar in which he used to drink. It is the one where they named a special drink for him, not the fancy one where he used to meet flashy literary lights such as K-K-Kenneth Tynan and, er, Tennessee W-Williams (as Mr. Tynan would say it). No, it is not the Floridita; it is a shirt-sleeves place with plain wooden tables, sawdust on the floor, and a big mirror like a dirty cloud behind the bar. Papa went there when there were too many tourists around the Floridita who wanted to meet Mr. Hemingway. And the thing that happened there was destined to be big news, bigger than the report of what he said to Fitzgerald about the rich, even bigger than the story of his swing at Max Eastman on that long-ago day in Charlie Scribner's office. This news had to do with an ancient parrot.

That senior bird lived in a cage right atop the bar in the Cuba Libre. He had "kept his cage" in that place for roughly twenty-nine years, which means that the old parrot had been there almost as long as Papa had lived in Cuba.

And that adds up to this monumental fact: All during the time Papa had lived in Finca Vigía, he had known the parrot and had talked to him and the parrot had talked back. As the years passed, people said that Hemingway began to talk like the parrot and others said no, the parrot learned to talk like *him!* Papa used to line the drinks up on the counter and sit near the cage and involve that bird in the best kind of conversation you ever heard, four nights running. By the end of the second year, that parrot knew more about Hem and Thomas Wolfe and Sherwood Anderson than Gertrude Stein did. In fact, the parrot even knew who Gertrude Stein *was*. All you had to say was "Gertrude" and the parrot said:

"Pigeons on the grass alas."

At other times, pressed, the parrot would say, "There was this old man and this boy and this boat and this sea and this big fish in the sea. . . ." And then it would take time out to eat a cracker.

Well, this fabled creature, this parrot, this odd bird, vanished, cage and all, from the Cuba Libre late one Sunday afternoon.

And that's why my phone was ringing itself off the hook. And that's why one of the big magazines got a special State Department clearance and flew me down to Cuba to see if I could find so much as the cage, anything remaining of the bird or anyone resembling a kidnaper. They wanted a light and amiable article, with overtones, as they said. And, very honestly, I was curious. I had heard rumors of the bird. In a strange kind of way, I was concerned.

I got off the jet from Mexico City and taxied straight across Havana to that strange little café-bar.

I almost failed to get in the place. As I stepped through the door, a dark little man jumped up from a chair and cried, "No, no! Go away! We are closed!"

He ran out to jiggle the lock on the door, showing that he really meant to shut the place down. All the tables were empty and there was no one around. He had probably just been airing out the bar when I arrived.

"I've come about the parrot," I said.

"No, no," he cried, his eyes looking wet. "I won't talk. It's too much. If I were not Catholic, I would kill myself. Poor Papa. Poor El Córdoba!"

"El Córdoba?" I murmured.

"That," he said fiercely, "was the parrot's name!"

"Yes," I said, recovering quickly. "El Córdoba. I've come to rescue him."

That made him stop and blink. Shadows and then sunlight went over his face and then shadows again. "Impossible! Could you? No, no. How could anyone! Who *are* you?"

"A friend to Papa and the bird," I said quickly. "And the more time we talk, the farther away goes the criminal. You want El Córdoba back tonight? Pour us several of Papa's good drinks and talk."

My bluntness worked. Not two minutes later, we were drinking Papa's special, seated in the bar near the empty place where the cage used to sit. The little man, whose name was Antonio, kept wiping that empty place and then wiping his eyes with the bar rag. As I finished the first drink and started on the second, I said:

"This is no ordinary kidnaping."

"You're telling me!" cried Antonio. "People came from all over the world to see that parrot, to talk to El Córdoba, to hear him, ah, God, speak with the voice of Papa. May his abductors sink and burn in hell, yes, hell."

"They will," I said. "Whom do you suspect?"

"Everyone. No one."

"The kidnaper," I said, eyes shut for a moment, savoring the drink, "had to be educated, a book reader, I mean, that's obvious, isn't it? Anyone like that around the last few days?"

"Educated. No education. *Señor*, there have always been strangers the last ten, the last twenty years, always asking for Papa. When Papa was here, they met him. With Papa gone, they met El Córdoba, the great one. So it was always strangers and strangers."

"But think, Antonio," I said, touching his trembling elbow. "Not only educated, a reader, but someone in the last few days who was—how shall I put it?—odd. Strange. Someone so peculiar, *muy eccéntrico*, that you remember him above all others. Someone who—"

"*¡Madre de Dios!*" cried Antonio, leaping up. His eyes stared off into memory. He seized his head as if it had just exploded. "Thank you, *señor*. *¡Si, si!* What a creature! In the name of

Christ, there was such a one yesterday! He was very small. And he spoke like this: very high—*eeeee.* Like a *muchacha* in a school play, eh? Like a canary swallowed by a witch! And he wore a blue-velvet suit with a big yellow tie."

"Yes, yes!" I had leaped up now and was almost yelling. "Go on!"

"And he had a small very round face, *señor,* and his hair was yellow and cut across the brow like this—*zitt!* And his mouth small, very pink, like candy, yes? He—he was like, yes, *uno muñeco,* of the kind one wins at carnivals."

"Kewpie dolls!"

"*¡Sí!* At Coney Island, yes, when I was a child, Kewpie dolls! And he was so high, you see? To my elbow. Not a midget, no— but—and how old? Blood of Christ, who can say? No lines in his face, but—thirty, forty, fifty. And on his feet he was wearing—"

"Green booties!" I cried.

"*¿Qué?*"

"Shoes, boots!"

"*Sí.*" He blinked, stunned. "But how did you *know?*"

I exploded, "Shelley Capon!"

"That is the name! And his friends with him, *señor,* all laughing—no, giggling. Like the nuns who play basketball in the late afternoons near the church. Oh, *señor,* do you think that they, that he—"

"I don't think, Antonio, I *know.* Shelley Capon, of all the writers in the world, hated Papa. Of course he would snatch El Córdoba. Why, wasn't there a rumor once that the bird had memorized Papa's last, greatest, and as-yet-not-put-down-on-paper novel?"

"There was such a rumor, *señor.* But I do not write books, I tend bar. I bring crackers to the bird. I—"

"You bring me the phone, Antonio, please."

"You know where the bird is, *señor?*"

"I have the hunch beyond intuition, the big one. *Gracias*." I dialed the Havana Libre, the biggest hotel in town.

"Shelley Capon, please."

The phone buzzed and clicked.

Half a million miles away, a midget boy Martian lifted the receiver and played the flute and then the bell chimes with his voice: "Capon here."

"Damned if you aren't!" I said. And got up and ran out of the Cuba Libre bar.

Racing back to Havana by taxi, I thought of Shelley as I'd seen him before. Surrounded by a storm of friends, living out of suitcases, ladling soup from other people's plates, borrowing money from billfolds seized from your pockets right in front of you, counting the lettuce leaves with relish, leaving rabbit pellets on your rug, gone. Dear Shelley Capon.

Ten minutes later, my taxi with no brakes dropped me running and spun on to some ultimate disaster beyond town.

Still running, I made the lobby, paused for information, hurried upstairs, and stopped short before Shelley's door. It pulsed in spasms like a bad heart. I put my ear to the door. The wild calls and cries from inside might have come from a flock of birds, feather-stripped in a hurricane. I felt the door. Now it seemed to tremble like a vast laundromat that had swallowed and was churning an acid-rock group and a lot of very dirty linen. Listening, my underwear began to crawl on my legs.

I knocked. No answer. I touched the door. It drifted open. I stepped in upon a scene much too dreadful for Bosch to have painted.

Around the pigpen living room were strewn various life-size dolls, eyes half-cracked open, cigarettes smoking in burned, limp fingers, empty Scotch glasses in hands, and all the while the radio belted them with concussions of music broadcast from some Stateside asylum. The place was sheer carnage. Not ten seconds ago, I felt, a large dirty locomotive must have plunged through here. Its victims had been hurled in all directions and now lay upside down in various parts of the room, moaning for first aid.

In the midst of this hell, seated erect and proper, well dressed in velveteen jerkin, persimmon bow tie, and bottle-green booties, was, of course, Shelley Capon. Who with no surprise at all waved a drink at me and cried:

"I *knew* that was you on the phone. I am absolutely telepathic! Welcome, Raimundo!"

He always called me Raimundo. Ray was plain bread and butter. Raimundo made me a don with a breeding farm full of bulls. I let it be Raimundo.

"Raimundo, sit down! No . . . fling yourself into an *interesting* position."

"Sorry," I said in my best Dashiell Hammett manner, sharpening my chin and steeling my eyes. "No time."

I began to walk around the room among his friends Fester and Soft and Ripply and Mild Innocuous and some actor I remembered who, when asked how he would do a part in a film, had said, "I'll play it like a doe."

I shut off the radio. That made a lot of people in the room stir: I yanked the radio's roots out of the wall. Some people sat up. I raised a window. I threw the radio out. They all screamed as if I had thrown their mothers down an elevator shaft.

The radio made a satisfying sound on the cement sidewalk below. I turned, with a beatific smile on my face. A number of people were on their feet, swaying toward me with faint menace. I pulled a twenty-dollar bill out of my pocket, handed it to someone without looking at him, and said, "Go buy a new one." He ran out the door slowly. The door slammed. I heard him fall down the stairs as if he were after his morning shot in the arm.

"All right, Shelley," I said, "where is it?"

"Where is *what*, dear boy?" he said, eyes wide with innocence.

"You know what I mean." I stared at the drink in his tiny hand.

Which was a Papa drink, the Cuba Libre's very own special blend of papaya, lime, lemon, and rum. As if to destroy evidence, he drank it down quickly.

I walked over to three doors in a wall and touched one.

"That's a closet, dear boy." I put my hand on the second door.

"Don't go in. You'll be sorry what you see." I didn't go in.

I put my hand on the third door. "Oh, dear, well, go ahead," said Shelley petulantly. I opened the door.

Beyond it was a small anteroom with a mere cot and a table near the window.

On the table sat a bird cage with a shawl over it. Under the shawl I could hear the rustle of feathers and the scrape of a beak on the wires.

Shelley Capon came to stand small beside me, looking in at the cage, a fresh drink in his little fingers.

"What a shame you didn't arrive at seven tonight," he said.

"Why seven?"

"Why, then, Raimundo, we would have just finished our curried fowl stuffed with wild rice. I wonder, is there much white meat, or any at all, under a parrot's feathers?"

"You wouldn't!?" I cried.

I stared at him.

"You would," I answered myself.

I stood for a moment longer at the door. Then, slowly, I walked across the small room and stopped by the cage with the shawl over it. I saw a single word embroidered across the top of the shawl: MOTHER.

I glanced at Shelley. He shrugged and looked shyly at his boot tips. I took hold of the shawl. Shelley said, "No. Before you lift it . . . ask something."

"Like what?"

"DiMaggio. Ask DiMaggio."

A small ten-watt bulb clicked on in my head. I nodded. I leaned near the hidden cage and whispered: "DiMaggio. 1939."

There was a sort of animal-computer pause. Beneath the word

MOTHER some feathers stirred, a beak tapped the cage bars. Then a tiny voice said:

"Home runs, thirty. Batting average, .381."

"I was stunned. But then I whispered: "Babe Ruth. 1927."

Again the pause, the feathers, the beak, and: "Home runs, sixty. Batting average, .356. Awk."

"My God," I said.

"My God," echoed Shelley Capon.

"That's the parrot who met Papa, all right."

"That's who it is."

And I lifted the shawl.

I don't know what I expected to find underneath the embroidery. Perhaps a miniature hunter in boots, bush jacket, and wide-brimmed hat. Perhaps a small, trim fisherman with a beard and turtleneck sweater perched there on a wooden slat. Something tiny, something literary, something human, something fantastic, but not really a parrot.

But that's all there was.

And not a very handsome parrot, either. It looked as if it had been up all night for years; one of those disreputable birds that never preens its feathers or shines its beak. It was a kind of rusty green and black with a dull-amber snout and rings under its eyes as if it were a secret drinker. You might see it half flying, half hopping out of café-bars at three in the morning. It was the bum of the parrot world.

Shelley Capon read my mind. "The effect is better," he said, "with the shawl over the cage."

I put the shawl back over the bars.

I was thinking very fast. Then I thought very slowly. I bent and whispered by the cage:

"Norman Mailer."

"Couldn't remember the alphabet," said the voice beneath the shawl.

"Gertrude Stein," I said.

"Suffered from undescended testicles," said the voice.

"My God," I gasped.

I stepped back. I stared at the covered cage. I blinked at Shelley Capon.

"Do you really *know* what you have here, Capon?"

" A *gold* mine, dear Raimundo!" he crowed.

"A *mint!*" I corrected.

"Endless opportunities for blackmail!"

"Causes for murder!" I added.

"Think!" Shelley snorted into his drink. "Think what Mailer's publishers *alone* would pay to shut this bird up!"

I spoke to the cage:

"F. Scott Fitzgerald."

Silence.

"Try 'Scottie,' " said Shelley.

"Ah," said the voice inside the cage. "Good left jab but couldn't follow through. Nice contender, but—"

"Faulkner," I said.

"Batting average fair, strictly a singles hitter."

"Steinbeck!"

"Finished last at end of season."

"Ezra Pound!"

"Traded off to the minor leagues in 1932."

"I think . . . I need . . . one of those drinks." Someone put a drink in my hand. I gulped it and nodded. I shut my eyes and felt the world give one turn, then opened my eyes to look at Shelley Capon, the classic son of a bitch of all time.

"There is something even more fantastic," he said. "You've heard only the first half."

"'You're lying," I said. "What could there be?"

He dimpled at me—in all the world, only Shelley Capon can dimple at you in a completely evil way. "It was like this," he said. "You remember that Papa had trouble actually getting his stuff down on paper in those last years while he lived here? Well, he'd planned another novel after *Islands in the Stream*, but somehow it just never seemed to get written."

"Oh, he had it in his mind, all right—the story was there and lots of people heard him mention it—but he just couldn't seem to write it. So he would go to the Cuba Libre and drink many drinks and have long conversations with the parrot. Raimundo, what Papa was telling El Córdoba all through those long drinking nights was the story of his last book. And, in the course of time, the bird has memorized it."

"*His very last book!*" I said. "The final Hemingway novel of all time! Never written but recorded in the brain of a parrot! Holy Jesus!"

Shelley was nodding at me with the smile of a depraved cherub.

"How much you want for this bird?"

"Dear, dear Raimundo." Shelley Capon stirred his drink with his pinkie. "What makes you think the creature is for sale?"

"You sold your mother once, then stole her back and sold her again under another name. Come off it, Shelley. You're onto something big." I brooded over the shawled cage. "How many telegrams have you sent out in the last four or five hours?"

"Really! You horrify me!"

"How many long-distance phone calls, reverse charges, have you made since breakfast?"

Shelley Capon mourned a great sigh and pulled a crumpled telegram duplicate from his velveteen pocket. I took it and read:

FRIENDS OF PAPA MEETING HAVANA TO REMINISCE OVER BIRD AND BOTTLE. WIRE BID OR BRING CHECKBOOKS AND OPEN MINDS. FIRST COME FIRST SERVED. ALL WHITE MEAT BUT CAVIAR PRICES. INTERNATIONAL PUBLICATION, BOOK, MAGAZINE, TV, FILM RIGHTS AVAILABLE. LOVE. SHELLEY YOU-KNOW-WHO.

My God again, I thought, and let the telegram fall to the floor as Shelley handed me a list of names the telegram had been sent to:

Time. Life. Newsweek. Scribner's. Simon & Schuster. *The New York Times. The Christian Science Monitor. The Times* of London. Le Monde. Paris-Match. One of the Rockefellers. Some of the Kennedys. CBS. NBC. MGM. Warner Bros. 20th Century-Fox. And on and on and on. The list was as long as my deepening melancholy.

Shelley Capon tossed an armful of answering telegrams onto the table near the cage. I leafed through them quickly.

Everyone, but everyone, was in the air, right now. Jets were streaming in from all over the world. In another two hours, four, six at the most, Cuba would be swarming with agents, publishers, fools, and plain damn fools, plus counterespionage kidnapers and blonde starlets who hoped to be in front-page photographs with the bird on their shoulders.

I figured I had maybe a good half-hour left in which to do something, I didn't know what.

Shelley nudged my arm. "Who sent you, dear boy? You *are* the very first, you know. Make a fine bid and you're in free, maybe. I must consider other offers, of course. But it might get thick and nasty here. I begin to panic at what I've done. I may wish to sell cheap and flee. Because, well, think, there's the problem of getting this bird out of the country, yes? And, simultaneously, Castro might declare the parrot a national monument or work of art, or, oh, hell, Raimundo, who *did* send you?"

"Someone, but now no one," I said, brooding. "I came on behalf of someone else. I'll go away on my own. From now on, anyway, it's just me and the bird. I've read Papa all my life. Now I know I came just because I had to."

"My God, an altruist!"

"Sorry to offend you, Shelley."

The phone rang. Shelley got it. He chatted happily for a moment, told someone to wait downstairs, hung up, and cocked an eyebrow at me: "NBC is in the lobby. They want an hour's taped interview with El Córdoba there. They're talking six figures."

My shoulders slumped. The phone rang. This time I picked it up, to my own surprise. Shelley cried out. But I said, "Hello. Yes?"

"*Señor*," said a man's voice. "There is a *Señor* Hobwell here from *Time*, he says, magazine." I could see the parrot's face on next week's cover, with six follow-up pages of text.

"Tell him to wait." I hung up.

"*Newsweek?*" guessed Shelley.

"The other one," I said.

"The snow was fine up in the shadow of the hills," said the voice inside the cage under the shawl.

"Shut up," I said quietly, wearily. "Oh, shut up, damn you."

Shadows appeared in the doorway behind us. Shelley Capon's friends were beginning to assemble and wander into the room. They gathered and I began to tremble and sweat.

For some reason, I began to rise to my feet. My body was going to do something, I didn't know what. I watched my hands. Suddenly, the right hand reached out. It knocked the cage over, snapped the wire-frame door wide, and darted in to seize the parrot.

"No!"

There was a great gasping roar, as if a single thunderous wave had come in on a shore. Everyone in the room seemed knocked in the stomach by my action. Everyone exhaled, took a step, began to yell, but by then I had the parrot out. I had it by the throat.

"No! No!" Shelley jumped at me. I kicked him in the shins. He sat down, screaming.

"Don't anyone move!" I said and almost laughed, hearing myself use the old cliché. "You ever see a chicken killed? This parrot has a thin neck. One twist, the head comes off. Nobody move a hair." Nobody moved.

"You son of a bitch," said Shelley Capon, on the floor.

For a moment, I thought they were all going to rush me. I saw myself beaten and chased along the beach, yelling, the cannibals ringing me in and eating me, Tennessee Williams style, shoes and all. I felt sorry for my skeleton, which would be found in the main Havana plaza at dawn tomorrow.

But they did not hit, pummel, or kill. As long as I had my fingers around the neck of the parrot who met Papa, I knew I could stand there forever.

I wanted with all my heart, soul, and guts to wring the bird's neck and throw its disconnected carcass into those pale and gritty faces. I wanted to stop up the past and destroy Papa's preserved memory forever, if it was going to be played with by feeble-minded children like these.

But I could not, for two reasons. One dead parrot would mean one dead duck: me. And I was weeping inside for Papa. I simply could not shut off his voice transcribed here, held in my hands, still alive, like an old Edison record. I could not kill.

If these ancient children had known that, they would have swarmed over me like locusts. But they didn't know. And, I guess, it didn't show in my face.

"Stand back!" I cried.

It was that beautiful last scene from *The Phantom of the Opera* where Lon Chaney, pursued through midnight Paris, turns upon the mob, lifts his clenched fist as if it contained an explosive, and holds the mob at bay for one terrific instant. He laughs, opens his hand to show it empty, and then is driven to his death in the river. . . . Only I had no intention of letting them see an empty hand. I kept it close around El Córdoba's scrawny neck.

"Clear a path to the door!" They cleared a path.

"Not a move, not a breath. If anyone so much as swoons, this bird is dead forever and no rights, no movies, no photos. Shelley, bring me the cage and the shawl."

Shelley Capon edged over and brought me the cage and its cover. "Stand off!" I yelled.

Everyone jumped back another foot.

"Now, hear this," I said. "After I've got away and have hidden out, one by one each of you will be called to have his chance to meet Papa's friend here again and cash in on the headlines."

I was lying. I could hear the lie. I hoped they couldn't. I

spoke more quickly now, to cover the lie: "I'm going to start walking now. Look. See? I have the parrot by the neck. He'll stay alive as long as you play 'Simon says' my way. Here we go, now. One, two. One, two. Halfway to the door." I walked among them and they did not breathe. "One, two," I said, my heart beating in my mouth. "At the door. Steady. No sudden moves. Cage in one hand. Bird in the other—"

"The lions ran along the beach on the yellow sand," said the parrot, his throat moving under my fingers.

"Oh, my God," said Shelley, crouched there by the table. Tears began to pour down his face. Maybe it wasn't all money. Maybe some of it was Papa for him, too. He put his hands out in a beckoning, come-back gesture to me, the parrot, the cage. "Oh, God, oh, God." He wept.

"There was only the carcass of the great fish lying by the pier, its bones picked clean in the morning light," said the parrot.

"Oh," said everyone softly.

I didn't wait to see if any more of them were weeping. I stepped out. I shut the door. I ran for the elevator. By a miracle, it was there, the operator half-asleep inside. No one tried to follow. I guess they knew it was no use.

On the way down, I put the parrot inside the cage and put the shawl marked MOTHER over the cage. And the elevator moved slowly down through the years. I thought of those years ahead and where I might hide the parrot and keep him warm against any weather and feed him properly and once a day go in and talk through the shawl, and nobody ever to see him, no papers, no magazines, no cameramen, no Shelley Capon, not even Antonio from the Cuba Libre. Days might go by or weeks and sudden fears might come over me that the parrot had gone dumb. Then, in the middle of the night, I might wake and shuffle in and stand by his cage and say:

"Italy, 1918 . . . ?"

And beneath the word MOTHER, an old voice would say: "The snow drifted off the edges of the mountain in a fine white dust that winter. . . ."

"Africa, 1932."

"We got the rifles out and oiled the rifles and they were blue and fine and lay in our hands and we waited in the tall grass and smiled—"

"Cuba. The Gulf Stream."

"That fish came out of the water and jumped as high as the sun. Everything I had ever thought about a fish was in that fish. Everything I had ever thought about a single leap was in that leap. All of my life was there. It was a day of sun and water and being alive. I wanted to hold it all still in my hands. I didn't want it to go away, ever. Yet there, as the fish fell and the waters moved over it white and then green, there it went. . . ."

By that time, we were at the lobby level and the elevator doors opened and I stepped out with the cage labeled MOTHER and walked quickly across the lobby and out to a taxicab.

The trickiest business—and my greatest danger—remained. I knew that by the time I got to the airport, the guards and the Castro militia would have been alerted. I wouldn't put it past Shelley Capon to tell them that a national treasure was getting away. He might even cut Castro in on some of the Book-of-the-Month Club revenue and the movie rights. I had to improvise a plan to get through customs.

I am a literary man, however, and the answer came to me quickly. I had the taxi stop long enough for me to buy some shoe polish. I began to apply the disguise to El Córdoba. I painted him black all over.

"Listen," I said, bending down to whisper into the cage as we drove across Havana. "Nevermore."

I repeated it several times to give him the idea. The sound would be new to him, because, I guessed, Papa would never have quoted a middleweight contender he had knocked out years ago. There was silence under the shawl while the word was recorded.

Then, at last, it came back to me. "Nevermore," in Papa's old, familiar, tenor voice, "nevermore," it said.

The Burning Man

The rickety Ford came along a road that plowed up dust in yellow plumes which took an hour to lie back down and move no more in that special slumber that stuns the world in mid-July. Far away, the lake waited, a cool-blue gem in a hot-green lake of grass, but it was indeed still far away, and Neva and Doug were bucketing along in their barrelful of red-hot bolts with lemonade slopping around in a thermos on the back seat and deviled-ham sandwiches fermenting on Doug's lap. Both boy and aunt sucked in hot air and talked out even hotter.

"Fire-eater," said Douglas. "I'm eating fire. Heck, I can hardly *wait* for that lake!"

Suddenly, up ahead, there was a man by the side of the road.

Shirt open to reveal his bronzed body to the waist, his hair ripened to wheat color by July, the man's eyes burned fiery blue in a nest of sun wrinkles. He waved, dying in the heat.

Neva tromped on the brake. Fierce dust clouds rose to make the man vanish. When the golden dust sifted away his hot yellow eyes glared balefully, like a cat's, defying the weather and the burning wind.

He stared at Douglas.

Douglas glanced away, nervously.

For you could see where the man had come across a field high with yellow grass baked and burnt by eight weeks of no rain. There was a path where the man had broken the grass and cleaved a passage to the road. The path went as far as one could see down to a dry swamp and an empty creek bed with nothing but baked hot stones in it and fried rock and melting sand.

"I'll be damned, you stopped!" cried the man, angrily.

"I'll be damned, I did," Neva yelled back. "Where you going?"

"I'll think of someplace." The man hopped up like a cat and swung into the rumble seat. "Get going. It's *after* us! The sun, I mean, of course!" He pointed straight up. "Git! Or we'll *all* go mad!"

Neva stomped on the gas. The car left gravel and glided on pure white-hot dust, coming down only now and then to careen off a boulder or kiss a stone. They cut the land in half with racket. Above it, the man shouted:

"Put 'er up to seventy, eighty, hell, why not ninety!"

Neva gave a quick, critical look at the lion, the intruder in the back seat, to see if she could shut his jaws with a glance. They shut.

And that, of course, is how Doug felt about the beast. Not a stranger, no, not hitchhiker, but intruder. In just two minutes of leaping into the red-hot car, with his jungle hair and jungle smell, he had managed to disingratiate himself with the climate, the automobile, Doug, and the honorable and perspiring aunt. Now she hunched over the wheel and nursed the car through further storms of heat and backlashes of gravel.

Meanwhile, the creature in the back, with his great lion ruff of hair and mint-fresh yellow eyes, licked his lips and looked straight on at Doug in the rearview mirror. He gave a wink. Douglas tried to wink back, but somehow the lid never came down.

"You ever try to figure—" yelled the man.

"What?" cried Neva.

"You ever try to figure," shouted the man, leaning forward between them "—whether or not the weather is driving you crazy, or you're crazy *already?*"

It was a surprise of a question, which suddenly cooled them on this blast-furnace day.

"I don't quite understand—" said Neva.

"Nor does anyone!" The man smelled like a lion house. His thin arms hung over and down between them, nervously tying and untying an invisible string. He moved as if there were nests of burning hair under each armpit. "Day like today, all hell breaks loose inside your head. Lucifer was born on a day like this, in a wilderness like this," said the man. "With just fire and flame and smoke everywhere," said the man. "And everything so hot you can't touch it, and people not wanting to be touched," said the man.

He gave a nudge to her elbow, a nudge to the boy.

They jumped a mile.

"You see?" The man smiled. "Day like today, you get to thinking lots of things." He smiled. "Ain't this the summer when the seventeen-year locusts are supposed to come back like pure holocaust? Simple but multitudinous plagues?"

"Don't know!" Neva drove fast, staring ahead.

"This *is* the summer. Holocaust just around the bend. I'm thinking so swift it hurts my eyeballs, cracks my head. I'm liable to explode in a fireball with just plain disconnected thought. Why—why—why—"

Neva swallowed hard. Doug held his breath.

Quite suddenly they were terrified. For the man simply idled on with his talk, looking at the shimmering green fire trees that burned by on both sides, sniffing the rich hot dust that flailed up around the tin car, his voice neither high nor low, but steady and calm now in describing his life:

"Yes, sir, there's more to the world than people appreciate. If there can be seventeen-year locusts, why not seventeen-year people? Ever *thought* of that?"

"Never did," said someone.

Probably me, thought Doug, for his mouth had moved like a mouse.

"Or how about twenty-four-year people, or fifty-seven-year people? I mean, we're all so used to people growing up, marrying, having kids, we never stop to think maybe there's other ways for people coming into the world, maybe like locusts, once in a while, who can tell, one hot day, middle of summer!"

"Who can tell?" There was the mouse again. Doug's lips trembled.

"And who's to say there ain't genetic evil in the world?" asked the man of the sun, glaring right up at it without blinking.

"*What* kind of evil?" asked Neva.

"Genetic, ma'am. In the blood, that is to say. People born evil, growed evil, died evil, no changes all the way down the line."

"Whew!" said Douglas. "You mean people who start out mean and stay *at* it?"

"You got the sum, boy. Why not? If there are people everyone thinks are angel-fine from their first sweet breath to their last pure declaration, why not sheer orneriness from January first to December, three hundred sixty-five days later?"

"I never thought of that," said the mouse.

"Think," said the man. "*Think.*"

They thought for above five seconds.

"Now," said the man, squinting one eye at the cool lake five miles ahead, his other eye shut into darkness and ruminating on coal-bins of fact there, "listen. What if the intense heat, I mean the really hot hot heat of a month like this, week like this, day like today, just baked the Ornery Man right out of the river mud. Been there buried in the mud for forty-seven years, like a damn larva, waiting to be born. And he shook himself awake and looked around, full grown, and climbed out of the hot mud into the world and said, 'I think I'll eat me some summer.' "

"How's that again?"

"Eat me some summer, boy, summer, ma'am. Just devour it whole. Look at them trees, ain't they a whole dinner? Look at that field of wheat, ain't that a feast? Them sunflowers by the road, by golly, there's breakfast. Tarpaper on top that house, there's lunch. And the lake, way up ahead, Jehoshaphat, that's dinner wine, drink it all!"

"I'm thirsty, all right," said Doug.

"Thirsty, hell, boy, thirst don't begin to describe the state of a man, come to think about him, come to talk, who's been waiting in the hot mud thirty years and is born but to die in one day! Thirst! Ye Gods! Your ignorance is complete."

"Well," said Doug.

"Well," said the man. "Not only thirst but hunger. Hunger. Look around. Not only eat the trees and then the flowers blazing by the roads but then the white-hot panting dogs. There's one. There's another! And all the cats in the country. There's two, just passed three! And then just glutton-happy begin to why, why not, begin to get around to, let me tell you, how's this strike you, eat people? I mean—people! Fried, cooked, boiled, and parboiled people. Sunburnt beauties of people. Old men, young. Old ladies' hats and then old ladies under their hats and then young ladies' scarves and young ladies, and then young boys' swim-trunks, by God, and young boys, elbows, ankles, ears, toes, and eyebrows! Eyebrows, by God, men, women, boys, ladies, dogs, fill up the menu, sharpen your teeth, lick your lips, dinner's on!"

"Wait!" someone cried.

Not me, thought Doug. I said nothing.

"Hold on!" someone yelled.

It was Neva.

He saw her knee fly up as if by intuition and down as if by finalized gumption.

Stomp! went her heel on the floor.

The car braked. Neva had the door open, pointing, shouting, pointing, shouting, her mouth flapping, one hand seized out to grab the man's shirt and rip it.

"Out! Get out!"

"*Here*, ma'am?" The man was astonished.

"Here, here, here, out, out, out!"

"But, ma'am . . . !"

"Out, or you're finished, through!" cried Neva, wildly. "I got a load of Bibles in the back trunk, a pistol with a silver bullet here under the steering wheel. A box of crucifixes under the seat! A wooden stake taped to the axle, with a hammer. I got holy water in the carburetor, blessed before it boiled early this morning at three churches on the way: St. Matthew's Catholic, the Green Town Baptist, and the Zion City High Episcopal. The steam from that will get you alone. Following us, one mile behind, and due to arrive in one minute, is the Reverend Bishop Kelly from Chicago. Up at the lake is Father Rooney from Milwaukee, and Doug, why, Doug here has in his back pocket at this minute one sprig of wolfbane and two chunks of mandrake root. Out! out! out!"

"Why, ma'am," cried the man. "I *am!*"

And he was.

He landed and fell rolling in the road.

Neva banged the car into full flight.

Behind, the man picked himself up and yelled, "You must be nuts. You must be crazy. Nuts. Crazy."

"*I'm* nuts? *I'm* crazy? said Neva, and hooted. "Boy!"

". . . nuts . . . crazy . . ." The voice faded.

Douglas looked back and saw the man shaking his fist, then ripping off his shirt and hurling it to the gravel and jumping big puffs of white-hot dust out of it with his bare feet.

The car exploded, rushed, raced, banged pell-mell ahead, his aunt ferociously glued to the hot wheel, until the little sweating figure of the talking man was lost in sun-drenched marshland and burning air. At last Doug exhaled:

"Neva, I never heard you talk like that before."

"And never will again, Doug."

"Was what you said *true?*"

"Not a word."

"You lied, I mean, you *lied?*"

"I lied." Neva blinked. "Do you think *he* was lying, too?"

"I don't know."

"All I know is sometimes it takes a lie to kill a lie, Doug. This time, anyway. Don't let it become customary."

"No, ma'am." He began to laugh. "Say the thing about mandrake root again. Say the thing about wolfbane in my pocket. Say it about a pistol with a silver bullet, say it."

She said it. They both began to laugh.

Whooping and shouting, they went away in their tin-bucket-junking car over the gravel ruts and humps, her saying, him listening, eyes squeezed shut, roaring, snickering, raving.

They didn't stop laughing until they hit the water in their bathing suits and came up all smiles.

The sun stood hot in the middle of the sky and they dog-paddled happily for five minutes before they began to really swim in the menthol-cool waves.

Only at dusk when the sun was suddenly gone and the shadows moved out from the trees did they remember that now they had to go *back* down that lonely road through all the dark places and past that empty swamp to get to town.

They stood by the car and looked down that long road. Doug swallowed hard.

"*Nothing* can happen to us going home."

"Nothing."

"Jump!"

They hit the seats and Neva kicked the starter like it was a dead dog and they were off.

They drove along under plum-colored trees and among velvet purple hills.

And nothing happened.

They drove along a wide raw gravel road that was turning the color of plums and smelled the warm-cool air that was like lilacs and looked at each other, waiting.

And nothing happened.

Neva began at last to hum under her breath.

The road was empty.

And then it was not empty.

Neva laughed. Douglas squinted and laughed with her.

For there was a small boy, nine years old maybe, dressed in a vanilla-white summer suit, with white shoes and a white tie and his face pink and scrubbed, waiting by the side of the road. He waved.

Neva braked the car.

"Going in to town?" called the boy, cheerily. "Got lost. Folks at a picnic, left without me. Sure glad you came along. It's *spooky* out here."

"Climb in!"

The boy climbed and they were off, the boy in the back seat, and Doug and Neva up front glancing at him, laughing, and then getting quiet.

The small boy kept silent for a long while behind them, sitting straight upright and clean and bright and fresh and new in his white suit.

And they drove along the empty road under a sky that was dark now with a few stars and the wind getting cool.

And at last the boy spoke and said something that Doug didn't hear but he saw Neva stiffen and her face grow as pale as the ice cream from which the small boy's suit was cut.

"What?" asked Doug, glancing back.

The small boy stared directly at him, not blinking, and his mouth moved all to itself as if it were separate from his face.

The car's engine missed fire and died.

They were slowing to a dead stop.

Doug saw Neva kicking and fiddling at the gas and the starter. But most of all he heard the small boy say, in the new and permanent silence:

"Have either of you ever wondered—"

The boy took a breath and finished:

"—if there is such a thing as genetic evil in the world?"

A Piece of Wood

"Sit down, young man," said the Official.

"Thanks." The young man sat.

"I've been hearing rumors about you," the Official said pleasantly. "Oh, nothing much. Your nervousness. Your not getting on so well. Several months now I've heard about you, and I thought I'd call you in. Thought maybe you'd like your job changed. Like to go overseas, work in some other War Area? Desk job killing you off, like to get right in on the old fight?"

"I don't think so," said the young sergeant.

"What *do* you want?"

The sergeant shrugged and looked at his hands. "To live in peace. To learn that during the night, somehow, the guns of the world had rusted, the bacteria had turned sterile in their bomb casings, the tanks had sunk like prehistoric monsters into roads suddenly made tar pits. That's what I'd like."

"That's what we'd all like, of course," said the Official. "Now stop all that idealistic chatter and tell me where you'd like to be sent. You have your choice—the Western or the Northern War Zone." The Official tapped a pink map on his desk.

But the sergeant was talking at his hands, turning them over, looking at the fingers: "What would you officers do, what would we men do, what would the *world* do if we all woke tomorrow with the guns in flaking ruin?"

The Official saw that he would have to deal carefully with the sergeant. He smiled quietly. "That's an interesting question. I like to talk about such theories, and my answer is that there'd be mass panic. Each nation would think itself the only unarmed nation in the world, and would blame its enemies for the disaster. There'd be waves of suicide, stocks collapsing, a million tragedies."

"But *after* that," the sergeant said. "After they realized it was true, that every nation was disarmed and there was nothing more to fear, if we were all clean to start over fresh and new, what then?"

"They'd rearm as swiftly as possible."

"What if they could be stopped?"

"Then they'd beat each other with their fists. If it got down to that. Huge armies of men with boxing gloves of steel spikes would gather at the national borders. And if you took the gloves away they'd use their fingernails and feet. And if you cut their legs off they'd *spit* on each other. And if you cut off their tongues and stopped their mouths with corks they'd fill the atmosphere so full of hate that mosquitoes would drop to the ground and birds would fall dead from telephone wires."

"Then you don't think it would do any good?" the sergeant said.

"Certainly not. It'd be like ripping the carapace off a turtle. Civilization would gasp and die from the shock."

The young man shook his head. "Or are you lying to yourself and me because you've a nice comfortable job?"

"Let's call it ninety percent cynicism, ten percent rationalizing the situation. Go put your Rust away and forget about it."

The sergeant jerked his head up. "How'd you know I *had* it?" he said.

"Had what?"

"The Rust, of course."

"What're you talking about?"

"I *can* do it, you know. I could start the Rust tonight if I wanted to."

The Official laughed. "You can't be serious."

"I am. I've been meaning to come talk to you. I'm glad you called me in. I've worked on this invention for a long time. It's been a dream of mine. It has to do with the structure of certain atoms. If you study them you find that the arrangement of atoms in steel armor is such-and-such an arrangement. I was looking for an imbalance factor. I majored in physics and metallurgy, you know. It came to me, there's a Rust factor in the air all the time. Water vapor. I had to find a way to give steel a 'nervous breakdown.' Then the water vapor everywhere in the world would take over. Not on all metal, of course. Our civilization is built on steel, I wouldn't want to destroy most buildings. I'd just eliminate guns and shells, tanks, planes, battleships. I can set the machine to work on copper and brass and aluminum, too, if necessary. I'd just walk by all of those weapons and just being near them I'd make them fall away."

The Official was bending over his desk, staring at the sergeant. "May I ask you a question?"

"Yes."

"Have you ever thought you were Christ?"

"I can't say that I have. But I have considered that God was good to me to let me find what I was looking for, if that's what you mean."

The Official reached into his breast pocket and drew out an expensive ball-point pen capped with a rifle shell. He flourished the pen and started filling in a form. "I want you to take this to Dr. Mathews this afternoon, for a complete checkup. Not that I expect anything really bad, understand. But don't you feel you *should* see a doctor?"

"You think I'm lying about my machine," said the sergeant. "I'm not. It's so small it can be hidden in this cigarette package. The effect of it extends for nine hundred miles. I could tour this country in a few days, with the machine set to a certain type of steel. The other nations couldn't take advantage of us because I'd rust their weapons as they approach us. Then I'd fly to Europe. By this time next month the world would be free of war forever. I don't know how I found this invention. It's impossible. Just as impossible as the atom bomb. I've waited a month now, trying to think it over. I worried about what would happen if I did rip off the carapace, as you say. But now I've just about decided. My talk with you has helped clarify things. Nobody thought an airplane would ever fly, nobody thought an atom would ever explode, and nobody thinks that there can ever be Peace, but there *will* be."

"Take that paper over to Dr. Mathews, will you?" said the Official hastily.

The sergeant got up. "You're not going to assign me to any new Zone then?"

"Not right away, no. I've changed my mind. We'll let Mathews decide."

"I've decided then," said the young man. "I'm leaving the Post within the next few minutes. I've a pass. Thank you very much for giving me your valuable time, sir."

"Now look here, Sergeant, don't take things so seriously. You don't have to leave. Nobody's going to hurt you."

"That's right. Because nobody would believe me. Good-bye, sir." The sergeant opened the office door and stepped out.

The door shut and the Official was alone. He stood for a moment looking at the door. He sighed. He rubbed his hands over his face. The phone rang. He answered it abstractedly.

"Oh, *hello,* Doctor. I was just going to call you." A pause. "Yes, I was going to send him over to you. Look, is it all right for that young man to be wandering about? It *is* all right? If you say so, Doctor. Probably needs a rest, a good long one. Poor boy has a delusion of rather an interesting sort. Yes, yes. It's a shame. But that's what a Sixteen-Year War can do to you, I suppose."

The phone voice buzzed in reply.

The Official listened and nodded. "I'll make a note on that. Just a second." He reached for his ball-point pen. "Hold on a moment. Always mislaying things." He patted his pocket. "Had my pen here a moment ago. Wait." He put down the phone and searched his desk, pulling out drawers. He checked his blouse pocket again. He stopped moving. Then his hands twitched slowly into his pocket and probed down. He poked his thumb and forefinger deep and brought out a pinch of something.

He sprinkled it on his desk blotter: a small filtering powder of yellow-red rust.

He sat staring at it for a moment. Then he picked up the phone. "Mathews," he said, "get off the line, quick." There was a click of someone hanging up and then he dialed another call. "Hello, Guard Station, listen, there's a man coming past you any minute now, you know him, name of Sergeant Hollis, stop him, shoot him down, kill him if necessary, don't ask any questions, kill the son of a bitch, you heard me, this is the Official talking! Yes, kill him, you hear!"

"But, sir," said a bewildered voice on the other end of the line. "I can't, I just *can't....*"

"What do you mean you can't, God damn it!"

"Because . . ." The voice faded away. You could hear the guard breathing into the phone a mile away.

The Official shook the phone. "Listen to me, listen, get your gun ready!"

" I can't shoot anyone," said the guard.

The Official sank back in his chair. He sat blinking for half a minute, gasping.

Out there even now—he didn't have to look, no one had to tell him—the hangars were dusting down in soft red rust, and the airplanes were blowing away on a brown-rust wind into nothingness, and the tanks were sinking, sinking slowly into the hot asphalt roads, like dinosaurs (isn't that what the man had said?) sinking into primordial tar pits. Trucks were blowing away into ocher puffs of smoke, their drivers dumped by the road, with only the tires left running on the highways.

"Sir . . ." said the guard, who was seeing all this, far away. "Oh, God . . ."

"Listen, listen!" screamed the Official. "Go after him, get him, with your hands, choke him, with your fists, beat him, use your feet, kick his ribs in, kick him to death, do anything, but get that man. I'll be right out!" He hung up the phone.

By instinct he jerked open the bottom desk drawer to get his service pistol. A pile of brown rust filled the new leather holster. He swore and leaped up.

On the way out of the office he grabbed a chair. It's wood, he thought. Good old-fashioned wood, good old-fashioned maple. He hurled it against the wall twice, and it broke. Then he seized one of the legs, clenched it hard in his fist, his face bursting red, the breath snorting in his nostrils, his mouth wide. He struck the palm of his hand with the leg of the chair, testing it. "All right, God damn it, come on!" he cried.

He rushed out, yelling, and slammed the door.

The Messiah

"We all have that special dream when we are young," said Bishop Kelly.

The others at the table murmured, nodded.

"There is no Christian boy," the Bishop continued, "who does not some night wonder: am I Him? Is this the Second Coming at long last, and am I It? What, what, oh, what, dear God, if I *were* Jesus? How grand!"

The Priests, the Ministers, and the one lonely Rabbi laughed gently, remembering things from their own childhoods, their own wild dreams, and being great fools.

"I suppose," said the young Priest, Father Niven, "that Jewish boys imagine themselves Moses?"

"No, no, my dear friend," said Rabbi Nittler. "The Messiah! The *Messiah!*"

More quiet laughter, from all.

"Of course," said Father Niven out of his fresh pink-and-cream face, "how stupid of me. Christ *wasn't* the Messiah, was he? And your people are still waiting for Him to arrive. Strange. Oh, the ambiguities."

"And nothing more ambiguous than this." Bishop Kelly rose to escort them all out onto a terrace which had a view of the Martian hills, the ancient Martian towns, the old highways, the rivers of dust, and Earth, sixty million miles away, shining with a clear light in this alien sky.

"Did we ever in our wildest dreams," said the Reverend Smith, "imagine that one day each of us would have a Baptist Church, a St. Mary's Chapel, a Mount Sinai Synagogue here, here on Mars?"

The answer was no, no, softly, from them all.

Their quiet was interrupted by another voice which moved among them. Father Niven, as they stood at the balustrade, had tuned his transistor radio to check the hour. News was being broadcast from the small new American-Martian wilderness colony below. They listened:

"—rumored near the town. This is the first Martian reported in our community this year. Citizens are urged to respect any such visitor. If—"

Father Niven shut the news off.

"Our elusive congregation," sighed the Reverend Smith. "I must confess, I came to Mars not only to work with Christians, but hoping to invite *one* Martian to Sunday supper, to learn of his theologies, *his* needs."

"We are still too new to them," said Father Lipscomb. "In another year or so I think they will understand we're not buffalo hunters in search of pelts. Still, it *is* hard to keep one's curiosity in hand. After all, our *Mariner* photographs indicated no life whatsoever here. Yet life there is, very mysterious and half-resembling the human."

"Half, Your Eminence?" The Rabbi mused over his coffee. "I feel they are even more human than ourselves. They have *let* us come in. They have hidden in the hills, coming among us only on occasion, we guess, disguised as Earthmen—"

"Do you really believe they have telepathic powers, then, and hypnotic abilities which allow them to walk in our towns, fooling us with masks and visions, and none of us the wiser?"

"I do so believe."

"Then this," said the Bishop, handing around brandies and crème-de-menthes, "is a true evening of frustrations. Martians who will not reveal themselves so as to be Saved by Us the Enlightened—"

Many smiles at this.

"—and Second Comings of Christ delayed for several thousand years. How long must we wait, O Lord?"

"As for myself," said young Father Niven, "I never wished to *be* Christ, the Second Coming. I just always wanted, with all my heart, to *meet* Him. Ever since I was eight I have thought on that. It might well be the first reason I became a priest."

"To have the inside track just in case He ever *did* arrive again?" suggested the Rabbi, kindly.

The young Priest grinned and nodded. The others felt the urge to reach and touch him, for he had touched some vague small sweet nerve in each. They felt immensely gentle.

"With your permission, Rabbi, gentlemen," said Bishop Kelly, raising his glass. "To the First Coming of the Messiah, or the Second Coming of Christ. May they be more than some ancient, some foolish dreams."

They drank and were quiet.

The Bishop blew his nose and wiped his eyes.

———•———

The rest of the evening was like many another for the Priests, the Reverends, and the Rabbi. They fell to playing cards and arguing St. Thomas Aquinas, but failed under the onslaught of Rabbi Nittler's educated logic. They named him Jesuit, drank nightcaps, and listened to the late radio news:

"—it is feared this Martian may feel trapped in our community. Anyone meeting him should turn away, so as to let the Martian pass. Curiosity seems his motive. No cause for alarm. That concludes our—"

While heading for the door, the Priests, Ministers, and Rabbi discussed translations they had made into various tongues from Old and New Testaments. It was then that young Father Niven surprised them:

"Did you know I was once asked to write a screenplay on the Gospels? They needed an *ending* for their film!"

"Surely," protested the Bishop, "there's only *one* ending to Christ's life?"

"But, Your Holiness, the Four Gospels tell it with four variations. I compared. I grew excited. Why? Because I rediscovered something I had almost forgotten. The Last Supper isn't really the Last Supper!"

"Dear me, what is it then?"

"Why, Your Holiness, the first of several, sir. The first of several! After the Crucifixion and Burial of Christ, did not Simon-called-Peter, with the Disciples, fish the Sea of Galilee?"

"They did."

"And their nets were filled with a miracle of fish?"

"They were."

"And seeing on the shore of Galilee a pale light, did they not land and approach what seemed a bed of white-hot coals on which fresh-caught fish were baking?"

"Yes, ah, yes," said the Reverend Smith.

"And there beyond the glow of the soft charcoal fire, did they not sense a Spirit Presence and call out to it?"

"They did."

"Getting no answer, did not Simon-called-Peter whisper again, 'Who is there?' And the unrecognized Ghost upon the shore of Galilee put out its hand into the firelight, and in the palm of that hand, did they not see the mark where the nail had gone in, the stigmata that would never heal?

"They would have fled, but the Ghost spoke and said, 'Take of these fish and feed thy brethren.' And Simon-called-Peter took the fish that baked upon the white-hot coals and fed the Disciples. And Christ's frail Ghost then said, 'Take of my word and tell it among the nations of all the world and preach therein forgiveness of sin.'

"And then Christ left them. And, in my screenplay, I had Him walk along the shore of Galilee toward the horizon. And when anyone walks toward the horizon, he seems to ascend, yes? For all land rises at a distance. And He walked on along the shore until He was just a small mote, far away. And then they could see Him no more.

"And as the sun rose upon the ancient world, all His thousand footprints that lay along the shore blew away in the dawn winds and were as nothing.

"And the Disciples left the ashes of that bed of coals to scatter in sparks, and with the taste of Real and Final and True Last Supper upon their mouths, went away. And in my screenplay, I had my CAMERA drift high above to watch the Disciples move some north, some south, some to the east, to tell the world what Needed to Be Told about One Man. And their footprints, circling in all directions, like the spokes of an immense wheel, blew away out of the sand in the winds of morn. And it was a new day. THE END."

The young Priest stood in the center of his friends, cheeks fired with color, eyes shut. Suddenly he opened his eyes, as if remembering where he was:

"Sorry."

"For what?" cried the Bishop, brushing his eyelids with the back of his hand, blinking rapidly. "For making me weep twice in one night? What, self-conscious in the presence of your own love for Christ? Why, you have given the Word back to me, *me!* who has known the Word for what seems a thousand years! You have freshened my soul, oh good young man with the heart of a boy. The eating of fish on Galilee's shore *is* the True Last Supper. Bravo. You deserve to meet Him. The Second Coming, it's only fair, must be for you!"

"I am unworthy!" said Father Niven.

"So are we all! But if a trade of souls were possible, I'd loan mine out on this instant to borrow yours fresh from the laundry. Another toast, gentlemen? To Father Niven! And then, good night, it's late, good night."

The toast was drunk and all departed; the Rabbi and the Ministers down the hill to their holy places, leaving the Priests to stand a last moment at their door looking out at Mars, this strange world, and a cold wind blowing.

Midnight came and then one and two, and at three in the cold deep morning of Mars, Father Niven stirred. Candles flickered in soft whispers. Leaves fluttered against his window.

Suddenly he sat up in bed, half-startled by a dream of mob-cries and pursuits. He listened.

Far away, below, he heard the shutting of an outside door.

Throwing on a robe, Father Niven went down the dim rectory stairs and through the church where a dozen candles here or there kept their own pools of light.

He made the rounds of all the doors, thinking: Silly, why lock churches? What is there to steal? But still he prowled the sleeping night . . .

. . . and found the front door of the church unlocked, and softly being pushed in by the wind.

Shivering, he shut the door.

Soft running footsteps.

He spun about.

The church lay empty. The candle flames leaned now this way, now that in their shrines. There was only the ancient smell of wax and incense burning, stuffs left over from all the market-places of time and history; other suns, and other noons.

In the midst of glancing at the crucifix above the main altar, he froze.

There was a sound of a single drop of water falling in the night.

Slowly he turned to look at the baptistery in the back of the church.

There were no candles there, yet—

A pale light shone from that small recess where stood the baptismal font.

"Bishop Kelly?" he called, softly.

Walking slowly up the aisle, he grew very cold, and stopped because—

Another drop of water had fallen, hit, dissolved away.

It was like a faucet dripping somewhere. But there were no faucets. Only the baptismal font itself, into which, drop by drop, a slow liquid was falling, with three heartbeats between each sound.

At some secret level, Father Niven's heart told itself something and raced, then slowed and almost stopped. He broke into a wild perspiration. He found himself unable to move, but move he must, one foot after the other, until he reached the arched doorway of the baptistery.

There was indeed a pale light within the darkness of the small place.

No, not a light. A shape. A figure.

The figure stood behind and beyond the baptismal font. The sound of falling water had stopped.

His tongue locked in his mouth, his eyes flexed wide in a kind of madness, Father Niven felt himself struck blind. Then vision returned, and he dared cry out:

"Who!"

A single word, which echoed back from all around the church, which made candle flames flutter in reverberation, which stirred the dust of incense, which frightened his own heart with its swift return in saying: Who!

The only light within the baptistery came from the pale garments of the figure that stood there facing him. And this light was enough to show him an incredible thing.

As Father Niven watched, the figure moved. It put a pale hand out upon the baptistery air.

The hand hung there as if not wanting to, a separate thing from the Ghost beyond, as if it were seized and pulled forward, resisting, by Father Niven's dreadful and fascinated stare to reveal what lay in the center of its open white palm.

There was fixed a jagged hole, a cincture from which, slowly, one by one, blood was dripping, falling away down and slowly down, into the baptismal font.

The drops of blood struck the holy water, colored it, and dissolved in slow ripples.

The hand remained for a stunned moment there before the Priest's now-blind, now-seeing eyes.

As if struck a terrible blow, the Priest collapsed to his knees with an outgasped cry, half of despair, half of revelation, one hand over his eyes, the other fending off the vision.

"No, no, no, no, no, no, no, it *can't!*"

It was as if some dreadful physician of dentistry had come upon him without narcotic and with one seizure entire-extracted his soul, bloodied raw, out of his body. He felt himself prized, his life yanked forth, and the roots, O God, were . . . *deep!*

"No, no, no, no!"

But, yes.

Between the lacings of his fingers, he looked again.

And the Man was there.

And the dreadful bleeding palm quivered dripping upon the baptistery air.

"Enough!"

The palm pulled back, vanished. The Ghost stood waiting.

And the face of the Spirit was good and familiar. Those strange beautiful deep and incisive eyes were as he knew they always must be. There was the gentleness of the mouth, and the paleness framed by the flowing locks of hair and beard. The Man was robed in the simplicity of garments worn upon the shores and in the wilderness near Galilee.

The Priest, by a great effort of will, prevented his tears from spilling over, stopped up his agony of surprise, doubt, shock, these clumsy things which rioted within and threatened to break forth. He trembled.

And then saw that the Figure, the Spirit, the Man, the Ghost, Whatever, was trembling, too.

No, thought the Priest, He can't be! Afraid? Afraid of . . . *me?*

And now the Spirit shook itself with an immense agony not unlike his own, like a mirror image of his own concussion, gaped wide its mouth, shut up its own eyes, and mourned:

"Oh, please, let me go."

At this the young Priest opened his eyes wider and gasped. He thought: But you're free. No one keeps you here!

And in that instant: "Yes!" cried the Vision. "*You* keep me! Please! Avert your gaze! The more you look the more I become *this!* I am *not* what I seem!"

But, thought the Priest, I did not speak! My lips did not move! How does this Ghost know my mind?

"I know all you think," said the Vision, trembling, pale, pulling back in baptistery gloom. "Every sentence, every word. I did not mean to come. I ventured into town. Suddenly I was many things to many people. I ran. They followed. I escaped here. The door was open. I entered. And then and then—oh, and then was trapped."

No, thought the Priest.

"Yes," mourned the Ghost. "By you."

Slowly now, groaning under an even more terrible weight of

revelation, the Priest grasped the edge of the font and pulled himself, swaying, to his feet. At last he dared force the question out:

"You are not . . . what you seem?"

"I am not," said the other. "Forgive me."

I, thought the Priest, shall go mad.

"Do not," said the Ghost, "or I shall go down to madness with you."

"I can't give you up, oh, dear God, now that you're here, after all these years, all my dreams, don't you see, it's asking too *much*. Two thousand years, a whole race of people have waited for your return! And I, I am the one who meets you, sees you—"

"You meet only your own dream. You see only your own need. Behind all this—" the figure touched its own robes and breast, "I am another thing."

"What must I *do!*" the Priest burst out, looking now at the heavens, now at the Ghost which shuddered at his cry. "*What?*"

"Avert your gaze. In that moment I will be out the door and gone."

"Just—just like that?"

"Please," said the Man.

The Priest drew a series of breaths, shivering.

"Oh, if this moment could last for just an hour."

"Would you kill me?"

"No!"

"If you keep me, force me into this shape some little while longer, my death will be on your hands."

The Priest bit his knuckles, and felt a convulsion of sorrow rack his bones.

"You—you are a Martian, then?"

"No more. No less."

"And I have done this to you with my thoughts?"

"You did not mean. When you came downstairs, your old dream seized and made me over. My palms still bleed from the wounds you gave out of your secret mind."

The Priest shook his head, dazed.

"Just a moment more . . . wait . . ."

He gazed steadily, hungrily, at the darkness where the Ghost stood out of the light. That face was beautiful. And, oh, those hands were loving and beyond all description.

The Priest nodded, a sadness in him now as if he had within the hour come back from the true Calvary. And the hour was gone. And the coals strewn dying on the sand near Galilee.

"If—if I let you go—"

"You must, oh you must!"

"If I let you go, will you promise—"

"What?"

"Will you promise to come back?"

"Come back?" cried the figure in the darkness.

"Once a year, that's all I ask, come back once a year, here to this place, this font, at the same time of night—"

"Come back . . . ?"

"Promise! Oh, I must know this moment again. You don't know how important it is! Promise, or I won't let you go!"

"I—"

"Say it! Swear it!"

"I promise," said the pale Ghost in the dark. "I swear."

"Thank you, oh thanks."

"On what day a year from now must I return?"

The tears had begun to roll down the young Priest's face now. He could hardly remember what he wanted to say and when he said it he could hardly hear:

"Easter, oh, God, yes, Easter, a year from now!"

"Please, don't weep," said the figure. "I will come. Easter, you say? I know your calendar. Yes. Now—" The pale wounded hand moved in the air, softly pleading. "May I go?"

The Priest ground his teeth to keep the cries of woe from exploding forth. "Bless me, and go."

"Like this?" said the voice.

And the hand came out to touch him ever so quietly.

"Quick!" cried the Priest, eyes shut, clenching his fists hard against his ribs to prevent his reaching out to seize. "Go before I keep you forever. Run. Run!"

The pale hand touched him a last time upon his brow. There was a soft run of naked feet.

A door opened upon stars; the door slammed.

There was a long moment when the echo of the slam made its way through the church, to every altar, into every alcove and up like a blind flight of some single bird seeking and finding release in the apse. The church stopped trembling at last, and the Priest laid his hands on himself as if to tell himself how to behave, how to breathe again; be still, be calm, stand tall. . . .

Finally, he stumbled to the door and held to it, wanting to throw it wide, look out at the road which must be empty now, with perhaps a figure in white, far fleeing. He did not open the door.

He went about the church, glad for things to do, finishing out the ritual of locking up. It was a long way around to all the doors. It was a long way to next Easter.

He paused at the font and saw the clear water with no trace of red. He dipped his hand and cooled his brow and temples and cheeks and eyelids.

Then he went slowly up the aisle and laid himself out before the altar and let himself burst forth and really weep. He heard the sound of his sadness go up and come back in agonies from the tower where the bell hung silent.

And he wept for many reasons.

For himself.

For the Man who had been here a moment ago.

For the long time until the rock was rolled back and the tomb found empty again.

Until Simon-Called-Peter once more saw the Ghost upon the Martian shore, and himself Simon-Peter.

And most of all he wept because, oh, because, because . . . never in his life could he speak of this night to anyone. . . .

G. B. S.—Mark V

"Charlie! Where you going?"

Members of the rocket crew, passing, called.

Charles Willis did not answer.

He took the vacuum tube down through the friendly humming bowels of the spaceship. He fell, thinking: This is the grand hour.

"Chuck! Where traveling?" someone called.

To meet someone dead but alive, cold but warm, forever untouchable but reaching out somehow to touch.

"Idiot! Fool!"

The voice echoed. He smiled.

Then he saw Clive, his best friend, drifting up in the opposite chute. He averted his gaze, but Clive sang out through his sea-shell ear-pack radio:

"I want to see you!"

"Later!" Willis said.

"I *know* where you're going. Stupid!"

And Clive was gone up away while Willis fell softly down, his hands trembling.

His boots touched surface. On the instant he suffered renewed delight.

He walked down through the hidden machineries of the rocket. Lord, he thought, crazy. Here we are one hundred days gone away from the Earth in Space, and, this very hour, most of the crew, in fever, dialing their aphrodisiac animatronic devices that touched and hummed to them in their shut clamshell beds. While, what do *I* do? he thought. *This.*

He moved to peer into a small storage pit.

There, in an eternal dusk, sat the old man.

"Sir," he said, and waited.

"Shaw," he whispered. "Oh, Mr. George Bernard Shaw."

The old man's eyes sprang wide as if he had swallowed an Idea.

He seized his bony knees and gave a sharp cry of laughter.

"By God, I *do* accept it *all!*"

"Accept *what*, Mr. Shaw?"

Mr. Shaw flashed his bright blue gaze upon Charles Willis.

"The Universe! *It* thinks, therefore I *am!* So I had *best* accept, eh? Sit."

Willis sat in the shadowed areaway, clasping his knees and his own warm delight with being here again.

"Shall I read your mind, young Willis, and tell you what you've been up to since last we conversed?"

"*Can* you read minds, Mr. Shaw?"

"No, thank God. Wouldn't it be awful if I were not only the cuneiform-tablet robot of George Bernard Shaw, but could also scan your head-bumps and spell your dreams? Unbearable."

"You already *are*, Mr. Shaw."

"*Touché!* Well, now." The old man raked his reddish beard with his thin fingers, then poked Willis gently in the ribs. "How is it you are the only one aboard this starship who ever visits me?"

"Well, sir, you see—"

The young man's cheeks burnt themselves to full blossom.

"Ah, yes, I do see," said Shaw. "Up through the honeycomb of the ship, all the happy male bees in their hives with their syrupy wind-up soft-singing nimble-nibbling toys, their bright female puppets."

"Mostly *dumb*."

"Ah, well. It was not always thus. On my last trip the Captain wished to play Scrabble using only names of characters, concepts and ideas from my plays. Now, strange boy, why do *you* squat here with this hideous old ego? Have you no need for that soft and gentle company abovestairs?"

"It's a long journey, Mr. Shaw, two years out beyond Pluto and back. Plenty of time for abovestairs company. Never enough for this. I have the dreams of a goat but the genetics of a saint."

"Well said!" The old man sprang lightly to his feet and paced about, pointing his beard now toward Alpha Centauri, now toward the nebula in Orion.

"How runs our menu today, Willis? Shall I preface Saint Joan for you? Or . . . ?"

"Chuck . . . ?"

Willis's head jerked. His seashell radio whispered in his ear. "Willis! Clive calling. You're late for dinner. I know where you are. I'm coming down. Chuck—"

Willis thumped his ear. The voice cut off.

"Quick, Mr. Shaw! Can you—well—*run?*"

"Can Icarus fall from the sun? Jump! I shall pace you with these spindly cricket legs!"

They ran.

Taking the corkscrew staircase instead of the air-tube, they looked back from the top platform in time to see Clive's shadow dart into that tomb where Shaw had died but to wake again.

"Willis!" cried his voice.

"To hell with him," said Willis.

Shaw beamed. "Hell? I know it well. Come. I'll show you around!"

Laughing, they jumped into the feather-tube and fell *up*.

This was the place of stars.

Which is to say the one place in all the ship where, if one wished, one could come and truly look at the Universe and the billion billion stars which poured across it and never stopped pouring, cream from the mad dairies of the gods. Delicious frights or outcrops, on the other hand, if you thought it so, from the sickness of Lord God Jehovah turned in his sleep, upset with Creation, and birthing dinosaur worlds spun about satanic suns.

"It's all in the thinking," observed Mr. Shaw, sidling his eyes at his young consort.

"Mr. Shaw! You *can* read minds?"

"Poppycock. I merely read faces. Yours is clear glass. I glanced just now and saw Job afflicted, Moses and the Burning Bush. Come. Let us look at the Deeps and see what God has been up to in the ten billion years since He collided with Himself and procreated Vastness."

They stood now, surveying the Universe, counting the stars to a billion and beyond.

"Oh," moaned the young man, suddenly, and tears fell from his eyes. "How I wish I had been alive when you were alive, sir. How I wish I had *truly* known you."

"*This* Shaw is best," retorted the old man, "all of the mincemeat and none of the tin. The coattails are better than the man. Hang to them and survive."

Space lay all about, as vast as God's first thought, as deep as His primal breathing.

They stood, one of them tall, one short, by the scanning window, with a fine view of the great Andromeda Nebula whenever they wished to focus it near with a touch of the button which made the Eye magnify and suck things close.

After a long moment of drinking stars, the young man let out his breath.

"Mr. Shaw . . . ? *Say* it. You know what I like to hear."

"Do I, my boy?" Mr. Shaw's eyes twinkled.

All of Space was around them, all of the Universe, all of the night of the celestial Being, all the stars and all the places between the stars, and the ship moving on its silent course, and the crew of the ship busy at work or games or touching their amorous toys, so these two were alone with their talk, these two stood viewing the Mystery and saying what must be said.

"Say it, Mr. Shaw."

"Well, now . . ."

Mr. Shaw fixed his eyes on a star some twenty light-years away.

"What *are* we?" he asked. "Why, we are the miracle of force and matter making itself over into imagination and will. Incredible. The Life Force experimenting with forms. You for one. Me for another. The Universe has shouted itself alive. We are one of the shouts. Creation turns in its abyss. We have bothered it, dreaming ourselves to shapes. The void is filled with slumbers; ten billion on a billion on a billion bombardments of light and material that know not themselves, that sleep moving and move but finally to make an eye and waken on themselves. Among so much that is flight and ignorance, we are the blind force that gropes like Lazarus from a billion-light-year tomb. We summon ourselves. We say, O Lazarus Life Force, truly come ye forth. So the Universe, a motion of deaths, fumbles to reach across Time to feel its own flesh and know it to be ours. We touch both ways and find each other miraculous because we are One."

Mr. Shaw turned to glance at his young friend.

"There you have it. Satisfied?"

"Oh, yes! I—"

The young man stopped.

Behind them, in the viewing-cabin door, stood Clive. Beyond him, they could hear music pulsing from the far cubicles where crewmen and their huge toys played at amorous games.

"Well," said Clive, "what goes on—?"

"Here?" interjected Shaw, lightly. "Why, only the confounding of two energies making do with puzzlements. This contraption—" he touched his own breast, "speaks from computerized elations. That genetic conglomeration—" he nodded at his young friend, "responds with raw, beloved, and true emotions. The sum of us? Pandemonium spread on biscuits and devoured at high tea."

Clive swiveled his gaze to Willis.

"Damn, you're nuts. At dinner you should have *heard* the laughter! You and this old man, and just talk! they said. Just talk, talk! Look, idiot, it's your stand-watch in ten minutes. Be there! God!"

And the door was empty. Clive was gone.

Silently, Willis and Mr. Shaw floated down the drop-tube to the storage pit beneath the vast machineries.

The old man sat once again on the floor.

"Mr. Shaw." Willis shook his head, snorting softly. "Hell. Why is it you seem more alive to me than anyone I have ever known?"

"Why, my dear young friend," replied the old man, gently, "what you warm your hands at are Ideas, eh? I am a walking monument of concepts, scrimshaws of thought, electric deliriums of philosophy and wonder. You love concepts. I am their receptacle. You love dreams in motion. I move. You love palaver and jabber. I am the consummate palaverer and jabberer. You and I, together, masticate Alpha Centauri and spit forth universal myths. We chew upon the tail of Halley's Comet and worry the Horsehead Nebula until it cries a monstrous Uncle and gives over to our creation. You love libraries. I am a library. Tickle my ribs and I vomit forth Melville's Whale, Spirit Spout and all. Tic my ear and I'll build Plato's Republic with my tongue for you to run and live in. You love Toys. I am a Toy, a fabulous plaything, a computerized—"

"—friend," said Willis, quietly.

Mr. Shaw gave him a look less of fire than of hearth.

"Friend," he said.

Willis turned to leave, then stopped to gaze back at that strange old figure propped against the dark storage wall.

"I—I'm afraid to go. I have this fear something may *happen* to you."

"I shall survive," replied Shaw tartly, "but only if you warn your Captain that a vast meteor shower approaches. He must shift course a few hundred thousand miles. Done?"

"Done." But still Willis did not leave.

"Mr. Shaw," he said, at last. "What . . . what do you *do* while the rest of us sleep?"

"Do? Why, bless you. I listen to my tuning fork. Then, I write symphonies between my ears."

Willis was gone.

In the dark, alone, the old man bent his head. A soft hive of dark bees began to hum under his honey-sweet breath.

Four hours later, Willis, off watch, crept into his sleep-cubicle.

In half-light, the mouth was waiting for him.

Clive's mouth. It licked its lips and whispered:

"Everyone's talking. About you making an ass out of yourself visiting a two-hundred-year-old intellectual relic, you, you, you. Jesus, the psycho-med'll be out tomorrow to X-ray your stupid skull!"

"Better that than what you men do all night every night," said Willis.

"What we do is us."

"Then why not let me be *me?*"

"Because it's unnatural." The tongue licked and darted. "We all *miss* you. Tonight we piled all the grand toys in the midst of the wild room and—"

"I don't want to hear it!"

"Well, then," said the mouth, "I might just trot down and tell all this to your old gentleman friend—"

"Don't go *near* him!"

"I might." The lips moved in the shadows. "You can't stand guard on him forever. Some night soon, when you're asleep, someone might—tamper with him, eh? Scramble his electronic eggs so he'll talk vaudeville instead of *Saint Joan?* Ha, yes. Think. Long journey. Crew's bored. Practical joke like that, worth a million to see you froth. Beware, Charlie. Best come play with us."

Willis, eyes shut, let the blaze out of him.

"Whoever dares to touch Mr. Shaw, so help me God, I'll kill!"

He turned violently on his side, gnawing the back of his fist. In the half-dark, he could sense Clive's mouth still moving.

"Kill? Well, well. Pity. Sweet dreams."

An hour later, Willis gulped two pills and fell stunned into sleep.

In the middle of the night he dreamed that they were burning good Saint Joan at the stake and, in the midst of burning, the plain-potato maiden turned to an old man stoically wrapped around with ropes and vines. The old man's beard was fiery red even before the flames reached it, and his bright blue eyes were fixed fiercely upon Eternity, ignoring the fire.

"Recant!" cried a voice. "Confess and recant! Recant!"

"There is nothing to confess, therefore no need for recantation," said the old man quietly.

The flames leaped up his body like a mob of insane and burning mice.

"Mr. Shaw!" screamed Willis.

He sprang awake.

Mr. Shaw.

The cabin was silent. Clive lay asleep.

On his face was a smile.

The smile made Willis pull back, with a cry. He dressed. He ran.

Like a leaf in autumn he fell down the air-tube, growing older and heavier with each long instant.

The storage pit where the old man "slept" was much more quiet than it had a right to be.

Willis bent. His hand trembled. At last, he touched the old man.

"Sir—?"

There was no motion. The beard did not bristle. Nor the eyes fire themselves to blue flames. Nor the mouth tremble with gentle blasphemies . . .

"Oh, Mr. Shaw," he said. "Are you dead, then, oh God, are you really dead?"

The old man was what they called dead when a machine no longer spoke or tuned an electric thought or moved. His dreams and philosophies were snow in his shut mouth.

Willis turned the body this way and that, looking for some cut, wound, or bruise on the skin.

He thought of the years ahead, the long traveling years and no Mr. Shaw to walk with, gibber with, laugh with. Women in the storage shelves, yes, women in the cots late at night, laughing their strange taped laughters and moving their strange machined motions, and saying the same dumb things that were said on a thousand worlds on a thousand nights.

"Oh, Mr. Shaw," he murmured at last. "Who *did* this to you?"

Silly boy, whispered Mr. Shaw's memory voice. You *know.*

I know, thought Willis.

He whispered a name and ran away.

———————•———————

"Damn you, you killed him!"

Willis seized Clive's bedclothes, at which instant Clive, like a robot, popped wide his eyes. The smile remained constant.

"You can't kill what was never alive," he said.

"Son of a bitch!"

He struck Clive once in the mouth, after which Clive was on his feet, laughing in some strange wild way, wiping blood from his lips.

"What did you do to him?" cried Willis.

"Not much, just—"

But that was the end of their conversation.

"On posts!" a voice cried. "Collision course!"

Bells rang. Sirens shrieked.

In the midst of their shared rage, Willis and Clive turned cursing to seize emergency spacesuits and helmets off the cabin walls.

"Damn, oh, damn, oh—d—"

Half-through his last damn, Clive gasped. He vanished out a sudden hole in the side of the rocket.

The meteor had come and gone in a billionth of a second. On its way out, it had taken all the air in the ship with it through a hole the size of a small car.

My God, thought Willis, he's gone forever.

What saved Willis was a ladder he stood near, against which the swift river of air crushed him on its way into Space. For a moment he could not move or breathe. Then the suction was finished, all the air in the ship gone. There was only time to adjust the pressure in his suit and helmet, and glance wildly around at the veering ship which was being bombarded now as in a space war. Men ran, or rather floated, shouting wildly, everywhere.

Shaw, thought Willis unreasonably, and had to laugh. Shaw.

A final meteor in a tribe of meteors struck the motor section of the rocket and blew the entire ship apart. Shaw, Shaw, oh, Shaw, thought Willis.

He saw the rocket fly apart like a shredded balloon, all its gases only impelling it to more disintegration. With the bits and pieces went wild crowds of men, dismissed from school, from life, from all and everything, never to meet face to face again, not even to say farewell, the dismissal was so abrupt and their deaths and isolation such a swift surprise.

Good-bye, thought Willis.

But there was no true good-bye. He could hear no weeping and no laments over his radio. Of all the crew, he was the last and final and only one alive, because of his suit, his helmet, his oxygen, miraculously spared. For what? To be alone and fall?

To be alone. To fall.

Oh, Mr. Shaw, oh, sir, he thought.

"No sooner called then delivered," whispered a voice.

It was impossible, but . . .

Drifting, spinning, the ancient doll with the wild red beard and blazing blue eyes fell across darkness as if impelled by God's breath, on a whim.

Instinctively, Willis opened his arms.

And the old party landed there, smiling, breathing heavily, or pretending to breathe heavily, as was his bent.

"Well, well, Willis! Quite a treat, eh?"

"Mr. Shaw! You were *dead!*"

"Poppycock! Someone bent some wires in me. The collision knocked things back together. The disconnection is here below my chin. A villain cut me there. So if I fall dead again, jiggle under my jaw and wire me up, eh?"

"Yes, sir!"

"How much food do you carry at this moment, Willis?"

"Enough to last two hundred days in Space."

"Dear me, that's fine, fine! And self-recycling oxygen units, also, for two hundred days?"

"Yes, sir. Now, how long will *your* batteries last, Mr. Shaw?"

"Ten thousand years!" the old man sang out happily. "Yes, I vow, I swear! I am fitted with solar-cells which will collect God's universal light until I wear out my circuits."

"Which means you will outtalk me, Mr. Shaw, long after I have stopped eating and breathing."

"At which point you must dine on conversation, and breathe past participles instead of air. But, we must hold the thought of rescue uppermost. Are not the chances good?"

"Rockets *do* come by. And I am equipped with radio signals—"

"Which even now cry out into the deep night: I'm here with ramshackle Shaw, eh?"

I'm here with ramshackle Shaw, thought Willis, and was suddenly warm in winter.

"Well, then, while we're waiting to be rescued, Charles Willis, what next?"

"Next? Why—"

They fell away down Space alone but not alone, fearful but elated, and now grown suddenly quiet.

"*Say* it, Mr. Shaw."

"Say what?"

"You know. Say it again."

"Well, then." They spun lazily, holding to each other. "Isn't life miraculous? Matter and force, yes, matter and force making itself over into intelligence and will."

"Is *that* what we are, sir?"

"We are, bet ten thousand bright tin-whistles on it, we are. Shall I say *more*, young Willis?"

"Please, sir," laughed Willis. "I want some more!"

And the old man spoke and the young man listened and the young man spoke and the old man hooted and they fell around a corner of Universe away out of sight, eating and talking, talking and eating, the young man biting gumball foods, the old man devouring sunlight with his solar-cell eyes, and the last that was seen of them they were gesticulating and babbling and conversing and waving their hands until their voices faded into Time and the solar system turned over in its sleep and covered them with a blanket of dark and light, and whether or not a rescue ship named Rachel, seeking her lost children, ever came by and found them, who can tell, who would truly ever want to know?

The Utterly Perfect Murder

It was such an utterly perfect, such an incredibly delightful idea for murder, that I was half out of my mind all across America.

The idea had come to me for some reason on my forty-eighth birthday. Why it hadn't come to me when I was thirty or forty, I cannot say. Perhaps those were good years and I sailed through them unaware of time and clocks and the gathering of frost at my temples or the look of the lion about my eyes. . . .

Anyway, on my forty-eighth birthday, lying in bed that night beside my wife, with my children sleeping through all the other quiet moonlit rooms of my house, I thought:

I will arise and go now and kill Ralph Underhill.

Ralph Underhill! I cried, who in God's name is *he?*

Thirty-six years later, kill him? For *what?*

Why, I thought, for what he did to me when I was twelve.

My wife woke, an hour later, hearing a noise.

"Doug?" she called. "What are you doing?"

"Packing," I said. "For a journey."

"Oh," she murmured, and rolled over and went to sleep.

"Board! All aboard!" the porter's cries went down the train platform.

The train shuddered and banged.

"See you!" I cried, leaping up the steps.

"Someday," called my wife, "I wish you'd *fly!*"

Fly? I thought, and spoil thinking about murder all across the plains? Spoil oiling the pistol and loading it and thinking of Ralph Underhill's face when I show up thirty-six years late to settle old scores? Fly? Why, I would rather pack cross-country on foot, pausing by night to build fires and fry my bile and sour spit and eat again my old, mummified but still-living antagonisms and touch those bruises which have never healed. Fly? !

The train moved. My wife was gone.

I rode off into the Past.

Crossing Kansas the second night, we hit a beaut of a thunderstorm. I stayed up until four in the morning, listening to the rave of winds and thunders. At the height of the storm, I saw my face, a darkroom negative-print on the cold window glass, and thought:

Where is that fool going?

To kill Ralph Underhill!

Why? Because!

Remember how he hit my arm? Bruises. I was covered with bruises, both arms; dark blue, mottled black, strange yellow bruises. Hit and run, that was Ralph, hit and run—

And yet . . . you loved him?

Yes, as boys love boys when boys are eight, ten, twelve, and the world is innocent and boys are evil beyond evil because they know not what they do, but do it anyway. So, on some secret level, I *had* to be hurt. We dear fine friends needed each other. I to be hit. He to strike. My scars were the emblem and symbol of our love.

What else makes you want to murder Ralph so late in time?

The train whistle shrieked. Night country rolled by.

And I recalled one spring when I came to school in a new tweed knicker suit and Ralph knocking me down, rolling me in snow and fresh brown mud. And Ralph laughing and me going home, shame-faced, covered with slime, afraid of a beating, to put on fresh dry clothes.

Yes! And what *else?*

Remember those toy clay statues you longed to collect from the Tarzan radio show? Statues of Tarzan and Kala the Ape and Numa the Lion, for just twenty-five cents?! Yes, yes! Beautiful! Even now, in memory, O the sound of the Ape man swinging through green jungles far away, ululating! But who had twenty-five cents in the middle of the Great Depression? No one.

Except Ralph Underhill.

And one day Ralph asked you if you wanted one of the statues. Wanted! you cried. Yes! Yes!

That was the same week your brother in a strange seizure of love mixed with contempt gave you his old, but expensive, baseball-catcher's mitt.

"Well," said Ralph, "I'll give you my extra Tarzan statue if you'll give me that catcher's mitt."

Fool! I thought. The statue's worth twenty-five cents. The glove cost two dollars! No fair! Don't!

But I raced back to Ralph's house with the glove and gave it to him and he, smiling a worse contempt than my brother's, handed me the Tarzan statue and, bursting with joy, I ran home.

My brother didn't find out about his catcher's mitt and the statue for two weeks, and when he did he ditched me when we hiked out in farm country and left me lost because I was such a sap. "Tarzan statues! Baseball mitts!" he cried. "That's the last thing I *ever* give you!"

And somewhere on a country road I just lay down and wept and wanted to die but didn't know how to give up the final vomit that was my miserable ghost.

The thunder murmured.

The rain fell on the cold Pullman-car windows.

What *else?* Is that the list?

No. One final thing, more terrible than all the rest.

In all the years you went to Ralph's house to toss up small bits of gravel on his Fourth of July six-in-the-morning fresh dewy window or to call him forth for the arrival of dawn circuses in the cold fresh blue railroad stations in late June or late August, in all those years, never once did Ralph run to your house.

Never once in all the years did he, or anyone else, prove their friendship by coming by. The door never knocked. The window of your bedroom never faintly clattered and belled with a high-tossed confetti of small dusts and rocks.

And you always knew that the day you stopped going to Ralph's house, calling up in the morn, that would be the day your friendship ended.

You tested it once. You stayed away for a whole week. Ralph never called. It was as if you had died, and no one came to your funeral.

When you saw Ralph at school, there was no surprise, no query, not even the faintest lint of curiosity to be picked off your coat. Where *were* you, Doug? I need someone to beat. Where you *been,* Doug, I got no one to *pinch!*

Add all the sins up. But especially think on the last:

He never came to my house. He never sang up to my early-morning bed or tossed a wedding rice of gravel on the clear panes to call me down to joy and summer days.

And for this last thing, Ralph Underhill, I thought, sitting in the train at four in the morning, as the storm faded, and I found tears in my eyes, for this last and final thing, for that I shall kill you tomorrow night.

Murder, I thought, after thirty-six years. Why, God, you're madder than Ahab.

The train wailed. We ran cross-country like a mechanical Greek Fate carried by a black metal Roman Fury.

They say you can't go home again.

That is a lie.

If you are lucky and time it right, you arrive at sunset when the old town is filled with yellow light.

I got off the train and walked up through Green Town and looked at the courthouse, burning with sunset light. Every tree was hung with gold doubloons of color. Every roof and coping and bit of gingerbread was purest brass and ancient gold.

I sat in the courthouse square with dogs and old men until the sun had set and Green Town was dark. I wanted to savor Ralph Underhill's death.

No one in history had ever done a crime like this.

I would stay, kill, depart, a stranger among strangers.

How would anyone dare to say, finding Ralph Underhill's body on his doorstep, that a boy aged twelve, arriving on a kind of Time Machine train, traveled out of hideous self-contempt, had gunned down the Past? It was beyond all reason. I was safe in my pure insanity.

Finally, at eight-thirty on this cool October night, I walked across town, past the ravine.

I never doubted Ralph would still be there.

People do, after all, move away. . . .

I turned down Park Street and walked two hundred yards to a single streetlamp and looked across. Ralph Underhill's white two-story Victorian house waited for me.

And I could feel him *in* it.

He was there, forty-eight years old, even as I felt myself here, forty-eight, and full of an old and tired and self-devouring spirit.

I stepped out of the light, opened my suitcase, put the pistol in my right-hand coat pocket, shut the case, and hid it in the bushes where, later, I would grab it and walk down into the ravine and across town to the train.

I walked across the street and stood before his house and it was the same house I had stood before thirty-six years ago. There were the windows upon which I had hurled those spring bouquets of rock in love and total giving. There were the sidewalks, spotted with firecracker burn marks from ancient July Fourths when Ralph and I had just blown up the whole damned world, shrieking celebrations.

I walked up on the porch and saw on the mailbox in small letters: UNDERHILL.

What if his wife answers?

No, I thought, he himself, with absolute Greek-tragic perfection, will open the door and take the wound and almost gladly die for old crimes and minor sins somehow grown to crimes.

I rang the bell.

Will he know me, I wondered, after all this time? In the instant before the first shot, *tell* him your name. He must know who it is.

Silence.

I rang the bell again.

The doorknob rattled.

I touched the pistol in my pocket, my heart hammering, but did not take it out.

The door opened.

Ralph Underhill stood there.

He blinked, gazing out at me.

"Ralph?" I said.

"Yes—?" he said.

We stood there, riven, for what could not have been more than five seconds. But, O Christ, many things happened in those five swift seconds.

I saw Ralph Underhill.

I saw him clearly.

And I had not seen him since I was twelve.

Then, he had towered over me to pummel and beat and scream.

Now he was a little old man.

I am five foot eleven.

But Ralph Underhill had not grown much from his twelfth year on.

The man who stood before me was no more than five feet two inches tall.

I *towered* over him.

I gasped. I stared. I saw more.

I was forty-eight years old.

But Ralph Underhill, forty-eight, had lost most of his hair, and what remained was threadbare gray, black and white. He looked sixty or sixty-five.

I was in good health.

Ralph Underhill was waxen pale. There was a knowledge of sickness in his face. He had traveled in some sunless land. He had a ravaged and sunken look. His breath smelled of funeral flowers.

All this, perceived, was like the storm of the night before, gathering all its lightnings and thunders into one bright concussion. We stood in the explosion.

So this is what I came for? I thought. This, then, is the truth. This dreadful instant in time. Not to pull out the weapon. *Not* to kill. No, no. But simply—

To see Ralph Underhill as he *is* in this hour.

That's all.

Just to be here, stand here, and look at him as he has become.

Ralph Underhill lifted one hand in a kind of gesturing wonder. His lips trembled. His eyes flew up and down my body, his mind measured this giant who shadowed his door. At last his voice, so small, so frail, blurted out:

"Doug—?"

I recoiled.

"Doug?" he gasped, "is that *you?*"

I hadn't expected that. People don't remember! They can't! Across the years? Why would he know, bother, summon up, recognize, call?

I had a wild thought that what had happened to Ralph Underhill was that after I left town, half of his life had collapsed. I had been the center of his world, someone to attack, beat, pummel, bruise. His whole life had cracked by my simple act of walking away thirty-six years ago.

Nonsense! Yet, some small crazed mouse of wisdom scuttered about my brain and screeched what it knew: You needed Ralph, but, *more!* he needed *you!* And you did the only unforgivable, the wounding, thing! You vanished.

"Doug?" he said again, for I was silent there on the porch with my hands at my sides. "Is that you?"

This was the moment I had come for.

At some secret blood level, I had always known I would not use the weapon. I had brought it with me, yes, but Time had gotten here before me, and age, and smaller, more terrible deaths. . . .

Bang.

Six shots through the heart.

But I didn't use the pistol. I only whispered the sound of the shots with my mouth. With each whisper, Ralph Underhill's face aged another ten years. By the time I reached the last shot he was one hundred and ten years old.

"Bang," I whispered. "Bang. Bang. Bang. Bang. Bang."

His body shook with the impact.

"You're dead. Oh, God, Ralph, you're dead."

I turned and walked down the steps and reached the street before he called:

"Doug, is that *you?*"

I did not answer, walking.

"Answer me?" he cried, weakly. "Doug! Doug Spaulding, is that you? Who is that? Who are you?"

I got my suitcase and walked down into the cricket night and darkness of the ravine and across the bridge and up the stairs, going away.

"Who is that?" I heard his voice wail a last time.

A long way off, I looked back.

All the lights were on all over Ralph Underhill's house. It was as if he had gone around and put them all on after I left.

On the other side of the ravine I stopped on the lawn in front of the house where I had been born.

Then I picked up a few bits of gravel and did the thing that had never been done, ever in my life.

I tossed the few bits of gravel up to tap that window where I had lain every morning of my first twelve years. I called my own name. I called me down in friendship to play in some long summer that no longer was.

I stood waiting just long enough for my other young self to come down to join me.

Then swiftly, fleeing ahead of the dawn, we ran out of Green Town and back, thank you, dear Christ, back toward Now and Today for the rest of my life.

Punishment Without Crime

"You wish to kill your wife?" said the dark man at the desk.

"Yes. No . . . not exactly. I mean . . ."

"Name?"

"Hers or mine?"

"Yours."

"George Hill."

"Address?"

"Eleven South St. James, Glenview."

The man wrote this down, emotionlessly. "Your wife's name?"

"Katherine."

"Age?"

"Thirty-one."

Then came a swift series of questions. Color of hair, eyes, skin, favorite perfume, texture and size index. "Have you a dimensional photo of her? A tape recording of her voice? Ah, I see you do. Good. Now—"

An hour later, George Hill was perspiring.

"That's all." The dark man arose and scowled. "You still want to go through with it."

"Yes."

"Sign here."

He signed.

"You know this is illegal?"

"Yes."

"And that we're in no way responsible for what happens to you as a result of your request?"

"For God's sake!" cried George. "You've kept me long enough. Let's get on!"

The man smiled faintly. "It'll take nine hours to prepare the marionette of your wife. Sleep awhile, it'll help your nerves. The third mirror room on your left is unoccupied."

George moved in a slow numbness to the mirror room. He lay on the blue velvet cot, his body pressure causing the mirrors in the ceiling to whirl. A soft voice sang, "Sleep . . . sleep . . . sleep . . ."

George murmured, "Katherine, I didn't want to come here. You forced me into it. You made me do it. God, I wish I weren't here. I wish I could go back. I don't want to kill you."

The mirrors glittered as they rotated softly.

He slept.

He dreamed he was forty-one again, he and Katie running on a green hill somewhere with a picnic lunch, their helicopter beside them. The wind blew Katie's hair in golden strands and she was laughing. They kissed and held hands, not eating. They read poems; it seemed they were always reading poems.

Other scenes. Quick changes of color, in flight. He and Katie flying over Greece and Italy and Switzerland, in that clear, long autumn of 1997! Flying and never stopping!

And then—nightmare. Katie and Leonard Phelps. George cried out in his sleep. How had it happened? Where had Phelps sprung from? Why had he interfered? Why couldn't life be simple and good? Was it the difference in age? George touching fifty, and Katie so young, so very young. Why, why?

The scene was unforgettably vivid. Leonard Phelps and Katherine in a green park beyond the city. George himself appearing on a path only in time to see the kissing of their mouths.

The rage. The struggle. The attempt to kill Leonard Phelps.

More days, more nightmares.

George Hill awoke, weeping.

"Mr. Hill, we're ready for you now."

Hill arose clumsily. He saw himself in the high and now-silent mirrors, and he looked every one of his years. It had been a wretched error. Better men than he had taken young wives only to have them dissolve away in their hands like sugar crystals under water. He eyed himself, monstrously. A little too much stomach. A little too much chin. Somewhat too much pepper in the hair and not enough in the limbs . . .

The dark man led him to a room.

George Hill gasped. "This is *Katie's* room!"

"We try to have everything perfect."

"It *is*, to the last detail!"

George Hill drew forth a signed check for ten thousand dollars. The man departed with it.

The room was silent and warm.

George sat and felt for the gun in his pocket. A lot of money. But rich men can afford the luxury of cathartic murder. The violent unviolence. The death without death. The murder without murdering. He felt better. He was suddenly calm. He watched the door. This was a thing he had anticipated for six months and now it was to be ended. In a moment the beautiful robot, the stringless marionette, would appear, and . . .

"Hello, George."

"Katie!"

He whirled.

"Katie." He let his breath out.

She stood in the doorway behind him. She was dressed in a feather-soft green gown. On her feet were woven gold-twine sandals. Her hair was bright about her throat and her eyes were blue and clear.

He did not speak for a long while. "You're beautiful," he said at last, shocked.

"How else could I be?"

His voice was slow and unreal. "Let me look at you."

He put out his vague hands like a sleepwalker. His heart pounded sluggishly. He moved forward as if walking under a deep pressure of water. He walked around and around her, touching her.

"Haven't you seen enough of me in all these years?"

"Never enough," he said, and his eyes were filled with tears.

"What did you want to talk to me about?"

"Give me time, please, a little time." He sat down weakly and put his trembling hands to his chest. He blinked. "It's incredible. Another nightmare. How did they *make* you?"

"We're not allowed to talk of that; it spoils the illusion."

"It's magic!"

"Science."

Her touch was warm. Her fingernails were perfect as seashells. There was no seam, no flaw. He looked upon her. He remembered again the words they had read so often in the good days. *Thou art fair, my love. Behold, thou art fair; thou hast doves' eyes within thy locks. Thy lips are like a thread of scarlet. And thy speech is comely. Thy two breasts are like two young roes that are twins, which feed among the lilies. There is no spot in thee.*

"George?"

"What?" His eyes were cold glass.

He wanted to kiss her lips.

Honey and milk are under thy tongue.

And the smell of thy garments is like the smell of Lebanon.

"George."

A vast humming. The room began to whirl.

"Yes, yes, a moment, a moment." He shook his humming head.

How beautiful are thy feet with shoes, O prince's daughter! The joints of thy thighs are like jewels, the work of the hands of a cunning workman. . . .

"How did they do it?" he cried. In so short a time. Nine hours, while he slept. Had they melted gold, fixed delicate watch springs, diamonds, glitter, confetti, rich rubies, liquid silver, copper thread? Had metal insects spun her hair? Had they poured yellow fire in molds and set it to freeze?

"No," she said. "If you talk that way, I'll go."

"Don't!"

"Come to business, then," she said, coldly. "You want to talk to me about Leonard."

"Give me time, I'll get to it."

"Now," she insisted.

He knew no anger. It had washed out of him at her appearance. He felt childishly dirty.

"Why did you come to see me?" She was not smiling.

"Please."

"I insist. Wasn't it about Leonard? You know I love him, don't you?"

"Stop it!" He put his hands to his ears.

She kept at him. "You know, I spend all of my time with him now. Where you and I used to go, now Leonard and I stay. Remember the picnic green on Mount Verde? We were there last week. We flew to Athens a month ago, with a case of champagne."

He licked his lips. "You're not guilty, you're *not.*" He rose and held her wrists. "You're fresh, you're not her. She's guilty, not you. You're different!"

"On the contrary," said the woman. "I *am* her. I can act only as she acts. No part of me is alien to her. For all intents and purposes we are one."

"But you did not do what she has done!"

"I did all those things. I kissed him."

"You can't have, you're just born!"

"Out of her past and from your mind."

"Look," he pleaded, shaking her to gain her attention. "Isn't there some way, can't I—pay more money? Take you away with me? We'll go to Paris or Stockholm or any place you like!"

She laughed. "The marionettes only rent. They never sell."

"But I've money!"

"It was tried, long ago. It leads to insanity. It's not possible. Even this much is illegal, you *know* that. We exist only through governmental sufferance."

"All I want is to live with you, Katie."

"That can never be, because I am Katie, every bit of me is her. We do not want competition. Marionettes can't leave the premises; dissection might reveal our secrets. Enough of this. I warned you, we mustn't speak of these things. You'll spoil the illusion. You'll feel frustrated when you leave. You paid your money, now do what you came to do."

"I don't want to kill you."

"One part of you does. You're walling it in, you're trying not to let it out."

He took the gun from his pocket. "I'm an old fool, I should never have come. You're so beautiful."

"I'm going to see Leonard tonight."

"Don't talk."

"We're flying to Paris in the morning."

"You heard what I said!"

"And then to Stockholm." She laughed sweetly and caressed his chin. "My little fat man."

Something began to stir in him. His face grew pale. He knew what was happening. The hidden anger and revulsion and hatred in him were sending out faint pulses of thought. And the delicate telepathic web in her wondrous head was receiving the death impulse. The marionette. The invisible strings. He himself manipulating her body.

"Plump, odd little man, who once was so fair."

"Don't," he said.

"Old while I am only thirty-one, ah, George, you were blind, working years to give me time to fall in love again. Don't you think Leonard is lovely?"

He raised the gun blindly.

"Katie."

"*His head is as the most fine gold—*" she whispered.

"Katie, don't!" he screamed.

"*His locks are bushy and black as a raven, his hands are as gold rings set with the beryl!*"

How could she speak those words! It was in *his* mind, how could *she* mouth it!

"Katie, don't make me do this!"

"*His cheeks are as a bed of spices,*" she murmured, eyes closed, moving about the room softly. "*His belly is as bright ivory overlaid with sapphires; his legs are as pillars of marble—*"

"Katie!" he shrieked.

"*His mouth is most sweet—*"

One shot.

"*—this is my beloved—*"

Another shot.

She fell.

"Katie, Katie, Katie!"

Four more times he pumped bullets into her body.

She lay shuddering. Her senseless mouth clicked wide and some insanely warped mechanism had caused her to repeat again and again, "Beloved, beloved, beloved, beloved, beloved . . ."

George Hill fainted.

———•———

He awakened to a cool cloth on his brow.

"It's all over," said the dark man.

"Over?" George Hill whispered.

The dark man nodded.

George Hill looked weakly down at his hands. They had been covered with blood. When he fainted he had dropped to the floor. The last thing he remembered was the feeling of the real blood pouring upon his hands in a freshet.

His hands were now clean washed.

"I've got to leave," said George Hill.

"If you feel capable."

"I'm all right." He got up. "I'll go to Paris now, start over. I'm not to try to phone Katie or anything, am I."

"Katie is dead."

"Yes. I killed her, didn't I? God, the blood, it was *real!*"

"We are proud of that touch."

He went down in the elevator to the street. It was raining, and he wanted to walk for hours. The anger and destruction were purged away. The memory was so terrible that he would never wish to kill again. Even if the real Katie were to appear before him now, he would only thank God, and fall senselessly to his knees. She was dead now. He had had his way. He had broken the law and no one would know.

The rain fell cool on his face. He must leave immediately, while the purge was in effect. After all, what was the use of such purges if one took up the old threads? The marionettes' function was primarily to prevent actual crime. If you wanted to kill, hit, or torture someone, you took it out on one of those unstringed automatons. It wouldn't do to return to the apartment now. Katie might be there. He wanted only to think of her as dead, a thing attended to in deserving fashion.

He stopped at the curb and watched the traffic flash by. He took deep breaths of the good air and began to relax.

"Mr. Hill?" said a voice at his elbow.

"Yes?"

A manacle was snapped to Hill's wrist. "You're under arrest."

"But—"

"Come along. Smith, take the other men upstairs, make the arrests!"

"You can't do this to me," said George Hill.

"For murder, yes, we can."

Thunder sounded in the sky.

It was eight-fifteen at night. It had been raining for ten days. It rained now on the prison walls. He put his hands out to feel the drops gather in pools on his trembling palms.

A door clanged and he did not move but stood with his hands in the rain. His lawyer looked up at him on his chair and said, "It's all over. You'll be executed tonight."

George Hill listened to the rain.

"She wasn't real. I didn't kill her."

"It's the law, anyhow. You remember. The others are sentenced, too. The president of Marionettes, Incorporated, will die at midnight. His three assistants will die at one. You'll go about one-thirty."

"Thanks," said George. "You did all you could. I guess it was murder, no matter how you look at it, image or not. The idea was there, the plot and the plan were there. It lacked only the real Katie herself."

"It's a matter of timing, too," said the lawyer. "Ten years ago you wouldn't have got the death penalty. Ten years from now you wouldn't, either. But they had to have an object case, a whipping boy. The use of marionettes has grown so in the last year it's fantastic. The public must be scared out of it, and scared badly. God knows where it would all wind up if it went on. There's the spiritual side of it, too, where does life begin or end? are the robots alive or dead? More than one church has been split up the seams on the question. If they aren't alive, they're the next thing to it; they react, they even think. You know the 'live robot' law that was passed two months ago; you come under that. Just bad timing, is all, bad timing."

"The government's right. I see that now," said George Hill.

"I'm glad you understand the attitude of the law."

"Yes. After all, they can't let murder be legal. Even if it's done with machines and telepathy and wax. They'd be hypocrites to let me get away with my crime. For it *was* a crime. I've felt guilty about it ever since. I've felt the need of punishment. Isn't that odd? That's how society gets to you. It makes you feel guilty even when you see no reason to be...."

"I have to go now. Is there anything you want?"

"Nothing, thanks."

"Good-bye then, Mr. Hill."

The door shut.

George Hill stood up on the chair, his hands twisting together, wet, outside the window bars. A red light burned in the wall suddenly. A voice came over the audio: "Mr. Hill, your wife is here to see you."

He gripped the bars.

She's dead, he thought.

"Mr. Hill?" asked the voice.

"She's dead. I killed her."

"Your wife is waiting in the anteroom, will you see her?"

"I saw her fall, I shot her, I saw her fall dead!"

"Mr. Hill, do you hear me?"

"Yes!" he shouted, pounding at the wall with his fists. "I hear you. I hear you! She's dead, she's dead, can't she let me be! I killed her, I won't see her, she's dead!"

A pause. "Very well, Mr. Hill," murmured the voice.

The red light winked off.

Lightning flashed through the sky and lit his face. He pressed his hot cheeks to the cold bars and waited, while the rain fell. After a long time, a door opened somewhere onto the street and he saw two caped figures emerge from the prison office below. They paused under an arc light and glanced up.

It was Katie. And beside her, Leonard Phelps.

"Katie!"

Her face turned away. The man took her arm. They hurried across the avenue in the black rain and got into a low car.

"Katie!" He wrenched at the bars. He screamed and beat and pulled at the concrete ledge. "She's alive! Guard! Guard! I saw her! She's not dead, I didn't kill her, now you can let me out! I didn't murder anyone, it's all a joke, a mistake, I saw her, I saw her! Katie, come back, tell them, Katie, say you're alive! Katie!"

The guards came running.

"You can't kill me! I didn't do anything! Katie's alive, I saw her!"

"We saw her, too, sir."

"But let me free, then! Let me free!" It was insane. He choked and almost fell.

"We've been through all that, sir, at the trial."

"It's not fair!" He leaped up and clawed at the window, bellowing.

The car drove away, Katie and Leonard inside it. Drove away to Paris and Athens and Venice and London next spring and Stockholm next summer and Vienna in the fall.

"Katie, come back, you can't *do* this to me!"

The red taillight of the car dwindled in the cold rain. Behind him, the guards moved forward to take hold of him while he screamed.

Getting Through Sunday Somehow

Sunday in Dublin.

The words are Doom itself.

Sunday in Dublin.

Drop such words from a cliff and they never strike bottom. They just fall through emptiness toward five in the gray afternoon.

Sunday in Dublin. How to get through it somehow.

Sound the funeral bells. Yank the covers up over your ears. Hear the hiss of the black feathered wreath as it rustles, hung on your silent door. Listen to those empty streets below your hotel room waiting to gulp you if you venture forth before noon. Feel the mist sliding its wet flannel tongue under the window ledges, licking hotel roofs, its great bulk dripping of ennui.

Sunday, I thought. Dublin. The pubs shut tight save for a fleeting hour. The cinemas sold out two or three weeks in advance. Nothing to do but perhaps go stare at the uriny lions at the Phoenix Park Zoo, at the vultures looking like they'd fallen, covered with glue, into the rag-pickers' bin. Wander by the River Liffey, see the fog-colored waters. Wander in the alleys, see the Liffey-colored skies.

No, I thought wildly, stay in bed, wake me at sunset, feed me high tea, tuck me in again, good night, all!

But I staggered up, a hero, under the crashing blow of Sunday, shaved, and in a faint panic at noon considered the day ahead from the corner of my eye. There it lay, a deserted corridor of hours, colored like the upper side of my tongue on a dim morn. Even God must be bored with days like this, in northern lands. I could not resist thinking of Sicily, where any Sunday is a fete in regalia, a celebratory fireworks parade as springtime flocks of chickens and humans strut and pringle the warm pancake-batter alleys, waving their combs, their hands, their feet, tilting their sun-blazed eyes, while music in free gifts leaps or is thrown from each never-shut window.

But Dublin! Dublin! Ah, you great dead brute of a city! I thought, peering from my window at the snowed-on, sooted-over corpse. Here are two coins for your eyes!

Then I opened the door and stepped out into all of that criminal Sunday which awaited only me.

I shut another door. I stood in the deep silence of a Sabbath pub. I moved noiselessly to whisper for the best drink and stood a long while nursing my soul. Nearby, an old man was similarly engaged in finding the pattern of his life in the depths of his glass. Ten minutes must have passed, when, very slowly, the old man raised his head to stare deep beyond the fly specks on the mirror, beyond me, beyond himself.

"What have I done," he mourned, "for a single mortal soul this day? Nothing! And that's why I feel so terrible destroyed."

I waited.

"The older I get," said the man, "the less I do for people. The less I do, the more I feel a prisoner at the bar. Smash and grab, that's me!"

"Well—" said I.

"No!" cried the old man. "It's an awesome responsibility when the world runs to hand you things. For an instance: sunsets. Everything pink and gold, looking like those melons they ship up from Spain. That's a gift, ain't it?"

"It is."

"Well, who do you thank for sunsets? And don't drag the Lord in the bar, now! Any remarks to Him are too quiet. I mean someone to grab and slap their back and say thanks for the fine early light this morn, boyo, or, much obliged for the look of them damn wee flowers by the road this day, and the grass laying about in the wind. Those are gifts, too, who'll deny it?"

"Not me," I said.

"Have you ever waked middle of the night and felt summer coming on for the first time, through the window, after the long cold? Did you shake your wife and tell her your gratitude? No, you lay there, a clod, chortling to yourself alone, you and the new weather! Do you see the pattern I'm at, now?"

"Clearly," I said.

"Then ain't you horribly guilty, yourself? Don't the burden make you hunchback? All the lovely things you got from life and no penny down? Ain't they hid in your dark flesh somewhere, lighting up your soul, them fine summers and easy falls, or maybe just the clean taste of stout here, all gifts, and you feeling the fool to go thank any mortal man for your fortune. What befalls chaps like us, I ask, who coin up all their gratitude for a lifetime, and spend none of it, misers that we be? One day, don't we crack down the beam and show the dry rot? Some night, don't we smother?"

"I never thought . . ."

"Think, man!" he cried. "Before it's too late. You're American, ain't you, and young? Got the same natural gifts as me? But for lack of humbly thanking someone somewhere somehow you're getting round in the shoulder and short in the breath. Act, man, before you're the walking dead!"

With this he lapsed quietly into the final half of his reverie, with the Guinness lapping a soft lace mustache slowly along his upper lip.

I walked from the pub into the Sunday weather.

I stood looking at the gray stone streets and the gray stone clouds, watching the frozen people trudge by exhaling gray funeral plumes from their wintry mouths, dressed in their smoke-colored suits and soot-black coats, and I felt the white grow out in my hair.

Days like this, I thought, all the things you never did catch up with you, unravel your laces, itch your beard. God help any man who hasn't paid his debts this day.

Drearily, I turned like a weathercock in a slow wind, started my remote feet back toward the hotel.

Right then, it happened.

I stopped. I stood very still. I listened.

For it seemed the wind had shifted and now blew from the west country and brought with it a prickling and tingling: the strum of a harp.

"Well," I whispered.

As if a cork had been pulled, all the heavy gray sea waters vanished roaring down a hole in my shoe; I felt my sadness go.

And around the corner I went.

And there sat a little woman, not half so big as her harp, her hands held out in the shivering strings like a child feeling a fine clear rain.

The harp threads flurried; the sounds dissolved like shudders of disturbed water nudging a shore. "Danny Boy" leaped out of the harp. "Wearin' of the Green" sprang after, full-clothed. Then "Limerick Is My Town, Sean Liam Is My Name" and "The Loudest Wake That Ever Was." The harp sound was the kind of thing you feel when champagne, poured in a full big glass, prickles your eyelids, sprays soft on your cheeks.

My mouth was pinned high at both corners. Spanish oranges bloomed in my cheeks. My breath fifed my nostrils. My feet minced, hidden, a secret dancing in my motionless shoes.

The harp played "Yankee Doodle."

Had the lady seen me stand near with my idiot fever? No, I thought, coincidence.

And then I turned sad again.

For look, I thought, she doesn't see her harp. She doesn't hear her music!

True. Her hands, all alone, jumped and frolicked on the air, picked and pringled the strings, two ancient spiders busy at webs quickly built, then, torn by wind, rebuilt. She let her fingers play abandoned, to themselves, while her face turned this way and that, as if she lived in a nearby house and need only glance out on occasion to see her hands had come to no harm.

"Ah . . ." My soul sighed in me.

Then:

Here's your chance! I almost shouted. Good God, of course!

But I held to myself and let her reap out the last full falling sheaves of "Yankee Doodle."

Then, heartbeat in throat, I said:

"You play beautifully."

One hundred pounds melted from my body.

The woman nodded and began "Summer on the Shore," her fingers weaving mantillas from mere breath.

"You play very beautifully indeed," I said.

Another seventy pounds fell from my limbs.

"When you play forty years," she said, "you don't notice."

"You play well enough to be in a theater."

"Be off with you!" Two sparrows pecked in the shuttling loom. "Why should I think of orchestras and bands?"

"It's indoors work," I said.

"My father," she said, while her hands went away and returned, "made this harp, played it fine, taught me how. God's sake, he said, keep out from under roofs!"

The old woman blinked, remembering. "Play out back, in front, around the sides of theaters, Da said, but don't play in where the music gets snuffed. Might as well harp in a coffin!"

"Doesn't this rain hurt your instrument?"

"It's inside places hurt harps with heat and steam, Da said. Keep it out, let it breathe, take on fine tones and timbres from the air. Besides, Da said, when people buy tickets, each thinks it's in him to yell if you don't play up, down, sideways, for him alone. Shy off from that, Da said; they'll call you handsome one year, brute the next. Get where they'll pass on by; if they like your song—hurrah! Those that don't will run from your life. That way, girl, you'll meet just those who lean from natural bent in your direction. Why closet yourself with demon fiends when you can live in the streets' fresh wind with abiding angels? But I *do* go on. Ah, now, why?"

She peered at me for the first time, like someone come from a dark room, squinting.

"Who are you?" she asked. "You set my tongue loose! What're you up to?"

"Up to no good until a minute ago when I came around this corner," I said. "Ready to knock over Nelson's pillar. Ready to pick a theater queue and brawl along it, half weeping and half blasphemous . . ."

"I don't see you doing it." Her hands wove out another yard of song. "What changed your mind?"

"You," I said.

I might have fired a cannon in her face.

"Me?" she said.

"You picked the day up off the stones, gave it a whack, set it running with a yell again."

"*I* did that?"

For the first time, I heard a few notes missing from the tune.

"Or, if you like, those hands of yours that go about their work without your knowing."

"The clothes must be washed, so you wash them."

I felt the iron weights gather in my limbs.

"Don't!" I said. "Why should we, coming by, be happy with this thing, and not you?"

She cocked her head; her hands moved slower still.

"And why should you bother with the likes of *me?*"

I stood before her, and could I tell what the man told me in the lulling quiet of Dooley's Pub? Could I mention the hill of beauty that had risen to fill my soul through a lifetime, and myself with a toy sand-shovel doling it back to the world in dribs and drabs? Should I list all my debts to people on stages and silver screens who made me laugh or cry or just come alive, but no one in the dark theater to turn to and dare shout, "If you ever need help, I'm your friend!" Should I recall for her the man on a bus ten years before who chuckled so easy and light from the last seat that the sound of him melted everyone else to laughing warm and rollicking off out the doors, but with no one brave enough to pause and touch the man's arm and say, "Oh, man, you've favored us this night; Lord bless you!" Could I tell how she was just one part of a great account long owed and due? No, none of this could I tell. So I put it this way:

"Imagine something."

"I'm ready," she said.

"Imagine you're an American article writer, looking for material, far from home, wife, children, friends, in a hard winter, in a cheerless hotel, on a bad gray day with naught but broken glass, chewed tobacco, and sooty snow in your soul. Imagine you're walking in the damned winter streets and turn a corner, and there's this little woman with a golden harp and everything she plays is another season, autumn, spring, summer, coming, going in a free-for-all. And the ice melts, the fog lifts, the wind burns with June, and ten years shuck off your life. Imagine, if you please."

She stopped her tune.

She was shocked at the sudden silence.

"You *are* daft," she said.

"Imagine you're me," I said. "Going back to my hotel now. And on my way I'd like to hear anything, anything at all. Play. And when you play, walk off around the corner and listen."

She put her hands to the strings and paused, working her mouth. I waited. At last she sighed, she moaned. Then suddenly she cried:

"Go on!"

"What . . . ?"

"You've made me all thumbs! Look! You've spoilt it!"

"I just wanted to thank—"

"—me behind!" she cried. "What a clod, what a brute! Mind your business! Do your work! Let be, man! Ah, these poor fingers, ruint, ruint!"

She stared at them and at me with a terrible glaring fixity.

"Get!" she shouted.

I ran around the corner in despair.

There! I thought, you've done it! really done it! By thanks destroyed, that's her story. And yours, too, you must live with it! Fool, why didn't you keep your mouth shut?

I sank, I leaned, against a building. A minute must have ticked by.

Please, woman, I thought, come on. Play. Not for me. Play for yourself. Forget what I said! *Please.*

I heard a few faint, tentative harp whispers.

Another pause.

Then, when the wind blew again, it brought the sound of her very slow playing.

The song was an old one, and I knew the words. I said them to myself.

> *Tread lightly to the music,*
> *Nor bruise the tender grass,*
> *Life passes in the weather*
> *As the sand storms down the glass.*

Yes, I thought, go *on.*

> *Drift easy in the shadows,*
> *Bask lazy in the sun,*
> *Give thanks for thirsts and quenches,*
> *For dines and wines and wenches,*
> *Give thought to life soon over,*
> *Tread softly on the clover,*
> *So bruise not any lover.*
> *So exit from the living,*
> *Salute and make thanksgiving,*
> *Then sleep when all is done,*
> *That sleep so dearly won.*

Why, I thought, how wise the old woman is.
Tread lightly to the music.
And I'd almost squashed her with praise.
So bruise not any lover.
And she was covered with bruises from my kind thoughtlessness.

But now with a song that taught more than I could say, she was soothing herself.

I waited until she was well into the third chorus before I walked by again, tipping my hat.

But her eyes were shut and she was listening to what her hands were up to, moving in the strings like the fresh hands of a very young girl who has first known rain and washes her palms in its clear waterfalls.

She had gone through caring not at all, and then caring too much, and was now busy caring just the right way.

The corners of her mouth were pinned up, gently.

A close call, I thought. Very close.

I left them like two friends met in the street, the harp and herself.

I ran for the hotel to thank her the only way I knew how: to do my own work and do it well.

But on the way I stopped at Dooley's.

The music was still being treaded lightly and the clover was still being treaded softly, and no lover at all was being bruised as I let the pub door hush and looked all around for the man whose hand I most wanted to shake.

Drink Entire:
Against the Madness
of Crowds

It was one of those nights that are so damned hot you lie flat out lost until 2:00 A.M., then sway upright, baste yourself with your own sour brine, and stagger down into the great bake-oven subway where the lost trains shriek in.

"Hell," whispered Will Morgan.

And hell it was, with a lost army of beast people wandering the night from the Bronx on out to Coney and back, hour on hour, searching for sudden inhalations of salt ocean wind that might make you gasp with Thanksgiving.

Somewhere, God, somewhere in Manhattan or beyond was a cool wind. By dawn, it *must* be found. . . .

"Damn!"

Stunned, he saw maniac tides of advertisements squirt by with toothpaste smiles, his own advertising ideas pursuing him the whole length of the hot night island.

The train groaned and stopped.

Another train stood on the opposite track.

Incredible. There in the open train window across the way sat Old Ned Amminger. Old? They were the same age, forty, but . . .

Will Morgan threw his window up.

"Ned, you son of a bitch!"

"Will, you bastard. You ride late like this often?"

"Every damn hot night since 1946!"

"Me, too! Glad to see you!"

"Liar!"

Each vanished in a shriek of steel.

God, thought Will Morgan, two men who hate each other, who work not ten feet apart grinding their teeth over the next step up the ladder, knock together in Dante's Inferno here under a melting city at 3:00 A.M. Hear our voices echo, fading:

"Liar . . . !"

Half an hour later, in Washington Square, a cool wind touched his brow. He followed it into an alley where . . .

The temperature dropped ten degrees.

"Hold on," he whispered.

The wind smelled of the Ice House when he was a boy and stole cold crystals to rub on his cheeks and stab inside his shirt with shrieks to kill the heat.

The cool wind led him down the alley to a small shop where a sign read:

MELISSA TOAD, WITCH

LAUNDRY SERVICE:

CHECK YOUR PROBLEMS HERE BY NINE A.M.

PICK THEM UP, FRESH-CLEANED, AT DUSK

There was a smaller sign:

SPELLS, PHILTRES AGAINST DREAD CLIMATES, HOT OR COLD.
POTIONS TO INSPIRE EMPLOYERS AND ASSURE PROMOTIONS.
SALVES, UNGUENTS & MUMMY-DUSTS RENDERED DOWN FROM
ANCIENT CORPORATION HEADS. REMEDIES FOR NOISE. EMOL-
LIENTS FOR GASEOUS OR POLLUTED AIRS. LOTIONS FOR PARA-
NOID TRUCK DRIVERS. MEDICINES TO BE TAKEN BEFORE TRYING
TO SWIM OFF THE NEW YORK DOCKS.

A few bottles were strewn in the display window, labeled:

PERFECT MEMORY.
BREATH OF SWEET APRIL WIND.
SILENCE AND THE TREMOR OF FINE BIRDSONG.

He laughed and stopped.

For the wind blew cool and creaked a door. And again there was the memory of frost from the white Ice House grottoes of childhood, a world cut from winter dreams and saved on into August.

"Come in," a voice whispered.

The door glided back.

Inside, a cold funeral awaited him.

A six-foot-long block of clear dripping ice rested like a giant February remembrance upon three sawhorses.

"Yes," he murmured. In his hometown-hardware-store window, a magician's wife, MISS I. SICKLE, had been stashed in an immense rectangle of ice melted to fit her calligraphy. There she slept the nights away, a Princess of Snow. Midnights, he and other boys snuck out to see her smile in her cold crystal sleep. They stood half the summer nights staring, four or five fiery-furnace boys of some fourteen years, hoping their red-hot gaze might melt the ice. . . .

The ice had never melted.

"Wait," he whispered. "Look . . ."

He took one more step within this dark night shop.

Lord, yes. There, in *this* ice! Weren't those the outlines where, only moments ago, a woman of snow napped away in cool night dreams? Yes. The ice was hollow and curved and lovely. But . . . the woman was gone. Where?

"Here," whispered the voice.

Beyond the bright cold funeral, shadows moved in a far corner.

"Welcome. Shut the door."

He sensed that she stood not far away in shadows. Her flesh, if you could touch it, would be cool, still fresh from her time within the dripping tomb of snow. If he just reached out his hand—

"What are you doing here?" her voice asked, gently.

"Hot night. Walking. Riding. Looking for a cool wind. I think I need help."

"You've come to the right place."

"But this is *mad!* I don't believe in psychiatrists. My friends hate me because I say Tinkerbell *and* Freud died twenty years back, with the circus. I don't believe in astrologers, numerologists, or palmistry quacks—"

"I don't read palms. But . . . give me your hand."

He put his hand out into the soft darkness.

Her fingers tapped his. It felt like the hand of a small girl who had just rummaged an icebox. He said:

"Your sign reads MELISSA TOAD, WITCH. What would a Witch be doing in New York in the summer of 1974?"

"You ever know a city needed a Witch more than New York does this year?"

"Yes. We've gone mad. But, *you?*"

"A Witch is born out of the true hungers of her time," she said. "I was born out of New York. The things that are most wrong here summoned me. Now you come, not knowing, to find me. Give me your other hand."

Though her face was only a ghost of cool flesh in the shadows, he felt her eyes move over his trembling palm.

"Oh, why did you wait so *long?*" she mourned. "It's almost too late."

"Too late for what?"

"To be saved. To take the gift that I can give."

His heart pounded. "*What* can you give me?"

"Peace," she said. "Serenity. Quietness in the midst of bedlam. I am a child of the poisonous wind that copulated with the East River on an oil-slick, garbage-infested midnight. I turn about on my own parentage. I inoculate against those very biles that brought me to light. I am a serum born of venoms. I am the antibody of all Time. I am the Cure. You die of the City, do you not? Manhattan is your punisher. Let me be your shield."

"How?"

"You would be my pupil. My protection could encircle you, like an invisible pack of hounds. The subway train would never violate your ear. Smog would never blight your lung or nostril or fever your vision. I could teach your tongue, at lunch, to taste the rich fields of Eden in the merest cut-rate too-ripe frankfurter. Water, sipped from your office cooler, would be a rare wine of a fine family. Cops, when you called, would answer. Taxis, off-duty rushing nowhere, would stop if you so much as blinked one eye. Theater tickets would appear if you stepped to a theater window. Traffic signals would change, at high noon, mind you! if you dared to drive your car from fifty-eighth down to the Square, and not one light red. Green all the way, if you go with me.

"If you go with me, our apartment will be a shadowed jungle glade full of bird cries and love calls from the first hot sour day of June till the last hour after Labor Day when the living dead, heat-beat, go mad on stopped trains coming back from the sea. Our rooms will be filled with crystal chimes. Our kitchen an Eskimo hut in July where we might share out a provender of Popsicles made of Mumm's and Château Lafite Rothschild. Our larder?—fresh apricots in August or February. Fresh orange juice each morning, cold milk at breakfast, cool kisses at four in the afternoon, my mouth always the flavor of chilled peaches, my body the taste of rimed plums. The flavor begins at the elbow, as Edith Wharton said.

"Any time you want to come home from the office the middle of a dreadful day, I will call your boss and it will be so. Soon after, you will be the boss and come home, anyway, for cold chicken, fruit wine punch, and me. Summer in the Virgin Isles. Autumns so ripe with promise you will indeed go lunatic in the right way. Winters, of course, will be the reverse. I will be your hearth. Sweet dog, lie there. I will fall upon you like snowflakes.

"In sum, everything will be given you. I ask little in return. Only your soul."

He stiffened and almost let go of her hand.

"Well, isn't that what you *expected* me to demand?" She laughed. "But souls can't be sold. They can only be lost and never found again. Shall I tell you what I really want from you?"

"Tell."

"Marry me," she said.

Sell me your soul, he thought, and did not say it.

But she read his eyes. "Oh, dear," she said. "Is that *so* much to ask? For all I give?"

"I've got to think it over!"

Without noticing, he had moved back one step.

Her voice was very sad. "If you have to think a thing over, it will never be. When you finish a book you know if you like it, yes? At the end of a play you are awake or asleep, yes? Well, a beautiful woman is a beautiful woman, isn't she, and a good life a good life?"

"Why won't you come out in the light? How do I know you're beautiful?"

"You can't know unless you step into the dark. Can't you tell by my voice? No? Poor man. If you don't trust me now, you can't have me, ever."

"I need time to think? I'll come back tomorrow night! What can twenty-four hours mean?"

"To someone your age, everything."

"I'm only forty!"

"I speak of your soul, and *that* is late."

"Give me one more night!"

"You'll take it, anyway, at your own risk."

"Oh, God, oh, God, oh, God, God," he said, shutting his eyes.

"I wish He could help you right now. You'd better go. You're an ancient child. Pity. Pity. Is your mother alive?"

"Dead ten years."

"No, alive," she said.

He backed off toward the door and stopped, trying to still his confused heart, trying to move his leaden tongue:

"How long have you been in this place?"

She laughed, with the faintest touch of bitterness.

"Three summers now. And, in those three years, only six men have come into my shop. Two ran immediately. Two stayed awhile but left. One came back a second time, and vanished. The sixth man finally had to admit, after three visits, he didn't Believe. You see, no one Believes a really all-encompassing and protective love when they see it clear. A farmboy might have stayed forever, in his simplicity, which is rain and wind and seed. A New Yorker? Suspects everything.

"Whoever, whatever, you are, O good sir, stay and milk the cow and put the fresh milk in the dim cooling shed under the shade of the oak tree which grows in my attic. Stay and pick the watercress to clean your teeth. Stay in the North Pantry with the scent of persimmons and kumquats and grapes. Stay and stop my tongue so I can cease talking this way. Stay and stop my mouth so I can't breathe. Stay, for I am weary of speech and must need love. Stay. Stay."

So ardent was her voice, so tremulous, so gentle, so sweet, that he knew he was lost if he did not run.

"Tomorrow night!" he cried.

His shoe struck something. There on the floor lay a sharp icicle fallen from the long block of ice.

He bent, seized the icicle, and ran.

The door *slammed*. The lights blinked out. Rushing, he could not see the sign: MELISSA TOAD, WITCH.

Ugly, he thought, running. A beast, he thought, she *must* be a beast and ugly. Yes, that's it! Lies! All of it, lies! She—

He collided with someone.

In the midst of the street, they gripped, they held, they stared. Ned Amminger! My God, it was Old Ned!

It was four in the morning, the air still white-hot. And here was Ned Amminger sleepwalking after cool winds, his clothes scrolled on his hot flesh in rosettes, his face dripping sweat, his eyes dead, his feet creaking in their hot baked leather shoes.

They swayed in the moment of collision.

A spasm of malice shook Will Morgan. He seized Old Ned Amminger, spun him about, and pointed him into the dark alley. Far off deep in there, had that shop-window light blinked *on* again? Yes!

"Ned! *That* way! Go *there!*"

Heat-blinded, dead-weary Old Ned Amminger stumbled off down the alley.

"Wait!" cried Will Morgan, regretting his malice.

But Amminger was gone.

In the subway, Will Morgan tasted the icicle.

It was Love. It was Delight. It was Woman.

By the time his train roared in, his hands were empty, his body rusted with perspiration. And the sweet taste in his mouth? Dust.

Seven A.M. and no sleep.

Somewhere a huge blast furnace opened its door and burned New York to ruins.

Get up, thought Will Morgan. Quick! Run to the Village!

For he remembered that sign:

LAUNDRY SERVICE: CHECK YOUR PROBLEMS
HERE BY NINE A.M.
PICK THEM UP, FRESH-CLEANED, AT NIGHT.

He did not go to the Village. He rose, showered, and went off into the furnace to lose his job forever.

He knew this as he rode up in the raving-hot elevator with Mr. Binns, the sunburned and furious personnel manager. Binns's eyebrows were jumping, his mouth worked over his teeth with unspoken curses. Beneath his suit, you could feel porcupines of boiled hair needling to the surface. By the time they reached the fortieth floor, Binns was anthropoid.

Around them, employees wandered like an Italian army coming to attend a lost war.

"Where's Old Amminger?" asked Will Morgan, staring at an empty desk.

"Called in sick. Heat prostration. Be here at noon," someone said.

Long before noon the water cooler was empty, and the air-conditioning system?—committed suicide at 11:32. Two hundred people became raw beasts chained to desks by windows which had been invented not to open.

At one minute to twelve, Mr. Binns, over the intercom, told them to line up by their desks. They lined up. They waited, swaying. The temperature stood at ninety-seven. Slowly, Binns began to stalk down the long line. A white-hot sizzle of invisible flies hung about him.

"All right, ladies and gentlemen," he said. "You all know there is a recession, no matter how happily the President of the United States put it. I would rather knife you in the stomach than stab you in the back. Now, as I move down the line, I will nod and whisper, 'You.' To those of you who hear this single word, turn, clean out your desks, and be gone. Four weeks' severance pay awaits you on the way out. Hold on! Someone's missing!"

"Old Ned Amminger," said Will Morgan, and bit his tongue.

"*Old* Ned?" said Mr. Binns, glaring. "Old? *Old?*"

Mr. Binns and Ned Amminger were exactly the same age. Mr. Binns waited, ticking.

"Ned," said Will Morgan, strangling on self-curses, "should be here—"

"Now," said a voice.

They all turned.

At the far end of the line, in the door, stood Old Ned or Ned Amminger. He looked at the assembly of lost souls, read destruction in Binns's face, flinched, but then slunk into line next to Will Morgan.

"All right," said Binns. "Here goes."

He began to move, whisper, move, whisper, move, whisper. Two people, four, then six turned to clean out their desks.

Will Morgan took a deep breath, held it, waited.

Binns came to a full stop in front of him.

Don't say it? thought Morgan. Don't!

"You," whispered Binns.

Morgan spun about and caught hold of his heaving desk. *You*, the word cracked in his head, *you!*

Binns stepped to confront Ned Amminger.

"Well, *old* Ned," he said.

Morgan, eyes shut, thought: Say it, say it to him, you're fired, Ned, *fired!*

"Old Ned," said Binns, lovingly.

Morgan shrank at the strange, the friendly, the sweet sound of Binns's voice.

An idle South Seas wind passed softly on the air. Morgan blinked and stood up, sniffing. The sun-blasted room was filled with scent of surf and cool white sand.

"Ned, why dear old Ned," said Mr. Binns, gently.

Stunned, Will Morgan waited. I am mad, he thought.

"Ned," said Mr. Binns, gently. "Stay with us. Stay on."
Then, swiftly: "That's all, everyone. Lunch!"

And Binns was gone and the wounded and dying were leaving the field. And Will Morgan turned at last to look full at Old Ned Amminger, thinking, Why, God, *why?*

And got his answer . . .

Ned Amminger stood there, not old, not young, but somehow in-between. And he was not the Ned Amminger who had leaned crazily out a hot train window last midnight or shambled in Washington Square at four in the morning.

This Ned Amminger stood quietly, as if hearing far green country sounds, wind and leaves and an amiable time which wandered in a fresh lake breeze.

The perspiration had dried on his fresh pink face. His eyes were not bloodshot but steady, blue, and quiet. He was an island oasis in this dead and unmoving sea of desks and typewriters which might start up and scream like electric insects. He stood watching the walking-dead depart. And he cared not. He was kept in a splendid and beautiful isolation within his own calm cool beautiful skin.

"No!" cried Will Morgan, and fled.

He didn't know where he was going until he found himself in the men's room frantically digging in the wastebasket.

He found what he knew he would find, a small bottle with the label:

DRINK ENTIRE: AGAINST THE MADNESS OF CROWDS.

Trembling, he uncorked it. There was the merest cold blue drop left inside. Swaying by the shut hot window, he tapped it to his tongue.

In the instant, his body felt as if he had leaped into a tidal wave of coolness. His breath gusted out in a fount of crushed and savored clover.

He gripped the bottle so hard it broke. He gasped, watching the blood.

The door opened. Ned Amminger stood there, looking in. He stayed only a moment, then turned and went out. The door shut.

A few moments later, Morgan, with the junk from his desk rattling in his briefcase, went down in the elevator.

Stepping out, he turned to thank the operator.

His breath must have touched the operator's face.

The operator smiled.

A wild, an incomprehensible, a loving, a *beautiful* smile!

The lights were out at midnight in the little alley, in the little shop. There was no sign in the window which said MELISSA TOAD, WITCH. There were no bottles.

He beat on the door for a full five minutes, to no answer. He kicked the door for another two minutes.

And at last, with a sigh, not wanting to, the door opened.

A very tired voice said: "Come in."

Inside he found the air only slightly cool. The huge ice slab, in which he had seen the phantom shape of a lovely woman, had dwindled, had lost a good half of its weight, and now was dripping steadily to ruin.

Somewhere in the darkness, the woman waited for him. But he sensed that she was clothed now, dressed and packed, ready to leave. He opened his mouth to cry out, to reach, but her voice stopped him:

"I warned you. You're too late."

"It's never too late!" he said.

"Last night it wouldn't have been. But in the last twenty hours, the last little thread snapped in you. I feel. I know. I tell. It's gone, gone, gone."

"What's gone, God damn it?"

"Why, your soul, of course. Gone. Eaten up. Digested. Vanished. You're empty. Nothing there."

He saw her hand reach out of darkness. It touched at his chest. Perhaps he imagined that her fingers passed through his ribs to probe about his lights, his lungs, his beating and pitiful heart.

"Oh, yes, gone," she mourned. "How sad. The city unwrapped you like a candy bar and ate you all up. You're nothing but a dusty milk bottle left on a tenement porch, a spider building a nest across the top. Traffic din pounded your marrow to dust. Subway sucked your breath like a cat sucks the soul of a babe. Vacuum cleaners got your brain. Alcohol dissolved the rest. Typewriters and computers took your final dregs in and out their tripes, printed you on paper, punched you in confettis, threw you down a sewer vent. TV scribbled you in nervous tics on old ghost screens. Your final bones will be carried off by a big angry bulldog crosstown bus holding you munched in its big rubber-lipped mouth door."

"No!" he cried. "I've changed my mind! Marry me! Marry—"

His voice cracked the ice tomb. It shattered on the floor behind him. The shape of the beautiful woman melted into the floor. Spinning about, he plunged into darkness.

He fell against the wall just as a panel slammed shut and locked.

It was no use screaming. He was alone.

At dusk in July, a year later, in the subway, he saw Ned Amminger for the first time in 365 days.

In all the grind and ricochet and pour of fiery lava as trains banged through, taking a billion souls to hell, Amminger stood as cool as mint leaves in green rain. Around him wax people melted. He waded in his own private trout stream.

"Ned!" cried Will Morgan, running up to seize his hand and pump it. "Ned, Ned! The best friend I ever had!"

"Yes, that's true, isn't it?" said young Ned, smiling.

And oh God, how true it was! Dear Ned, fine Ned, friend of a lifetime! Breathe upon me, Ned! Give me your life's breath!

"You're president of the company, Ned! I heard!"

"Yes. Come along home for a drink?"

In the raging heat, a vapor of iced lemonade rose from his creamy fresh suit as they looked for a cab. In all the curses, yells, horns, Ned raised his hand.

A cab pulled up. They drove in serenity.

At the apartment house, in the dusk, a man with a gun stepped from the shadows.

"Give me everything," he said.

"Later," said Ned, smiling, breathing a scent of fresh summer apples upon the man.

"Later." The man stepped back to let them pass. "Later."

On the way up in the elevator, Ned said, "Did you know I'm married? Almost a year. Fine wife."

"Is she," said Will Morgan, and stopped, ". . . beautiful?"

"Oh, yes. You'll love her. You'll love the apartment."

Yes, thought Morgan; a green glade, crystal chimes, cool grass for a carpet. I know, I know.

They stepped out into an apartment that was indeed a tropic isle. Young Ned poured huge goblets of iced champagne.

"What shall we drink to?"

"To you, Ned. To your wife. To me. To midnight, tonight."

"Why midnight?"

"When I go back down to that man who is waiting downstairs with his gun. That man you said 'later' to. And he agreed 'later.' I'll be there alone with him. Funny, ridiculous, funny. And *my* breath just ordinary breath, not smelling of melons or pears. And him waiting all those long hours with his sweaty gun, irritable with heat. What a grand joke. Well . . . a toast?"

"A toast!"

They drank.

At which moment, the wife entered. She heard each of them laughing in a different way, and joined in their laughter.

But her eyes, when she looked at Will Morgan, suddenly filled with tears.

And he knew whom she was weeping for.

Interval in Sunlight

They moved into the Hotel de Las Flores on a hot green afternoon in late October. The inner patio was blazing with red and
yellow and white flowers, like flames, which lit their small room.
The husband was tall and black-haired and pale and looked as
if he had driven ten thousand miles in his sleep; he walked
through the tile patio, carrying a few blankets, he threw himself
on the small bed of the small room with an exhausted sigh and
lay there. While he closed his eyes, his wife, about twenty-four,
with yellow hair and horn-rim glasses, smiling at the manager,
Mr. Gonzales, hurried in and out from the room to the car. First
she carried two suitcases, then a typewriter, thanking Mr. Gonzales, but steadily refusing his help. And then she carried in a

huge packet of Mexican masks they had picked up in the lake town of Patzcuaro, and then out to the car again and again for more small cases and packages, and even an extra tire which they were afraid some native might roll off down the cobbled street during the night. Her face pink from the exertion, she hummed as she locked the car, checked the windows, and ran back to the room where her husband lay, eyes closed, on one of the twin beds.

"Good God," he said, without opening his eyes, "this is one hell of a bed. Feel it. I told you to pick one with a Simmons mattress." He gave the bed a weary slap. "It's as hard as a rock."

"I don't speak Spanish," said the wife, standing there, beginning to look bewildered. "You should have come in and talked to the landlord yourself."

"Look," he said, opening his gray eyes just a little and turning his head, "I've done all the driving on this trip. You just sit there and look at the scenery. You're supposed to handle the money, the lodgings, the gas and oil, and all that. This is the second place we've hit where you got hard beds."

"I'm sorry," she said, still standing, beginning to fidget.

"I like to at least sleep nights, that's all I ask."

"I said I was sorry."

"Didn't you even *feel* the beds?"

"They looked all right."

"You've got to feel them." He slapped the bed and punched it at his side.

The woman turned to her own bed and sat on it, experimentally. "It feels all right to me."

"Well, it isn't."

"Maybe my bed is softer."

He rolled over tiredly and reached out to punch the other bed. "You can have this one if you want," she said, trying to smile.

"That's hard, too," he said, sighing, and fell back and closed his eyes again.

No one spoke, but the room was turning cold, while outside

the flowers blazed in the green shrubs and the sky was immensely blue. Finally, she rose and grabbed the typewriter and suitcase and turned toward the door.

"Where're you going?" he said.

"Back out to the car," she said. "We're going to find another place."

"Put it down," said the man. "I'm tired."

"We'll find another place."

"Sit down, we'll stay here tonight, my God, and move tomorrow."

She looked at all the boxes and crates and luggage, the clothes, and the tire, her eyes flickering. She put the typewriter down.

"Damn it!" she cried, suddenly. "You can have the mattress off my bed. "I'll sleep on the springs."

He said nothing.

"You can have the mattress off my bed," she said. "Only don't talk about it. Here!" She pulled the blanket off and yanked at the mattress.

"That might be better," he said, opening his eyes, seriously.

"You can have both mattresses, my God, I can sleep on a bed of nails!" she cried. "Only stop yapping."

"I'll manage." He turned his head away. "It wouldn't be fair to you."

"It'd be plenty fair just for you to keep quiet about the bed; it's not that hard, good God, you'll sleep if you're tired. Jesus God, Joseph!"

"Keep your voice down," said Joseph. "Why don't you go find out about Paricutin volcano?"

"I'll go in a minute." She stood there, her face red.

"Find out what the rates are for a taxi out there and a horse up the mountain to see it, and look at the sky; if the sky's blue that means the volcano isn't erupting today, and don't let them gyp you."

"I guess I can do that."

She opened the door and stepped out and shut the door and *Señor* Gonzales was there. Was everything all right? he wished to know.

She walked past the town windows, and smelled the soft charcoal air. Beyond the town all of the sky was blue except north (or east or west, she couldn't be certain) where the huge broiling black cloud rose up from the terrible volcano. She looked at it with a small tremoring inside. Then she sought out a large fat taxi driver and the arguments began. The price started at sixty pesos and dwindled rapidly, with expressions of mournful defeat upon the buck-toothed fat man's face, to thirty-seven pesos. So! He was to come at three tomorrow afternoon, did he understand? That would give them time to drive out through the gray snows of land where the flaking lava ash had fallen to make a great dusty winter for mile after mile, and arrive at the volcano as the sun was setting. Was this very clear?

"*¡Si, señora, esta es muy claro, si!*"

"*Bueno.*" She gave him their hotel room number and bade him good-bye.

She idled into little lacquer shops, alone; she opened the little lacquer boxes and sniffed the sharp scent of camphor wood and cedar and cinnamon. She watched the craftsmen, enchanted, razor blades flashing in the sun, cutting the flowery scrolls and filling these patterns with red and blue color. The town flowed about her like a silent slow river and she immersed herself in it, smiling all of the time, and not even knowing she smiled.

Suddenly she looked at her watch. She'd been gone half an hour. A look of panic crossed her face. She ran a few steps and then slowed to a walk again, shrugging.

As she walked in through the tiled cool corridors, under the silvery tin candelabra on the adobe walls, a caged bird fluted high and sweet, and a girl with long soft dark hair sat at a piano painted sky blue and played a Chopin nocturne.

She looked at the windows of their room, the shades pulled down. Three o'clock of a fresh afternoon. She saw a soft-drinks box at the end of the patio and bought four bottles of Coke. Smiling, she opened the door to their room.

"It certainly took you long enough," he said, turned on his side toward the wall.

"We leave tomorrow afternoon at three," she said.

"How much?"

She smiled at his back, the bottles cold in her arms. "Only thirty-seven pesos."

"Twenty pesos would have done it. You can't let these Mexicans take advantage of you."

"I'm richer than they are; if anyone *deserves* being taken advantage of, it's us."

"That's not the idea. They *like* to bargain."

"I feel like a bitch, doing it."

"The guide book says they double their price and expect you to halve it."

"Let's not quibble over a dollar."

"A dollar is a dollar."

"I'll pay the dollar from my own money," she said. "I brought some cold drinks—do you want one?"

"What've you got?" He sat up in bed.

"Cokes."

"Well, you know I don't like Cokes much; take two of those back, will you, and get some Orange Crush?"

"Please?" she said, standing there.

"Please," he said, looking at her. "Is the volcano active?"

"Yes."

"Did you ask?"

"No, I looked at the sky. Plenty of smoke."

"You should have asked."

"The damn sky is just exploding with it."

"But how do we know it's good tomorrow?"

"We don't know. If it's not, we put it off."

"I guess that's right." He lay down again.

She brought back two bottles of Orange Crush.

"It's not very cold," he said, drinking it.

They had supper in the patio: sizzling steak, green peas, a plate of Spanish rice, a little wine, and spiced peaches for dessert.

As he napkined his mouth, he said, casually, "Oh, I meant to tell you. I've checked your figures on what I owe you for the last six days, from Mexico City to here. You say I owe you one hundred twenty-five pesos, or about twenty-five American dollars, right?"

"Yes."

"I make it I owe you only twenty-two."

"I don't think that's possible," she said, still working on her spiced peaches with a spoon.

"I added the figures twice."

"So did I."

"I think you added them wrong."

"Perhaps I did." She jarred the chair back suddenly. "Let's go check."

In the room, the notebook lay open under the lighted lamp. They checked the figures together. "You see," said he, quietly. "You're three dollars off. How did that happen?"

"It just happened. I'm sorry."

"You're one hell of a bookkeeper."

"I do my best."

"Which isn't very good. I thought you could take a little responsibility."

"I try damned hard."

"You forgot to check the air in the tires, you get hard beds, you lose things, you lost a key in Acapulco, to the car trunk, you lost the air-pressure gauge, and you can't keep books. I have to drive—"

"I know, I know, you have to drive all day, and you're tired, and you just got over a strep infection in Mexico City, and you're afraid it'll come back and you want to take it easy on your heart, and the least I could do is to keep my nose clean and the arithmetic neat. I know it all by heart. I'm only a writer, and I admit I've got big feet."

"You won't make a very good writer this way," he said. "It's such a simple thing, addition."

"I didn't do it on purpose!" she cried, throwing the pencil down. "Hell! I wish I *had* cheated you now. I wish I'd done a lot of things now. I wish I'd lost that air-pressure gauge on purpose, I'd have some pleasure in thinking about it and knowing I did it to spite you, anyway. I wish I'd picked these beds for their hard mattresses, then I could laugh in my sleep tonight, thinking how hard they are for you to sleep on, I wish I'd done *that* on purpose. And now I wish I'd thought to fix the books. I could enjoy laughing about that, too."

"Keep your voice down," he said, as to a child.

"I'll be god-damned if I'll keep my voice down."

"All I want to know now is how much money you have in the kitty."

She put her trembling hands in her purse and brought out all the money. When he counted it, there was five dollars missing.

"Not only do you keep poor books, overcharging me on some item or other, but now there's five dollars gone from the kitty," he said. "Where'd it go?"

"I don't know. I must have forgotten to put it down, or if I did, I didn't say what for. Good God, I don't want to add this damned list again. I'll pay what's missing out of my own allowance to keep everyone happy. Here's five dollars! Now, let's go out for some air, it's hot in here."

She jerked the door wide and she trembled with a rage all out of proportion to the facts. She was hot and shaking and stiff and she knew her face was very red and her eyes bright, and when *Señor* Gonzales bowed to them and wished them a good evening, she had to smile stiffly in return.

"Here," said her husband, handing her the room key. "And don't, for God's sake, lose it."

The band was playing in the green zocalo. It hooted and blared and tooted and screamed up on the bronze-scrolled bandstand. The square was bloomed full with people and color, men and boys walking one way around the block, on the pink and blue tiles, women and girls walking the other way, flirting their dark olive eyes at one another, men holding each other's elbows and talking earnestly between meetings, women and girls twined like ropes of flowers, sweetly scented, blowing in a summer night wind over the cooling tile designs, whispering, past the vendors of cold drinks and tamales and enchiladas. The band precipitated "Yankee Doodle" once, to the delight of the blonde woman with the horn-rim glasses, who smiled wildly and turned to her husband. Then the band hooted "La Cumparsita" and "La Paloma Azul," and she felt a good warmth and began to sing a little, under her breath.

"Don't act like a tourist," said her husband.

"I'm just enjoying myself."

"Don't be a damned fool, is all I ask."

A vendor of silver trinkets shuffled by. "¿Señor?"

Joseph looked them over, while the band played, and held up one bracelet, very intricate, very exquisite. "How much?"

"Veinte pesos, señor."

"Ho ho," said the husband, smiling. "I'll give you five for it," in Spanish.

"Five," replied the man in Spanish. "I would starve."

"Don't bargain with him," said the wife.

"Keep out of this," said the husband, smiling. To the vendor, "Five pesos, señor."

"No, no, I would lose money. My last price is ten pesos."

"Perhaps I could give you six," said the husband. "No more than that."

The vendor hesitated in a kind of numbed panic as the husband tossed the bracelet back on the red velvet tray and turned away. "I am no longer interested. Good night."

"*¡Señor!* Six pesos, it is yours!"

The husband laughed. "Give him six pesos, darling."

She stiffly drew forth her wallet and gave the vendor some peso bills. The man went away. "I hope you're satisfied," she said.

"Satisfied?" Smiling, he flipped the bracelet in the palm of his pale hand. "For a dollar and twenty-five cents I buy a bracelet that sells for thirty dollars in the States!"

"I have something to confess," she said. "I gave that man ten pesos."

"What!" The husband stopped laughing.

"I put a five-peso note in with those one-peso bills. Don't worry, I'll take it out of my own money. It won't go on the bill I present you at the end of the week."

He said nothing, but dropped the bracelet in his pocket. He looked at the band thundering into the last bars of "*Ay, Jalisco.*" Then he said, "You're a fool. You'd let these people take all your money."

It was her turn to step away a bit and not reply. She felt rather good. She listened to the music.

"I'm going back to the room," he said. "I'm tired."

"We only drove a hundred miles from Patzcuaro."

"My throat is a little raw again. Come on."

They moved away from the music and the walking, whispering, laughing people. The band played the "Toreador Song." The drums thumped like great dull hearts in the summery night. There was a smell of papaya in the air, and green thicknesses of jungle and hidden waters.

"I'll walk you back to the room and come back myself," she said. "I want to hear the music."

"Don't be naïve."

"I like it, damn it, I like it, it's good music. It's not fake, it's real, or as real as anything ever gets in this world, that's why I like it."

"When I don't feel well, I don't expect to have you out running around the town alone. It isn't fair you see things I don't."

They turned in at the hotel and the music was still fairly loud. "If you want to walk by yourself, go off on a trip by yourself and go back to the United States by yourself," he said. "Where's the key?"

"Maybe I lost it."

They let themselves into the room and undressed. He sat on the edge of the bed looking into the night patio. At last he shook his head, rubbed his eyes, and sighed. "I'm tired. I've been terrible today." He looked at her where she sat, next to him, and he put out his hand to take her arm. "I'm sorry. I get all riled up, driving, and then us not talking the language too well. By evening I'm a mess of nerves."

"Yes," she said.

Quite suddenly he moved over beside her. He took hold of her and held her tightly, his head over her shoulder, eyes shut, talking into her ear with a quiet, whispering fervency. "You know, we *must* stay together. There's only us, really, no matter what happens, no matter what trouble we have. I do love you so much, you know that. Forgive me if I'm difficult. We've got to make it go."

She stared over his shoulder at the blank wall and the wall was like her life in this moment, a wide expanse of nothingness with hardly a bump, a contour, or a feeling to it. She didn't know what to say or do. Another time, she would have melted. But there was such a thing as firing metal too often, bringing it to a glow, shaping it. At last the metal refuses to glow or shape; it is nothing but a weight. She was a weight now, moving mechanically in his arms, hearing but not hearing, understanding but not understanding, replying but not replying. "Yes, we'll stay together." She felt her lips move. "We love each other." The lips said what they must say, while her mind was in her eyes and her eyes bored deep into the vacuum of the wall. "Yes." Holding but not holding him. "Yes."

The room was dim. Outside, someone walked in a corridor, perhaps glancing at this locked door, perhaps hearing their vital whispering as no more than something falling drop by drop from a loose faucet, a running drain perhaps, or a turned book-leaf under a solitary bulb. Let the doors whisper, the people of the world walked down tile corridors and did not hear.

"Only you and I know the things." His breath was fresh. She felt very sorry for him and herself and the world, suddenly. Every-one was infernally alone. He was like a man clawing at a statue. She did not feel herself move. Only her mind, which was a lightless, dim fluorescent vapor, shifted. "Only you and I re-member," he said, "and if one of us should leave, then half the memories are gone. So we must stay together because if one forgets the other remembers."

Remembers what? she asked herself. But she remembered instantly, in a linked series, those parts of incidents in their life together that perhaps he might not recall; the night at the beach, five years ago, one of the first fine nights beneath the canvas with the secret touchings, the days at Sunland sprawled together, taking the sun until twilight. Wandering in an abandoned silver mine, oh, a million things, one touched on and revealed another in an instant!

He held her tight back against the bed now. "Do you know how lonely I am? Do you know how lonely I make myself with these arguments and fights and all of it, when I'm tired?" He waited for her to answer, but she said nothing. She felt his eye-lid flutter on her neck. Faintly, she remembered when he had first flicked his eyelid near her ear. "Spider-eye," she had said, laughing, then. "It feels like a small spider in my ear." And now this small lost spider climbed with insane humor upon her neck. There was something in his voice which made her feel she was a woman on a train going away and he was standing in the sta-tion saying, "Don't go." And her appalled voice silently cried, "But *you're* the one on a train! *I'm* not going *anywhere!*"

She lay back, bewildered. It was the first time in two weeks he had touched her. And the touching had such an immediacy that she knew the wrong word would send him very far away again.

She lay and said nothing.

Finally, after a long while, she heard him get up, sighing, and move off. He got into his own bed and drew the covers up, silently. She moved at last, arranged herself on her bed, and lay listening to her watch tick in the small hot darkness. "My God," she whispered, finally, "it's only eight-thirty."

"Go to sleep," he said.

She lay in the dark, perspiring, naked, on her own bed, and in the distance, sweetly, faintly, so that it made her soul and heart ache to hear it, she heard the band thumping and brassing out its melodies. She wanted to walk among the dark moving people and sing with them and smell the soft charcoal air of October in a small summery town deep in the tropics of Mexico, a million miles lost from civilization, listening to the good music, tapping her foot and humming. But now she lay with her eyes wide, in bed. In the next hour, the band played *"La Golondrina,"* *"Marimba,"* *"Los Viejitos,"* *"Michoacan la Verde,"* *"Barca-rolle,"* and *"Luna Lunera."*

At three in the morning she awoke for no reason and lay, her sleep done and finished with, feeling the coolness that came with deep night. She listened to his breathing and she felt away and separate from the world. She thought of the long trip from Los Angeles to Laredo, Texas, like a silver-white boiling nightmare. And then the green technicolor, red and yellow and blue and purple, dream of Mexico arising like a flood about them to engulf their car with color and smell of rain forest and deserted town. She thought of all the small towns, the shops, the walking people, the burros, and all the arguments and near-fights. She thought of the five years she had been married. A long, long time. There had been no day in all that time that they had not seen each other; there had been no day when she had seen friends, sepa-rately; *he* was always there to see and criticize. There had been no day when she was allowed to be gone for more than an hour or so without a full explanation. Sometimes, feeling infinitely evil, she would sneak to a midnight show, telling no one, and sit, feeling free, breathing deeply of the air of freedom, watching the people, far realer than she, upon the screen, motioning and moving.

And now here they were, after five years. She looked over at his sleeping form. One thousand eight hundred and twenty-five days with you, she thought, my husband. A few hours each day at my typewriter, and then all the rest of each day and night with you. I feel quite like that man walled up in a vault in *The Cask of Amontillado*. I scream but no one hears.

There was a shift of footsteps outside, a knock on their door. "*Señora*," called a soft voice, in Spanish. "It is three o'clock."

Oh, my God, thought the wife. "Sh!" she hissed, leaping up to the door. But her husband was awake. "What *is* it?" he cried.

She opened the door the slightest crack. "You've come at the wrong time," she said to the man in the darkness.

"Three o'clock, *señora*."

"No, no," she hissed, her face wrenching with the agony of the moment. "I meant tomorrow afternoon."

"What is it?" demanded her husband, switching on a light. "Christ, it's only three in the morning. What does the fool want?"

She turned, shutting her eyes. "He's here to take us to Paricutin."

"My God, you can't speak Spanish at all!"

"Go away," she said to the guide.

"But I arose for this hour," said the guide.

The husband swore and got up. "I won't be able to sleep now, anyway. Tell the idiot we'll be dressed in ten minutes and go with him and get it over, my God!"

She did this and the guide slipped away into the darkness and out into the street where the cool moon burnished the fenders of his taxi.

"You *are* incompetent," snapped the husband, pulling on two pairs of pants, two T-shirts, a sport shirt, and a wool shirt over that. "Jesus, this'll fix my throat, all right. If I come down with another strep infection—"

"Get back into bed, damn you."

"I couldn't sleep now, anyway."

"Well, we've had six hours' sleep already, and you had at least three hours' this afternoon; that should be enough."

"Spoiling our trip," he said, putting on two sweaters and two pairs of socks. "It's cold up there on the mountain; dress warm, hurry up." He put on a jacket and a muffler and looked enormous in the heap of clothing he wore. "Get me my pills. Where's some water?"

"Get back to bed," she said. "I won't have you sick and whining." She found his medicine and poured some water.

"The least thing you could do was get the hour right."

"Shut up!" She held the glass.

"Just another of your thick-headed blunders."

She threw the water in his face. "Let me alone, damn you, let me alone. I didn't mean to do that!"

"You!" he shouted, face dripping. He ripped off his jacket. "You'll chill me, I'll catch cold!"

"I don't give a damn, let me alone!" She raised her hands into fists, and her face was terrible and red, and she looked like some animal in a maze who has steadily sought exit from an impossible chaos and has been constantly fooled, turned back, rerouted, led on, tempted, whispered to, lied to, led further, and at last reached a blank wall.

"Put your hands down!" he shouted.

"I'll kill you, by God, I'll kill you!" she screamed, her face contorted and ugly. "Leave me alone! I've tried my damnedest— beds, language, time, my God, the mistakes, you think I don't *know* it? You think I'm not *sorry?*"

"I'll catch cold, I'll catch cold." He was staring at the wet floor. He sat down with water on his face.

"Here. Wipe your face off!" She flung him a towel.

He began to shake violently. "I'm cold!"

"Get a chill, damn it, and die, but leave me alone!"

"I'm cold, I'm cold." His teeth chattered, he wiped his face with trembling hands. "I'll have another infection."

"Take off that coat! It's wet."

He stopped shaking after a minute and stood up to take off the soggy coat. She handed him a leather jacket. "Come on, he's waiting for us."

He began to shiver again. "I'm not going anywhere, to hell with you," he said, sitting down. "You owe me fifty dollars now."

"What for?"

"You remember, you promised."

And she remembered. They had had a fight about some silly thing, in California, the first day of the trip, yes, by God, the very first day out. And she for the first time in her life had lifted her hand to slap him. Then, appalled, she had dropped her hand, staring at her traitorous fingers. "You were going to slap me!" he had cried. "Yes," she replied. "Well," he said quietly, "the next time you do a thing like that, you'll hand over fifty dollars of your money." That's how life was, full of little tributes and ransoms and blackmails. She paid for all her errors, unmotivated or not. A dollar here, a dollar there. If she spoiled an evening, she paid the dinner bill from her clothing money. If she criticized a play they had just seen and he had liked it, he flew into a rage, and, to quiet him, she paid for the theater tickets. On and on it had gone, swifter and swifter over the years. If they bought a book together and she didn't like it but he did and she dared speak out, there was a fight, sometimes a small thing which grew for days, and ended with her buying the book plus another and perhaps a set of cufflinks or some other silly thing to calm the storm. Jesus!

"Fifty dollars. You promised if you acted up again with these tantrums and slappings."

"It was only water. I didn't hit you. All right, shut up, I'll pay the money, I'll pay anything just to be let alone; it's worth it. and five hundred dollars more, more than worth it. I'll pay."

She turned away. When you're sick for a number of years, when you're an *only* child, the *only* boy, all of your life, you get the way he is, she thought. Then you find yourself thirty-five years old and still undecided as to what you're to be—a ceramist, a social worker, a businessman. And your wife has always known what she would be—a writer. And it must be maddening to live with a woman with a single knowledge of herself, so sure of what she would do with her writing. And selling stories, at last, not many, no, but just enough to cause the seams of the marriage to rip. And so how natural that he must convince her that she was wrong and he was right, that she was an uncontrollable child and must forfeit money. Money was to be the weapon he held over her. When she had been a fool she would give up some of the precious gain—the product of her writing.

"Do you know," she said, suddenly, aloud, "since I made that big sale to the magazine, you seem to pick more fights and I seem to pay more money?"

"What do you mean by that?" he said.

It seemed to her to be true. Since the big sale he had put his special logic to work on situations, a logic of such a sort that she had no way to combat it. Reasoning with him was impossible. You were finally cornered, your explanations exhausted, your alibis depleted, your pride in tatters. So you struck out. You slapped at him or broke something, and then, there you were again, paying off, and he had won. And he was taking your success away from you, your single purpose, or he thought he was, anyway. But strangely enough, though she had never told him, she didn't care about forfeiting the money. If it made peace, if it made him happy, if it made him think he was causing her to suffer, that was all right. He had exaggerated ideas as to the value of money; it hurt him to lose it or spend it, therefore he thought it would hurt her as much. But I'm feeling no pain, she thought, I'd like to give him all of the money, for that's not why I write at all, I write to say what I have to say, and he doesn't understand that.

He was quieted now. "You'll pay?"

"Yes." She was dressing quickly now, in slacks and jacket. "In fact, I've been meaning to bring this up for some time. I'm giving all the money to you from now on. There's no need of my keeping my profits separate from yours, as it has been. I'll turn it over to you tomorrow."

"I don't ask that," he said, quickly.

"I insist. It all goes to you."

What I'm doing, of course, is unloading your gun, she thought. Taking your weapon away from you. Now you won't be able to extract the money from me, piece by piece, bit by painful bit. You'll have to find another way to bother me.

"I—" he said.

"No, let's not talk about it. It's yours."

"It's only to teach you a lesson. You've a bad temper," he said. "I thought you'd control it if you had to forfeit something."

"Oh, I just *live* for money," she said.

"I don't want all of it."

"Come on now." She was weary. She opened the door and listened. The neighbors hadn't heard, or if they had, they paid no attention. The lights of the waiting taxi illuminated the front patio.

They walked out through the cool moonlit night. She walked ahead of him for the first time in years.

Paricutin was a river of gold that night. A distant murmuring river of molten ore going down to some dead lava sea, to some volcanic black shore. Time and again if you held your breath, stilled your heart within you, you could hear the lava pushing rocks down the mountain in tumblings and roarings, faintly, faintly. Above the crater were red vapors and red light. Gentle brown and gray clouds arose suddenly as coronets or halos or puffs from the interior, their undersides washed in pink, their tops dark and ominous, without a sound.

The husband and the wife stood on the opposite mountain, in the sharp cold, the horses behind them. In a wooden hut nearby, the scientific observers were lighting oil lamps, cooking their evening meal, boiling rich coffee, talking in whispers because of the clear, night-explosive air. It was very far away from everything else in the world.

On the way up the mountain, after the long taxi drive from Uruapan, over moon-dreaming hills of ashen snow, through dry stick villages, under the cold clear stars, jounced in the taxi like dice in a gambling-tumbler, both of them had tried to make a better thing of it. They had arrived at a campfire on a sort of sea bottom. About the campfire were solemn men and small dark boys, and a company of seven other Americans, all men, in riding breeches, talking in loud voices under the soundless sky. The horses were brought forth and mounted. They proceeded across the lava river. She talked to the other Yankees and they responded. They joked together. After a while of this, the husband rode on ahead.

Now, they stood together, watching the lava wash down the dark cone summit.

He wouldn't speak.

"What's wrong now?" she asked.

He looked straight ahead, the lava glow reflected in his eyes. "You could have ridden with me. I thought we came to Mexico to see things together. And now you talk to those damned Texans."

"I felt lonely. We haven't seen any people from the States for eight weeks. I like the days in Mexico, but I don't like the nights. I just wanted someone to talk to."

"You wanted to tell them you're a writer."

"That's unfair."

"You're always telling people you're a writer, and how good you are, and you've just sold a story to a large-circulation magazine and that's how you got the money to come here to Mexico."

"One of them asked me what I did, and I told him. Damn right I'm proud of my work. I've waited ten years to sell some damn thing."

He studied her in the light from the fire mountain and at last he said, "You know, before coming up here tonight, I thought about that damned typewriter of yours and almost tossed in into the river."

"You didn't!"

"No, but I locked it in the car. I'm tired of it and the way you've ruined the whole trip. You're not with me, you're with yourself, you're the one who counts, you and that damned machine, you and Mexico, you and your reactions, you and your inspiration, you and your nervous sensitivity, and you and your aloneness. I knew you'd act this way tonight, just as sure as there was a First Coming! I'm tired of your running back from every excursion we make to sit at that machine and bang away at all hours. This is a vacation."

"I haven't touched the typewriter in a week, because it bothered you."

"Well, don't touch it for another week or a month, don't touch it until we get home. Your damned inspiration can wait!"

I should never have said I'd give him all the money, she thought. I should never have taken that weapon from him, it kept him away from my real life, the writing and the machine. And now I've thrown off the protective cloak of money and he's searched for a new weapon and he's gotten to the true thing— to the *machine!* Oh Christ!

Suddenly, without thinking, with the rage in her again, she pushed him ahead of her. She didn't do it violently. She just gave him a push. Once, twice, three times. She didn't hurt him. It was just a gesture of pushing away. She wanted to strike him, throw him off a cliff, perhaps, but instead she gave these three pushes, to indicate her hostility and the end of talking. Then they stood separately, while behind them the horses moved their hooves softly, and the night air grew colder and their breath hissed in white plumes on the air, and in the scientists' cabin the coffee bubbled on the blue gas jet and the rich fumes permeated the moonlit heights.

After an hour, as the first dim furnacings of the sun came in the cold East, they mounted their horses for the trip down through growing light, toward the buried city and the buried church under the lava flow. Crossing the flow, she thought, Why doesn't his horse fall, why isn't he thrown onto those jagged lava rocks, why? But nothing happened. They rode on. The sun rose red.

They slept until one in the afternoon. She was dressed and sitting on the bed waiting for him to waken for half an hour before he stirred and rolled over, needing a shave, very pale with tiredness.

"I've got a sore throat," was the first thing he said.

She didn't speak.

"You shouldn't have thrown water on me," he said.

She got up and walked to the door and put her hand on the knob.

"I want you to stay here," he said. "We're going to stay here in Uruapan three or four more days."

At last she said, "I thought we were going on to Guadalajara."

"Don't be a tourist. You ruined that trip to the volcano for us. I want to go back up tomorrow or the next day. Go look at the sky."

She went out to look at the sky. It was clear and blue. She reported this. "The volcano dies down, sometimes for a week. We can't afford to wait a week for it to boom again."

"Yes, we can. We will. And you'll pay for the taxi to take us up there and do the trip over and do it right and enjoy it."

"Do you think we can ever enjoy it now?" she asked .

"If it's the last thing we do, we'll enjoy it."

"You insist, do you?"

"We'll wait until the sky is full of smoke and go back up."

"I'm going out to buy a paper." She shut the door and walked into the town.

She walked down the fresh-washed streets and looked in the shining windows and smelled that amazingly clear air and felt very good, except for the tremoring, the continual tremoring in her stomach. At last, with a hollowness roaring in her chest, she went to a man standing beside a taxi.

"*Señor*," she said.

"Yes?" said the man.

She felt her heart stop beating. Then it began to thump again and she went on: "How much would you charge to drive me to Morelia?"

"Ninety pesos, *señora*."

"And I can get the train in Morelia?"

"There is a train *here, señora*."

"Yes, but there are reasons why I don't want to *wait* for it here."

"I will drive you, then, to Morelia."

"Come along, there are a few things I must do."

The taxi was left in front of the the Hotel de Las Flores. She walked in, alone, and once more looked at the lovely garden with its many flowers, and listened to the girl playing the strange blue-colored piano, and this time the song was the "Moonlight Sonata." She smelled the sharp crystalline air and shook her head, eyes closed, hands at her sides. She put her hand to the door, opened it softly.

Why today? she wondered. Why not some other day in the last five years? Why have I waited, why have I hung around? Because. A thousand becauses. Because you always hoped things would start again the way they were the first year. Because there were times, less frequent now, when he was splendid for days, even weeks, when you were both feeling well and the world was green and bright blue. There were times, like yesterday, for a moment, when he opened the armor-plate and showed her the fear beneath it and the small loneliness of himself and said, "I need and love you, don't ever go away, I'm afraid without you." Because sometimes it had seemed good to cry together, to make up, and the inevitable goodness of the night and the day following their making up. Because he was handsome. Because she had been alone all year every year until she met him. Because she didn't want to be alone again, but now knew that it would be better to be alone than be this way because only last night he destroyed the typewriter; not physically, no, but with thoughts and words. And he might as well have picked her up bodily and thrown her from the river bridge.

She could not feel her hand on the door. It was as if ten thousand volts of electricity had numbed all of her body. She could not feel her feet on the tiled floor. Her face was gone, her mind was gone.

He lay asleep, his back turned. The room was greenly dim. Quickly, soundlessly, she put on her coat and checked her purse. The clothes and typewriter were of no importance now. Everything was a hollowing roar. Everything was like a waterfall leaping into clear emptiness. There was no striking, no impact, just a clear water falling into a hollow and then another hollow, followed by an emptiness.

She stood by the bed and looked at the man there, the familiar black hair on the nape of his neck, the sleeping profile. The form stirred. "What?" he asked, still asleep.

"Nothing," she said. "Nothing. And nothing."

She went out and shut the door.

The taxi sped out of town at an incredible rate, making a great noise, and all the pink walls and blue walls fled past and people jumped out of the way and there were some few cars which almost exploded upon them, and there went most of the town and there went the hotel and that man sleeping in the hotel and there went—

Nothing.

The taxi motor died.

No, no, thought Marie, oh God, no, no, no.

The car must start again.

The taxi driver leaped out, glaring at God in his Heaven, and ripped open the hood and looked as if he might strangle the iron guts of the car with his clawing hands, his face smiling a pure sweet smile of incredible hatred, and then he turned to Marie and forced himself to shrug, putting away his hate and accepting the Will of God.

"I will walk you to the bus station," he said.

No, her eyes said. No, her mouth almost said. Joseph will wake and run and find me still here and drag me back. No.

"I will carry your bags, *señora*," the taxi driver said, and walked off with them, and had to come back and find her still there, motionless, saying no, no, to no one, and helped her out and showed her where to walk.

The bus was in the square and the Indians were getting into it, some silently and with a slow, certain dignity, and some chattering like birds and shoving bundles, children, chickens' baskets, and pigs in ahead of them. The driver wore a uniform that had not been pressed or laundered in twenty years, and he was leaning out the window shouting and laughing with people outside, as Marie stepped up into the interior of hot smoke and burning grease from the engine, the smell of gasoline and oil, the smell of wet chickens, wet children, sweating men and damp women, old upholstery which was down to the skeleton, and oily leather. She found a seat in the rear and felt the eyes follow her and her suitcase, and she was thinking: I'm going away, at last I'm going away, I'm free, I'll never see him again in my life, I'm free, I'm free.

She almost laughed.

The bus started and all of the people in it shook and swayed and cried out and smiled, and the land of Mexico seemed to whirl about outside the window, like a dream undecided whether to stay or go, and then the greenness passed away, and the town, and there was the Hotel de Las Flores with its open patio, and there, incredibly, hands in pockets, standing in the open door but looking at the sky and the volcano smoke, was Joseph, paying no attention to the bus or her and she was going away from him, he was growing remote already, his figure was dwindling like someone falling down a mine shaft, silently, without a scream. Now, before she had even the decency or inclination to wave, he was no larger than a boy, then a child, then a baby, in distance, in size, then gone around a corner, with the engine thundering, someone playing upon a guitar up front in the bus, and Marie, straining to look back, as if she might penetrate walls, trees, and distances, for another view of the man standing so quietly watching the blue sky.

At last, her neck tired, she turned and folded her hands and examined what she had won for herself. A whole lifetime loomed suddenly ahead, as quickly as the turns and whirls of the highway brought her suddenly to edges of cliffs, and each bend of the road, even as the years, could not be seen ahead. For a moment it was simply good to lie back here, head upon jouncing seat rest, and contemplate quietness. To know nothing, to think nothing, to feel nothing, to be as nearly dead for a moment as one could be, with the eyes closed, the heart unheard, no special temperature to the body, to wait for life to come get her rather than to seek, at least for an hour. Let the bus take her to the train, the train to the plane, the plane to the city, and the city to her friends, and then, like a stone dropped into a cement mixer, let that life in the city do with her as it would, she flowing along in the mix and solidifying in any new pattern that seemed best.

The bus rushed on with a plummeting and swerving in the sweet green air of the afternoon, between the mountains baked like lion pelts, past rivers as sweet as wine and as clear as vermouth, over stone bridges, under aqueducts where water ran like clear wind in the ancient channels, past churches, through dust, and suddenly, quite suddenly the speedometer in Marie's mind said, A million miles, Joseph is back a million miles and I'll never see him again. The thought stood up in her mind and covered the sky with a blurred darkness. Never, never again until the day I die or after that will I see him again, not for an hour or a minute or a second, not at all will I see him.

The numbness started in her fingertips. She felt it flow up through her hands, into her wrists and on along the arms to her shoulders and through her shoulders to her heart and up her neck to her head. She was a numbness, a thing of nettles and ice and prickles and a hollow thundering nothingness. Her lips were dry petals, her eyelids were a thousand pounds heavier than iron, and each part of her body was now iron and lead and copper and platinum. Her body weighed ten tons, each part of it was so incredibly heavy, and, in that heaviness, crushed and beating to survive, was her crippled heart, throbbing and tearing about like a headless chicken. And buried in the limestone and steel of her robot body was her terror and crying out, walled in, with someone tapping the trowel on the exterior wall, the job finished, and, ironically, it was her own hand she saw before her that had wielded the trowel, set the final brick in place, frothed on the thick slush of mortar and pushed everything into a tightness and a self-finished prison.

Her mouth was cotton. Her eyes were flaming with a dark flame the color of raven wings, the sound of vulture wings, and her head was so heavy with terror, so full of an iron weight, while her mouth was stuffed with invisible hot cotton, that she felt her head sag down into her immensely fat, but she could not see the fat, hands. Her hands were pillows of lead to lie upon, her hands were cement sacks crushing down upon her senseless lap, her ears, faucets in which ran cold winds, and all about her, not looking at her, not noticing, was the bus on its way through towns and fields, over hills and into corn valleys at a great racketing speed, taking her each and every instant one million miles and ten million years away from the familiar.

I must *not* cry out, she thought. No! No!

The dizziness was so complete, and the colors of the bus and her hands and skirt were now so blued over and sooted with lack of blood that in a moment she would be collapsed upon the floor, she would hear the surprise and shock of the riders bending over her. But she put her head far down and sucked the chicken air, the sweating air, the leather air, the carbon monoxide air, the incense air, the air of lonely death, and drew it back through the copper nostrils, down the aching throat, into her lungs which blazed as if she swallowed neon light. Joseph, Joseph, Joseph, Joseph.

It was a simple thing. All terror is a simplicity.

I cannot live without him, she thought. I have been lying to myself. I need him, oh Christ, I, I . . .

"Stop the bus! Stop it!"

The bus stopped at her scream, everyone was thrown forward. Somehow she was stumbling forward over the children, the dogs barking, her hands flailing heavily, falling; she heard her dress rip, she screamed again, the door was opening, the driver was appalled at the woman coming at him in a wild stumbling, and she fell out upon the gravel, tore her stockings, and lay while someone bent to her; then she was vomiting on the ground, a steady sickness; they were bringing her bags out of the bus to her, she was telling them in chokes and sobs that she wanted to go that way; she pointed back at the city a million years ago, a million miles ago, and the bus driver was shaking his head. She half sat, half lay there, her arms about the suitcase, sobbing, and the bus stood in the hot sunlight over her and she waved it on; go on, go on; they're all staring at me, I'll get a ride back, don't worry, leave me here, go on, and at last, like an accordion, the door folded shut, the Indian copper-mask faces were transported on away, and the bus dwindled from consciousness. She lay on the suitcase and cried, for a number of minutes, and she was not as heavy or sick, but her heart was fluttering wildly, and she was cold as someone fresh from a winter lake. She arose and dragged the suitcase in little moves across the highway and swayed there, waiting, while six cars hummed by, and at last a seventh car pulled up with a Mexican gentleman in the front seat, a rich car from Mexico City.

"You are going to Uruapan?" he asked politely, looking only at her eyes.

"Yes," she said at last, "I am going to Uruapan."

And as she rode in this car, her mind began a private dialogue:

"What is it to be insane?"

"I don't know."

"Do you know what insanity is?"

"I don't know."

"Can one tell? The coldness, was that the start?"

"No."

"The heaviness, wasn't that a part?"

"Shut up."

"Is insanity screaming?"

"I didn't mean to."

"But that came later. First there was the heaviness, and the silence, and the blankness. That terrible void, that space, that silence, that aloneness, that backing away from life, that being in upon oneself and not wishing to look at or speak to the world. Don't tell me that wasn't the start of insanity."

"Yes."

"You were ready to fall over the edge."

"I stopped the bus just short of the cliff."

"And what if you hadn't stopped the bus? Would they have driven into a little town or Mexico City and the driver turned and said to you through the empty bus, 'All right, señora, all out.' Silence. 'All right, señora, all out.' Silence. 'Señora?' A stare into space. 'Señora!' A rigid stare into the sky of life, empty, empty, oh, empty. 'Señora!' No move. 'Señora.' Hardly a breath. You sit there, you sit there, you sit there, you sit there, you sit there.

"You would not even hear. 'Señora,' he would cry, and tug at you, but you wouldn't feel his hand. And the police would be summoned beyond your circle of comprehension, beyond your eyes or ears or body. You could not even hear the heavy boots in the car. 'Señora, you must leave the bus.' You do not hear. 'Señora, what is your name?' Your mouth is shut. 'Señora, you must come with us.' You sit like a stone idol. 'Let us see her passport.' They fumble with your purse which lies untended in your stone lap. 'Señora Marie Elliott, from California. Señora Elliott?' You stare at the empty sky. 'Where are you coming from? Where is your husband?' You were never married. 'Where are you going?' Nowhere. 'It says she was born in Illinois.' You were never born. 'Señora, señora.' They have to carry you, like a stone, from the bus. You will talk to no one. No, no, no one. 'Marie, this is me, Joseph.' No, too late. 'Marie!' Too late. 'Don't you recognize me?' Too late. Joseph. No, Joseph, no nothing, too late, too late."

"That is what would have happened, is it not?"

"Yes." She trembled.

"If you had not stopped the bus, you would have been heavier and heavier, true? And silenter and silenter and more made up of nothing and nothing and nothing."

"Yes."

"Señora," said the Spanish gentleman driving, breaking in on her thoughts. "It is a nice day, isn't it?"

"Yes," she said, both to him and the thoughts in her mind.

The old Spanish gentleman drove her directly to her hotel and let her out and doffed his hat and bowed to her.

She nodded and felt her mouth move with thanks, but she did not see him. She wandered into the hotel and found herself with her suitcase back in her room, that room she had left a thousand years ago. Her husband was there.

He lay in the dim light of late afternoon with his back turned, seeming not to have moved in the hours since she had left. He had not even known that she was gone, and had been to the ends of the earth and had returned. He did not even know.

She stood looking at his neck and the dark hairs curling there like ash fallen from the sky.

She found herself on the tiled patio in the hot light. A bird rustled in a bamboo cage. In the cool darkness somewhere, the girl was playing a waltz on the piano.

She saw but did not see two butterflies which darted and

jumped and lit upon a bush near her hand, to seal themselves together. She felt her gaze move to see the two bright things, all gold and yellow on the green leaf, their wings beating in slow pulses as they were joined. Her mouth moved and her hand swung like a pendulum, senselessly.

She watched her fingers tumble on the air and close on the two butterflies, tight, tighter, tightest. A scream was coming up into her mouth. She pressed it back. Tight, tighter, tightest.

She felt her hand open all to itself. Two lumps of bright powder fell to the shiny patio tiles. She looked down at the small ruins, then snapped her gaze up.

The girl who played the piano was standing in the middle of the garden, regarding her with appalled and startled eyes.

The wife put out her hand, to touch the distance, to say something, to explain, to apologize to the girl, this place, the world, everyone. But the girl went away.

The sky was full of smoke which went straight up and veered away south toward Mexico City.

She wiped the wing-pollen from her numb fingers and talked over her shoulder, not knowing if that man inside heard, her eyes on the smoke and the sky.

"You know . . . we might try the volcano tonight. It looks good. I bet there'll be lots of fire."

Yes, she thought, and it will fill the air and fall all around us, and take hold of us tight, tighter, tightest, and then let go and let us fall and we'll be ashes blowing south, all fire.

"Did you hear me?"

She stood over the bed and raised a fist high but *never* brought it down to strike him in the face.

A Story of Love

That was the week Ann Taylor came to teach summer school at Green Town Central. It was the summer of her twenty-fourth birthday, and it was the summer when Bob Spaulding was just fourteen.

Everyone remembered Ann Taylor, for she was that teacher for whom all the children wanted to bring huge oranges or pink flowers, and for whom they rolled up the rustling green and yellow maps of the world without being asked. She was that woman who always seemed to be passing by on days when the shade was green under the tunnels of oaks and elms in the old town, her face shifting with the bright shadows as she walked, until it was all things to all people. She was the fine peaches of summer in the snow of winter, and she was cool milk for cereal on a hot early-June morning. Whenever you needed an opposite, Ann Taylor was there. And those rare few days in the world when the climate was balanced as fine as a maple leaf between winds that blew just right, those were the days like Ann Taylor, and should have been so named on the calendar.

As for Bob Spaulding, he was the cousin who walked alone through town on any October evening with a pack of leaves after him like a horde of Hallowe'en mice, or you would see him, like a slow white fish in spring in the tart waters of the Fox Hill Creek, baking brown with the shine of a chestnut to his face by autumn. Or you might hear his voice in those treetops where the wind entertained; dropping down hand by hand, there would come Bob Spaulding to sit alone and look at the world, and later you might see him on the lawn with the ants crawling over his books as he read through the long afternoons alone, or played himself a game of chess on Grandmother's porch, or picked out a solitary tune upon the black piano in the bay window. You never saw him with any other child.

That first morning, Miss Ann Taylor entered through the side door of the schoolroom and all of the children sat still in their seats as they saw her write her name on the board in a nice round lettering.

"My name is Ann Taylor," she said, quietly. "And I'm your new teacher."

The room seemed suddenly flooded with illumination, as if the roof had moved back; and the trees were full of singing birds. Bob Spaulding sat with a spitball he had just made, hidden in his hand. After a half-hour of listening to Miss Taylor, he quietly let the spitball drop to the floor.

That day, after class, he brought in a bucket of water and a rag and began to wash the boards.

"What's this?" She turned to him from her desk, where she had been correcting spelling papers.

"The boards are kind of dirty," said Bob, at work.

"Yes, I know. Are you sure you want to clean them?"

"I suppose I should have asked permission," he said, halting uneasily.

"I think we can pretend you did," she replied, smiling, and at this smile he finished the boards in an amazing burst of speed and pounded the erasers so furiously that the air was full of snow, it seemed, outside the open window.

"Let's see," said Miss Taylor. "You're Bob Spaulding, aren't you?"

"Yes'm."

"Well, thank you, Bob."

"Could I do them every day?" he asked.

"Don't you think you should let the others try?"

"I'd like to do them," he said. "Every day."

"We'll try it for a while and see," she said.

He lingered.

"I think you'd better run on home," she said, finally.

"Good night." He walked slowly and was gone.

The next morning he happened by the place where she took board and room just as she was coming out to walk to school.

"Well, here I am," he said.

"And do you know," she said, "I'm not surprised."

They walked together.

"May I carry your books?" he asked.

"Why, thank you, Bob."

"It's nothing," he said, taking them.

They walked for a few minutes and he did not say a word. She glanced over and slightly down at him and saw how at ease he was and how happy he seemed, and she decided to let him break the silence, but he never did. When they reached the edge of the school ground he gave the books back to her. "I guess I better leave you here," he said. "The other kids wouldn't understand."

"I'm not sure I do, either, Bob," said Miss Taylor.

"Why we're friends," said Bob earnestly and with a great natural honesty.

"Bob—" she started to say.

"Yes'm?"

"Never mind." She walked away.

"I'll be in class," he said.

And he was in class, and he was there after school every night for the next two weeks, never saying a word, quietly washing the boards and cleaning the erasers and rolling up the maps while she worked at her papers, and there was that clock silence of four o'clock, the silence of the sun going down in the slow sky, the silence with the catlike sound of erasers patted together, and the drip of water from a moving sponge, and the rustle and turn of papers and the scratch of a pen, and perhaps the buzz of a fly banging with a tiny high anger against the tallest clear pane of window in the room. Sometimes the silence would go on this way until almost five, when Miss Taylor would find Bob Spauld-ing in the last seat of the room, sitting and looking at her silently, waiting for further orders.

"Well, it's time to go home," Miss Taylor would say, getting up.

"Yes'm."

And he would run to fetch her hat and coat. He would also lock the schoolroom door for her unless the janitor was coming in later. Then they would walk out of the school and across the yard, which was empty, the janitor taking down the chain swings slowly on his stepladder, the sun behind the umbrella trees. They talked of all sorts of various things.

"And what are you going to be, Bob, when you grow up?"

"A writer," he said.

"Oh, that's a big ambition; it takes a lot of work."

"I know, but I'm going to try," he said. "I've read a lot."

"Bob, haven't you anything to do after school?"

"How do you mean?"

"I mean, I hate to see you kept in so much, washing the boards."

"I like it," he said. "I never do what I don't like."

"But nevertheless."

"No, I've got to do that," he said. He thought for a while and said, "Do me a favor, Miss Taylor?"

"It all depends."

"I walk every Saturday from out around Buetrick Street along the creek to Lake Michigan. They're a lot of butterflies and crayfish and birds. Maybe you'd like to walk, too."

"Thank you," she said.

"Then you'll come?"

"I'm afraid not."

"Don't you think it'd be fun?"

"Yes, I'm sure of that, but I'm going to be busy."

He started to ask doing what, but stopped.

"I take along sandwiches," he said. "Ham-and-pickle ones. And orange pop and just walk along, taking my time. I get down to the lake about noon and walk back and get home about three o'clock. It makes a real fine day, and I wish you'd come. Do you collect butterflies? I have a big collection. We could start one for you."

"Thanks, Bob, but no, perhaps some other time."

He looked at her and said, "I shouldn't have asked you, should I?"

"You have every right to ask anything you want to," she said.

A few days later she found an old copy of *Great Expectations*, which she no longer wanted, and gave it to Bob. He was very grateful and took it home and stayed up that night and read it through and talked about it the next morning. Each day now he met her just beyond sight of her boarding house and many days she would start to say, "Bob—" and tell him not to come to meet her anymore, but she never finished saying it, and he talked with her about Dickens and Kipling and Poe and others, coming and going to school. She found a butterfly on her desk on Friday morning. She almost waved it away before she found it was dead and had been placed there while she was out of the room. She glanced at Bob over the heads of her other students, but he was looking at his book; not reading, just looking at it.

It was about this time that she found it impossible to call on Bob to recite in class. She would hover her pencil about his name and then call the next person up or down the list. Nor would she look at him while they were walking to or from school. But on several late afternoons as he moved his arm high on the blackboard, sponging away the arithmetic symbols, she found herself glancing over at him for seconds at a time before she returned to her papers.

And then on Saturday morning he was standing in the middle of the creek with his overalls rolled up to his knees, kneeling down to catch a crayfish under a rock, when he looked up and there on the edge of the running stream was Miss Ann Taylor.

"Well, here I am," she said, laughing.

"And do you know," he said, "I'm not surprised."

"Show me the crayfish and the butterflies," she said.

They walked down to the lake and sat on the sand with a warm wind blowing softly about them, fluttering her hair and the ruffle on her blouse, and he sat a few yards back from her and they ate the ham-and-pickle sandwiches and drank the orange pop solemnly.

"Gee, this is swell," he said. "This is the swellest time ever in my life."

"I didn't think I would ever come on a picnic like this," she said.

"With some kid," he said.

"I'm comfortable, however," she said.

"That's good news."

They said little else during the afternoon.

"This is all wrong," he said, later. "And I can't figure why it should be. Just walking along and catching old butterflies and crayfish and eating sandwiches. But Mom and Dad'd rib the heck out of me if they knew, and the kids would, too. And the other teachers, I suppose, would laugh at you, wouldn't they?"

"I'm afraid so."

"I guess we better not do any more butterfly catching, then."

"I don't exactly understand how I came here at all," she said. And the day was over.

That was about all there was to the meeting of Ann Taylor and Bob Spaulding, two or three monarch butterflies, a copy of Dickens, a dozen crayfish, four sandwiches, and two bottles of Orange Crush. The next Monday, quite unexpectedly, though he waited a long time, Bob did not see Miss Taylor come out to walk to school. But discovered later that she had left earlier and was already at school. Also, Monday night, she left early, with a headache, and another teacher finished her last class. He walked by her boarding house but did not see her anywhere, and he was afraid to ring the bell and inquire.

On Tuesday night after school they were both in the silent room again, he sponging the board contentedly, as if this time might go on forever, and she seated, working on her papers as if she, too, would be in this room and this particular peace and happiness forever, when suddenly the courthouse clock struck. It was a block away and its great bronze boom shuddered one's body and made the ash of time shake away off your bones and slide through your blood, making you seem older by the minute. Stunned by that clock, you could not but sense the crashing flow of time, and as the clock said five o'clock, Miss Taylor suddenly looked up at it for a long time, and then she put down her pen.

"Bob," she said.

He turned, startled. Neither of them had spoken in the peaceful and good hour before.

"Will you come here?" she asked.

He put down the sponge slowly.

"Yes," he said.

"Bob, I want you to sit down."

"Yes'm."

She looked at him intently for a moment until he looked away. "Bob, I wonder if you know what I'm going to talk to you about. Do you know?"

"Yes."

"Maybe it'd be a good idea if you told me, first."

"About us," he said, at last.

"How old are you, Bob?"

"Going on fourteen."

"You're thirteen years old."

He winced. "Yes'm."

"And do you know how old I am?"

"Yes'm. I heard. Twenty-four."

"Twenty-four."

"I'll be twenty-four in ten years, almost," he said.

"But unfortunately you're not twenty-four now."

"No, but sometimes I feel twenty-four."

"Yes, and sometimes you almost act it."

"Do I, really!"

"Now sit still there; don't bound around, we've a lot to discuss. It's very important that we understand what is happening, don't you agree?"

"Yes, I guess so."

"First, let's admit we are the greatest and best friends in the world. Let's admit I have never had a student like you, nor have I had as much affection for any boy I've ever known." He flushed at this. She went on. "And let me speak for you—you've found me to be the nicest teacher of all the teachers you've ever known."

"Oh, more than that," he said.

"Perhaps more than that, but there are facts to be faced and an entire way of life to be examined, and a town and its people, and you and me to be considered. I've thought this over for a good many days, Bob. Don't think I've missed anything, or been unaware of my own feelings in the matter. Under some circumstances our friendship would be odd indeed. But then you are no ordinary boy. I know myself pretty well, I think, and I know I'm not sick, either mentally or physically, and that whatever has evolved here has been a true regard for your character and goodness, Bob; but those are not the things we consider in this world, Bob, unless they occur in a man of a certain age. I don't know if I'm saying this right."

"It's all right," he said. "It's just if I was ten years older and about fifteen inches taller it'd make all the difference, and that's silly," he said, "to go by how tall a person is."

"The world hasn't found it so."

"I'm not the world," he protested.

"I know it seems foolish," she said. "When you feel very grown up and right and have nothing to be ashamed of. You have nothing at all to be ashamed of, Bob, remember that. You have been very honest and good, and I hope I have been, too."

"You have," he said.

"In an ideal climate, Bob, maybe someday they will be able to judge the oldness of a person's mind so accurately that they can say, This is a man, though his body is only thirteen; by some miracle of circumstance and fortune, this is a man, with a man's recognition of responsibility and position and duty; but until that day, Bob, I'm afraid we're going to have to go by ages and heights in the ordinary way in an ordinary world."

"I don't like that," he said.

"Perhaps I don't like it, either, but do you want to end up far unhappier than you are now? Do you want both of us to be unhappy? Which we would certainly be. There really is no way to do anything about us—it is so strange even to try to talk about us."

"Yes'm."

"But at least we know all about us and the fact that we have been right and fair and good and there is nothing wrong with our knowing each other, nor did we ever intend that it should be, for we both understand how impossible it is, don't we?"

"Yes, I know. But I can't help it."

"Now we must decide what to do about it," she said. "Now only you and I know about this. Later, others might know. I can secure a transfer from this school to another one—"

"No!"

"Or I can have you transferred to another school."

"You don't have to do that," he said.

"Why?"

"We're moving. My folks and I, we're going to live in Madison. We're leaving next week."

"It has nothing to do with all this, has it?"

"No, no, everything's all right. It's just that my father has a new job there. It's only fifty miles away. I can see you, can't I, when I come to town?"

"Do you think that would be a good idea?"

"No, I guess not."

They sat awhile in the silent schoolroom.

"When did all of this happen?" he said, helplessly.

"I don't know," she said. "Nobody ever knows. They haven't known for thousands of years, and I don't think they ever will. People either like each other or don't, and sometimes two people like each other who shouldn't. I can't explain myself, and certainly you can't explain you."

"I guess I'd better get home," he said.

"You're not mad at me, are you?"

"Oh, gosh no, I could never be mad at you."

"There's one more thing. I want you to remember, there are compensations in life. There always are, or we wouldn't go on living. You don't feel well, now; neither do I. But something will happen to fix that. Do you believe that?"

"I'd like to."

"Well, it's true."

"If only," he said.

"What?"

"If only you'd wait for me," he blurted.

"Ten years?"

"I'd be twenty-four then."

"But I'd be thirty-four and another person entirely, perhaps. No, I don't think it can be done."

"Wouldn't you like it to be done?" he cried.

"Yes," she said quietly. "It's silly and it wouldn't work, but I would like it very much."

He sat there for a long time.

"I'll never forget you," he said.

"It's nice for you to say that, even though it can't be true, because life isn't that way. You'll forget."

"I'll never forget. I'll find a way of never forgetting you," he said.

She got up and went to erase the boards.

"I'll help you," he said.

"No, no," she said hastily. "You go on now, get home, and no more tending to the boards after school. I'll assign Helen Stevens to do it."

He left the school. Looking back, outside, he saw Miss Ann Taylor, for the last time, at the board, slowly washing out the chalked words, her hand moving up and down.

He moved away from the town the next week and was gone for sixteen years. Though he was only fifty miles away, he never got down to Green Town again until he was almost thirty and married, and then one spring they were driving through on their way to Chicago and stopped off for a day.

Bob left his wife at the hotel and walked around town and finally asked about Miss Ann Taylor, but no one remembered at first, and then one of them remembered.

"Oh, yes, the pretty teacher. She died in 1936, not long after you left."

Had she ever married? No, come to think of it, she never had.

He walked out to the cemetery in the afternoon and found her stone, which said, "Ann Taylor, born 1910, died 1936." And he thought, Twenty-six years old. Why, I'm three years older than you are now, Miss Taylor.

Later in the day the people in the town saw Bob Spaulding's wife strolling to meet him under the elm trees and the oak trees, and they all turned to watch her pass, for her face shifted with bright shadows as she walked; she was the fine peaches of summer in the snow of winter, and she was cool milk for cereal on a hot early-summer morning. And this was one of those rare few days in time when the climate was balanced like a maple leaf between winds that blow just right, one of those days that should have been named, everyone agreed, after Robert Spaulding's wife.

The Wish

A whisper of snow touched the cold window.

The vast house creaked in a wind from nowhere.

"What?" I said.

"I didn't say anything." Charlie Simmons, behind me at the fireplace, shook popcorn quietly in a vast metal sieve. "Not a word."

"Damn it, Charlie, I *heard* you. . . ."

Stunned, I watched the snow fall on far streets and empty fields. It was a proper night for ghosts of whiteness to visit windows and wander off.

"You're imagining things," said Charlie.

Am I? I thought. Does the weather have voices? Is there a language of night and time and snow? What goes on between that dark out there and my soul in here?

For there in the shadows, a whole civilization of doves seemed to be landing unseen, without benefit of moon or lamp.

And was it the snow softly whispering out there, or was it the past, accumulations of old time and need, despairs mounding themselves to panics and at last finding tongue?

"God, Charles. Just now, I could have sworn I heard you say—"

"Say what?"

"You said: 'Make a wish.' "

"*I* did?"

His laughter behind me did not make me turn; I kept on watching the snow fall and I told him what I must tell—

"You said, 'It's a special, fine, strange night. So make the finest, dearest, strangest wish ever in your life, deep from your heart. It will be yours.' That's what I heard you say."

"No." I saw his image in the glass shake its head. "But, Tom, you've stood there hypnotized by the snowfall for half an hour. The fire on the hearth talked. Wishes don't come true, Tom. But—" and here he stopped and added with some surprise, "by God, you *did* hear something, didn't you? Well, here. Drink."

The popcorn was done popping. He poured wine which I did not touch. The snow was falling steadily along the dark window in pale breaths.

"Why?" I asked. "Why would this *wish* jump into my head? If you didn't say it, what did?"

What indeed, I thought; what's out there, and who are we? Two writers late, alone, my friend invited for the night, two old companions used to much talk and gossip about ghosts, who've tried their hands at all the usual psychic stuffs, Ouija boards, tarot cards, telepathies, the junk of amiable friendship over years, but always full of taunts and jokes and idle fooleries.

But this out there tonight, I thought, ends the jokes, erases smiles. The snow—why, look! It's burying our laughter. . . .

"Why?" said Charlie at my elbow, drinking wine, gazing at

the red-green-blue Yule-tree lights and now at the back of my neck. "Why a *wish* on a night like this? Well, it is the night before Christmas, right? Five minutes from now, Christ is born. Christ and the winter solstice all in one week. This week, this night, proves that Earth won't die. The winter has touched bottom and now starts upward toward the light. That's special. That's incredible."

"Yes," I murmured, and thought of the old days when cavemen died in their hearts when autumn came and the sun went away and the ape-men cried until the world shifted in its white sleep and the sun rose earlier one fine morning and the universe was saved once more, for a little while. "Yes."

"So—" Charlie read my thoughts and sipped his wine. "Christ always was the promise of spring, wasn't he? In the midst of the longest night of the year, Time shook, Earth shuddered and calved a myth. And what did the myth yell? Happy New Year! God, yes, January first isn't New Year's Day. Christ's birthday is. His breath, sweet as clover, touches our nostrils, promises spring, this very moment before midnight. Take a deep breath, Thomas."

"Shut up!"

"Why? Do you hear voices again?"

Yes! I turned to the window. In sixty seconds, it would be the morn of His birth. What purer, rarer hour was there, I thought wildly, for wishes.

"Tom—" Charlie seized my elbow. But I was gone deep and very wild indeed. Is this a special time? I thought. Do holy ghosts wander on nights of falling snow to do us favors in this strange-held hour? If I make a wish in secret, will that perambulating night, strange sleeps, old blizzards give back my wish tenfold?

I shut my eyes. My throat convulsed.

"Don't," said Charlie.

But it trembled on my lips. I could not wait. Now, now, I thought, a strange star burns at Bethlehem.

"Tom," gasped Charlie, "for Christ's sake!"

Christ, yes, I thought, and said:

"My wish is, for one hour tonight—"

"No!" Charlie struck me, once, to shut my mouth.

"—please, make my father alive again."

The mantel clock struck twelve times to midnight.

"Oh, Thomas . . ." Charlie grieved. His hand fell away from my arm. "Oh, Tom."

A gust of snow rattled the window, clung like a shroud, unraveled away.

The front door exploded wide.

Snow sprang over us in a shower.

"What a sad wish. And . . . it has just come true."

"True?" I whirled to stare at that open door which beckoned like a tomb.

"Don't go, Tom," said Charlie.

The door slammed. Outside, I ran; oh, God, how I ran.

"Tom, come back!" The voice faded far behind me in the whirling fall of white. "Oh, God, *don't!*"

But in this minute after midnight I ran and ran, mindless, gibbering, yelling my heart on to beat, blood to move, legs to run and keep running, and I thought: Him! Him! I know where *he* is! If the gift is mine! If the wish comes true! I know his *place!* And all about in the night-snowing town the bells of Christmas began to clang and chant and clamor. They circled and paced and drew me on as I shouted and mouthed snow and knew maniac desire.

Fool! I thought. He's dead! Go back!

But what if he is alive, one hour tonight, and I *didn't* go to find him?

I was outside town, with no hat or coat, but so warm from running, a salty mask froze my face and flaked away with the jolt of each stride down the middle of an empty road, with the sound of joyous bells blown away and gone.

A wind took me around a final corner of wilderness where a dark wall waited for me.

The cemetery.

I stood by the heavy iron gates, looking numbly in.

The graveyard resembled the scattered ruins of an ancient fort, blown up lifetimes ago, its monuments buried deep in some new Ice Age.

Suddenly, miracles were not possible.

Suddenly the night was just so much wine and talk and dumb enchantments and I running for no reason save I believed, I truly believed, I had felt something *happen* out here in this snow-dead world. . . .

Now I was so burdened at the blind sight of those untouched graves and printless snow, I would gladly have sunk and died there myself. I could not go back to town to face Charlie. I began to think this was all some brutal humor and awful trick of his, his insane ability to guess someone's terrible need and toy with it. *Had* he whispered behind my back, made promises, nudged me toward this wish? Christ!

I touched the padlocked gate.

What was here? Only a flat stone with a name and BORN 1888, DIED 1957, an inscription that even on summer days was hard to find, for the grass grew thick and the leaves gathered in mounds.

I let go of the iron gate and turned. Then, in an instant, I gasped. An unbelieving shout tore from my throat.

For I had sensed something beyond the wall, near the small boarded-up gatekeeper's lodge.

Was there some faint breathing there? A muted cry?

Or just a hint of warmth on the wind?

I clenched the iron gate and stared beyond.

Yes, there! The faintest track, as if a bird had landed to run along between the buried stones. Another moment, and I would have missed it forever!

I yelled, I ran, I leaped.

I have never, oh, God, in all my life, leaped so high. I cleared the wall and fell down on the other side, a last shout bloodying my mouth. I scrambled around to the far side of the gatehouse.

There in shadows, hidden away from the wind, leaning against a wall, was a man, eyes shut, his hands crossed over his chest.

I stared at him, wildly. I leaned insanely close to peer, to find.

I did not know this man.

He was old, old, very old.

I must have groaned with fresh despair.

For now the old man opened his trembling eyes.

It was his eyes, looking at me, that made me shout:

"Dad!"

I lurched to seize him into dim lamplight and the falling snows of after-midnight.

Charlie's voice, a long way off in the snowy town, echoed and pleaded: No, don't, go, run. Nightmare. Stop.

The man who stood before me did not know me.

Like a scarecrow held up against the wind, this strange but familiar shape tried to make me out with his white-blind and cobwebbed eyes. Who? he seemed to be thinking.

Then an answering cry burst from his mouth:

"—om! —om!"

He could not pronounce the T.

But it was my name.

Like a man on a cliff edge, terrified that the earth might fall and drop him back to night and soil, he shuddered, grappled me.

"—om!"

I held him tight. He could not fall.

Riveted in a fierce embrace, not able to let go, we stood and rocked gently, strangely, two men made one, in a wilderness of shredding snow.

Tom, O Tom, he grieved brokenly, over and over.

Father, O dear Pa, Dad, I thought, I said.

The old man stiffened, for over my shoulder he must have truly seen for the first time the stones, the empty fields of death. He gasped as if to cry: What *is* this place?

Old as his face was, in the instant of recognition and remembrance, his eyes, his cheeks, his mouth withered and grew yet older, saying No.

He turned to me as if seeking answers, some guardian of his rights, some protector who might say No with him. But the cold truth was in my eyes.

We were both staring now at the dim path his feet had made blundering across the land from the place where he had been buried for many years.

No, no, no, no, no, no, *no!*

The words fired from his mouth.

But he could not pronounce the *n*.

So it was a wild explosion of: "...o ...o ...o ...o ... o ...o!"

A forlorn, dismayed, child-whistling cry.

Then, another question shadowed his face.

I know this place. But *why* am I here?

He clawed his arms. He stared down at his withered chest.

God gives us dreadful gifts. The most dreadful of all is memory.

He remembered.

And he began to melt away. He recalled his body shriveling, his dim heart gone to stillness; the slam of some eternal door of night.

He stood very still in my arms, his eyelids flickering over the stuffs that shifted grotesque furnitures within his head. He must have asked himself the most terrible question of all:

Who has done this thing to me?

He opened his eyes. His gaze beat at me.

You? it said.

Yes, I thought. *I* wished you alive this night.

You! his face and body cried.

And then, half-aloud, the final inquisition:

"Why . . . ?"

Now it was my turn to be blasted and riven.

Why, indeed, had I done this to him?

How had I dared to wish for this awful, this harrowing, confrontation?

What was I to do now with this man, this stranger, this old, bewildered, and frightened child? Why had I summoned him, just to send him back to soils and graves and dreadful sleeps?

Had I even bothered to think of the consequences? No. Raw impulse had shot me from home to this burial field like a mindless stone to a mindless goal. Why? Why?

My father, this old man, stood in the snow now, trembling, waiting for my pitiful answer.

A child again, I could not speak. Some part of me knew a truth I could not say. Inarticulate with him in life, I found myself yet more mute in his waking death.

The truth raved inside my head, cried along the fibers of my spirit and being, but could not break forth from my tongue. I felt my own shouts locked inside.

The moment was passing. This hour would soon be gone. I would lose the chance to say what must be said, what should have been said when he was warm and above the earth so many years ago.

Somewhere far off across country, the bells sounded twelve-thirty on this Christmas morn. Christ ticked in the wind. Snow flaked away at my face with time and cold, cold and time.

Why? my father's eyes asked me; why have you brought me here?

"I—" and then I stopped.

For his hand had tightened on my arm. His face had found its own reason.

This was his chance, too, *his* final hour to say what he should have said when I was twelve or fourteen or twenty-six. No matter if *I* stood mute. Here in the falling snow, he could make his peace and go his way.

His mouth opened. It was hard, so dreadfully hard, for him to force the old words out. Only the ghost within the withered shell could dare to agonize and gasp. He whispered three words, lost in the wind.

"Yes?" I urged.

He held me tight and tried to keep his eyes open in the blizzard-night. He wanted to sleep, but first his mouth gaped and whistled again and again:

". . . I........uvvv............yuuuuuuuu . . . !"

He stopped, trembled, wracked his body, and tried to shout it again, failing:

". . . I........vvv............yyy............u . . . !"

"Oh, Dad!" I cried. "Let me say it *for* you!"

He stood very still and waited.

"Were you trying to say I . . . love . . . you?"

"Esssss!" he cried. And burst out, very clearly, at long last: "Oh, *yes!*"

"Oh, Dad," I said, wild with miserable happiness, all gain and loss. "Oh, and Pa, dear Pa, *I* love *you.*"

We fell together. We held.

I wept.

And from some strange dry well within his terrible flesh I saw my father squeeze forth tears which trembled and flashed on his eyelids.

And the final question was thus asked and answered.

Why have you brought me here?

Why the wish, why the gifts, and why this snowing night?

Because we had had to say, before the doors were shut and sealed forever, what we never had said in life.

And now it had been said and we stood holding each other in the wilderness, father and son, son and father, the parts of the whole suddenly interchangeable with joy.

The tears turned to ice upon my cheeks.

———•———

We stood in the cold wind and falling snow for a long while until we heard the sound of the bells at twelve forty-five, and still we stood in the snowing night saying no more—no more ever need be said—until at last our hour was done.

All over the white world the clocks of one A.M. on Christmas morn, with Christ new in the fresh straw, sounded the end of that gift which had passed so briefly into and now out of our numb hands.

My father held me in his arms.

The last sound of the one-o'clock bells faded.

I felt my father step back, at ease now.

His fingers touched my cheek.

I heard him walking in the snow.

The sound of his walking faded even as the last of the crying faded within myself.

I opened my eyes only in time to see him, a hundred yards off, walking. He turned and waved, once, at me.

The snow came down in a curtain.

How brave, I thought, to go where you go now, old man, and no complaint.

I walked back into town.

I had a drink with Charles by the fire. He looked in my face and drank a silent toast to what he saw there.

Upstairs, my bed waited for me like a great fold of white snow.

The snow was falling beyond my window for a thousand miles to the north, five hundred miles to the east, two hundred miles west, a hundred miles to the south. The snow fell on everything, everywhere. It fell on two sets of footprints beyond the town: one set coming out and the other going back to be lost among the graves.

I lay on my bed of snow. I remembered my father's face as he waved and turned and went away.

It was the face of the youngest, happiest man I had ever seen.

With that I slept, and gave up weeping.

Forever and the Earth

After seventy years of writing short stories that never sold, Mr. Henry William Field arose one night at eleven-thirty and burned ten million words. He carried the manuscripts downstairs through his dark old mansion and threw them into the furnace.

"That's that," he said, and thinking about his lost art and his misspent life, he put himself to bed, among his rich antiques. "My mistake was in ever trying to picture this wild world of A.D. 2257. The rockets, the atom wonders, the travels to planets and double suns. Nobody can do it. Everyone's tried. All of our modern authors have failed."

Space was too big for them, and rockets too swift, and atomic science too instantaneous, he thought. But at least the other writers, while failing, had been published, while he, in his idle wealth, had used the years of his life for nothing.

After an hour of feeling this way, he fumbled through the night rooms to his library and switched on a green hurricane lamp. At random, from a collection untouched in fifty years, he selected a book. It was a book three centuries yellow and three centuries brittle, but he settled into it and read hungrily until dawn. . . .

At nine the next morning, Henry William Field staggered from his library, called his servants, televised lawyers, scientists, literateurs.

"Come at once!" he cried.

By noon, a dozen people had stepped into the study where Henry William Field sat, very disreputable and hysterical with an odd, feeding joy, unshaven and feverish. He clutched a thick book in his brittle arms and laughed if anyone even said good morning.

"Here you see a book," he said at last, holding it out, "written by a giant, a man born in Asheville, North Carolina, in the year 1900. Long gone to dust, he published four huge novels. He was a whirlwind. He lifted up mountains and collected winds. He left a trunk of penciled manuscripts behind when he lay in bed at Johns Hopkins Hospital in Baltimore in the year 1938, on September fifteenth, and died of pneumonia, an ancient and awful disease."

They looked at the book.

Look Homeward, Angel.

He drew forth three more. *Of Time and the River. The Web and the Rock. You Can't Go Home Again.*

"By Thomas Wolfe," said the old man. "Three centuries cold in the North Carolina earth."

"You mean you've called us simply to see four books by a dead man?" his friends protested.

"More than that! I've called you because I feel Tom Wolfe's the man, the necessary man, to write of space, of time, huge things like nebulae and galactic war, meteors and planets, all the dark things he loved and put on paper were like this. He was born out of his time. He needed really *big* things to play with and never found them on Earth. He should have been born this afternoon instead of one hundred thousand mornings ago."

"I'm afraid you're a bit late," said Professor Bolton.

"I don't intend to be late!" snapped the old man. "I will *not* be frustrated by reality. You, professor, have experimented with time-travel. I expect you to finish your time machine as soon as possible. Here's a check, a blank check, fill it in. If you need more money, ask for it. You've done *some* traveling already, haven't you?"

"A few years, yes, but nothing like centuries—"

"We'll *make* it centuries! You others"—he swept them with a fierce and shining glance—"will work with Bolton. I *must* have Thomas Wolfe."

"What!" They fell back before him.

"Yes," he said. "That's the plan. Wolfe is to be brought to me. We will collaborate in the task of describing the flight from Earth to Mars, as only he could describe it!"

They left him in his library with his books, turning the dry pages, nodding to himself. "Yes. Oh, dear Lord yes, Tom's the boy, Tom is the *very* boy for this."

The months passed slowly. Days showed a maddening reluctance to leave the calendar, and weeks lingered on until Mr. Henry William Field began to scream silently.

At the end of four months, Mr. Field awoke one midnight. The phone was ringing. He put his hand out in the darkness.

"Yes?"

"This is Professor Bolton calling."

"Yes, Bolton?"

"I'll be leaving in an hour," said the voice.

"Leaving? Leaving where? Are you quitting? You can't do that!"

"Please, Mr. Field, leaving means *leaving*."

"You mean, you're actually going?"

"Within the hour."

"To 1938? To September fifteenth?"

"Yes!"

"You're sure you've the date fixed correctly? You'll arrive before he dies? Be sure of it! Good Lord, you'd better get there a good hour before his death, don't you think?"

"*Two* hours. On the way back, we'll mark time in Bermuda, borrow ten days of free floating continuum, inject him, tan him, swim him, vitaminize him, make him well."

"I'm so excited I can't hold the phone. Good luck, Bolton. Bring him through safely!"

"Thank you, sir. Good-bye."

The phone clicked.

Mr. Henry William Field lay through the ticking night. He thought of Tom Wolfe as a lost brother to be lifted intact from under a cold, chiseled stone, to be restored to blood and fire and speaking. He trembled each time he thought of Bolton whirling on the time wind back to other calendars and other days, bearing medicines to change flesh and save souls.

Tom, he thought, faintly, in the half-awake warmth of an old man calling after his favorite and long-gone child, Tom, where are you tonight, Tom? Come along now, we'll help you through, you've got to come, there's need for you. I couldn't do it, Tom, none of us here can. So the next best thing to doing it myself, Tom, is helping you to do it. You can play with rockets like jackstraws, Tom, and you can have the stars, like a handful of crystals. Anything your heart asks, it's here. You'd like the fire and the travel, Tom, it was made for you. Oh, we've a pale lot of writers today, I've read them all, Tom, and they're not like you. I've waded in libraries of their stuff and they've never touched space, Tom; we need *you* for that! Give an old man his wish then, for God knows I've waited all my life for myself or some other to write the really great book about the stars, and

I've waited in vain. So, wherever you are tonight, Tom Wolfe, make yourself tall. It's that book you were going to write. It's that good book the critics said was in you when you stopped breathing. Here's your chance, will you do it, Tom? Will you listen and come through to us, will you do that tonight, and be here in the morning when I wake? Will you, Tom?

His eyelids closed down over the fever and the demand. His tongue stopped quivering in his sleeping mouth.

The clock struck four.

Awakening to the white coolness of morning, he felt the excitement rising and welling in himself. He did not wish to blink, for fear that the thing which awaited him somewhere in the house might run off and slam a door, gone forever. His hands reached up to clutch his thin chest.

Far away . . . footsteps . . .

A series of doors opened and shut. Two men entered the bedroom.

Field could hear them breathe. Their footsteps took on identities. The first steps were those of a spider, small and precise: Bolton. The second steps were those of a big man, a large man, a heavy man.

"Tom?" cried the old man. He did not open his eyes.

"Yes," said a voice, at last.

Tom Wolfe burst the seams of Field's imagination, as a huge child bursts the lining of a too-small coat.

"Tom Wolfe, let me look at you!" If Field said it once he said it a dozen times as he fumbled from bed, shaking violently. "Put up the blinds, for God's sake, I want to see this! Tom Wolfe, is that *you?*"

Tom Wolfe looked down from his tall thick body, with big hands out to balance himself in a world that was strange. He looked at the old man and the room and his mouth was trembling.

"You're just as they said you were, Tom!"

Thomas Wolfe began to laugh and the laughing was huge, for he must have thought himself insane or in a nightmare, and he came to the old man and touched him and he looked at Professor Bolton and felt of himself, his arms and legs, he coughed experimentally and touched his own brow. "My fever's gone," he said. "I'm not sick anymore."

"Of course not, Tom."

"What a night," said Tom Wolfe. "It hasn't been easy. I thought I was sicker than any man ever was. I felt myself floating and I thought, This is fever. I felt myself traveling, and thought, I'm dying fast. A man came to me. I thought, This is the Lord's messenger. He took my hands. I smelled electricity. I flew up and over, and I saw a brass city. I thought, I've arrived. This is the city of heaven, there is the Gate! I'm numb from head to toe, like someone left in the snow to freeze. I've got to laugh and do things or I might think myself insane. You're not God, are you? You don't look like Him."

The old man laughed. "No, no, Tom, not God, but playing at it. I'm Field." He laughed again. "Lord, listen to me. I said it as if you should know who Field is. Field, the financier, Tom, bow low, kiss my ring finger. I'm Henry Field. I like your work, I brought you here. Come along."

The old man drew him to an immense crystal window.

"Do you see those lights in the sky, Tom?"

"Yes, sir."

"Those fireworks?"

"Yes."

"They're not what you think, son. It's not July Fourth, Tom. Not in the usual way. Every day's Independence Day now. Man has declared his Freedom from Earth. Gravitation without representation has been overthrown. The Revolt has long since been successful. That green Roman Candle's going to Mars. That red fire, that's the Venus rocket. And the others, you see the yellow and the blue? Rockets, all of them!"

Thomas Wolfe gazed up like an immense child caught amid

the colorized glories of a July evening when the set-pieces are awhirl with phosphorous and glitter and barking explosion.

"What year is this?"

"The year of the rocket. Look here." And the old man touched some flowers that bloomed at his touch. The blossoms were like blue and white fire. They burned and sparkled their cold, long petals. The blooms were two feet wide, and they were the color of an autumn moon. "Moon-flowers," said the old man. "From the other side of the moon." He brushed them and they dripped away into a silver rain, a shower of white sparks on the air. "The year of the rocket. That's a title for you, Tom. That's why we brought you here, we've need of you. You're the only man could handle the sun without being burnt to a ridiculous cinder. We want you to juggle the sun, Tom, and the stars, and whatever else you see on your trip to Mars."

"Mars?" Thomas Wolfe turned to seize the old man's arm, bending down to him, searching his face in unbelief.

"Tonight. You leave at six o'clock."

The old man held a fluttering pink ticket on the air, waiting for Tom to think to take it.

It was five in the afternoon. "Of course, of course I appreciate what you've done," cried Thomas Wolfe.

"Sit down, Tom. Stop walking around."

"Let me finish, Mr. Field, let me get through with this, I've got to say it."

"We've been arguing for hours," pleaded Mr. Field, exhaustedly.

They had talked from breakfast until lunch until tea, they had wandered through a dozen rooms and ten dozen arguments, they had perspired and grown cold and perspired again.

"It all comes down to this," said Thomas Wolfe, at last. "I can't stay here, Mr. Field. I've got to go back. This isn't my time. You've no right to interfere—"

"But, I—"

"I was deep in my work, my best yet to come, and now you run me off three centuries. Mr. Field, I want you to call Mr. Bolton back. I want you to have him put me in his machine, whatever it is, and return me to 1938, my rightful place and year. That's all I ask of you."

"But, don't you *want* to see Mars?"

"With all my heart. But I know it isn't for me. It would throw my writing off. I'd have a huge handful of experience that I couldn't fit into my other writing when I went home."

"You don't understand, Tom, you don't understand at all."

"I understand that you're selfish."

"Selfish? Yes," said the old man. "For myself, and for others, very selfish."

"I want to go home."

"Listen to me, Tom."

"Call Mr. Bolton."

"Tom, I don't want to have to tell you this. I thought I wouldn't have to, that it wouldn't be necessary. Now, you leave me only this alternative." The old man's right hand fetched hold of a curtained wall, swept back the drapes, revealing a large white screen, and dialed a number, a series of numbers. The screen flickered into vivid color, the lights of the room darkened, darkened, and a graveyard took line before their eyes.

"What are you doing?" demanded Wolfe, striding forward, staring at the screen.

"I don't like this at all," said the old man. "Look there."

The graveyard lay in midafternoon light, the light of summer. From the screen drifted the smell of summer earth, granite, and the odor of a nearby creek. From the trees, a bird called. Red and yellow flowers nodded among the stones, and the screen moved, the sky rotated, the old man twisted a dial for emphasis, and in the center of the screen, growing large, coming closer, yet larger, and now filling their senses, was a dark granite mass; and Thomas Wolfe, looking up in the dim room, ran his eyes over the chiseled words, once, twice, three times, gasped, and read again, for there was his name:

THOMAS WOLFE.

And the date of his birth and the date of his death, and the flowers and green ferns smelling sweetly on the air of the cold room.

"Turn it off," he said.

"I'm sorry, Tom."

"Turn it off, turn it off! I don't believe it."

"It's there."

The screen went black and now the entire room was a midnight vault, a tomb, with the last faint odor of flowers.

"I didn't wake up again," said Thomas Wolfe.

"No. You died that September of 1938. So, you see. O God, the ironies, it's like the title of your book. Tom, you *can't* go home again."

"I never finished my book."

"It was edited for you, by others who went over it, carefully."

"I didn't finish my work, I didn't finish my work."

"Don't take it so badly, Tom."

"How else can I take it?"

The old man didn't turn on the lights. He didn't want to see Tom there. "Sit down, boy." No reply. "Tom?" No answer. "Sit down, son; will you have something to drink?" For answer there was only a sigh and a kind of brutal morning.

"Good Lord," said Tom, "it's not fair. I had so much left to do, it's not fair." He began to weep quietly.

"Don't do that," said the old man. "Listen. Listen to me. You're still alive, aren't you? Here? Now? You still *feel*, don't *you?*"

Thomas Wolfe waited for a minute and then he said, "Yes."

"All right, then." The old man pressed forward on the dark air. "I've brought you here, I've given you another chance, Tom. An extra month or so. Do you think *I* haven't grieved for you? When I read your books and saw your gravestone there, three

183

centuries worn by rains and wind, boy, don't you imagine how it killed me to think of your talent gone away? Well, it did! It killed me, Tom. And I spent my money to find a way to you. You've got a respite, not long, not long at all. Professor Bolton says that, with luck, he can hold the channels open through time for eight weeks. He can keep you here that long, and only that long. In that interval, Tom, you must write the book you've wanted to write—no, not the book you were working on for them, son, no, for they're dead and gone and it can't be changed. No, this time it's a book for us, Tom, for us the living, that's the book we want. A book you can leave with us, for you, a book bigger and better in every way than anything you ever wrote; say you'll *do* it, Tom, say you'll forget about that stone and that hospital for eight weeks and start to work for us, will you, Tom, will you?"

The lights came slowly on. Tom Wolfe stood tall at the window, looking out, his face huge and tired and pale. He watched the rockets on the sky of early evening. "I imagine I don't realize what you've done for me," he said. "You've given me a little more time, and time is the thing I love most and need, the thing I always hated and fought against, and the only way I can show my appreciation is by doing as you say." He hesitated. "And when I'm finished, then what?"

"Back to your hospital in 1938, Tom."

"Must I?"

"We can't change time. We borrowed you for five minutes. We'll return you to your hospital cot five minutes after you left it. That way, we upset nothing. It's all been written. You can't hurt us in the future by living here now with us, but, if you refused to go back, you could hurt the past, and resultantly, the future, make it into some sort of chaos."

"Eight weeks," said Thomas Wolfe.

"Eight weeks."

"And the Mars rocket leaves in an hour?"

"Yes."

"I'll need pencils and paper."

"Here they are."

"I'd better go get ready. Good-bye, Mr. Field."

"Good luck, Tom."

Six o'clock. The sun setting. The sky turning to wine. The big house quiet. The old man shivering in the heat until Professor Bolton entered. "Bolton, how is he getting on, how was he at the port; tell me?"

Bolton smiled. "What a monster he is, so big they had to make a special uniform for him! You should've seen him, walking around, lifting up everything, sniffing like a great hound, talking, his eyes looking at everyone, excited as a ten-year-old!"

"God bless him, oh, God bless him! Bolton, can you keep him here as long as you say?"

Bolton frowned. "He doesn't belong here, you know. If our power should falter, he'd be snapped back to his own time, like a puppet on a rubber band. We'll try and keep him, I assure you."

"You've got to, you understand, you can't let him go back until he's finished with his book. You've—"

"Look," said Bolton. He pointed to the sky. On it was a silver rocket.

"Is that him?" asked the old man.

"That's Tom Wolfe," replied Bolton. "Going to Mars."

"Give 'em hell, Tom, give 'em hell!" shouted the old man, lifting both fists.

They watched the rocket fire into space.

By midnight, the story was coming through.

Henry William Field sat in his library. On his desk was a machine that hummed. It repeated words that were being written out beyond the moon. It scrawled them in black pencil, in facsimile of Tom Wolfe's fevered hand a million miles away. The old man waited for a pile of them to collect and then he seized them and read them aloud to the room where Bolton and the servants stood listening. He read the words about space and time and travel, about a large man and a large journey and how it was in the long midnight and coldness of space, and how a man could be hungry enough to take all of it and ask for more. He read the words that were full of fire and thunder and mystery.

Space was like October, wrote Thomas Wolfe. He said things about its darkness and its loneliness and man so small in it. The eternal and timeless October, was one of the things he said. And then he told of the rocket itself, the smell and the feel of the metal of the rocket, and the sense of destiny and wild exultancy to at last leave Earth behind, all problems and all sadnesses, and go seeking a bigger problem and a bigger sadness. Oh, it was fine writing, and it said what had to be said about space and man and his small rockets out there alone.

The old man read until he was hoarse, and then Bolton read, and then the others, far into the night, when the machine stopped transcribing words and they knew that Tom Wolfe was in bed, then, on the rocket, flying to Mars, probably not asleep, no, he wouldn't sleep for hours yet, no, lying awake, like a boy the night before a circus, not believing the big jeweled black tent is up and the circus is on, with ten billion blazing performers on the high wires and the invisible trapezes of space.

"There," breathed the old man, gentling aside the last pages of the first chapter. "What do you think of that, Bolton?"

"It's good."

"Good hell!" shouted Field. "It's wonderful! Read it again, sit down, read it again, damn you!"

It kept coming through, one day following another, for ten hours at a time. The stack of yellow papers on the floor, scribbled on, grew immense in a week, unbelievable in two weeks, absolutely impossible in a month.

"Listen to this!" cried the old man, and read.

"And this!" he said.

"And this chapter here, and this little novel here, it just came through, Bolton, titled 'The Space War,' a complete novel on how it feels to fight a space war. Tom's been talking to people, soldiers, officers, men, veterans of space. He's got it all here. And here's a chapter called 'The Long Midnight,' and here's one on the Negro colonization of Mars, and here's a character sketch of a Martian, absolutely priceless!"

Bolton cleared his throat. "Mr. Field?"

"Yes, yes, don't bother me."

"I've some bad news, sir."

Field jerked his gray head up. "What? The time element?"

"You'd better tell Wolfe to hurry his work. The connection may break sometime this week," said Bolton, softly.

"I'll give you anything, anything if you keep it going!"

"It's not money, Mr. Field. It's just plain physics right now. I'll do everything I can. But you'd better warn him."

The old man shriveled in his chair and was small. "But you can't take him away from me now, not when he's doing so well. You should see the outline he sent through an hour ago, the stories, the sketches. Here, here's one on spatial tides, another on meteors. Here's a short novel begun, called 'Thistledown and Fire'—"

"I'm sorry."

"If we lose him now, can we get him again?"

"I'd be afraid to tamper too much."

The old man was frozen. "Only one thing to do then. Arrange to have Wolfe type his work, if possible, or dictate it, to save time; rather than have him use pencil and paper, he's got to use a machine of some sort. See to it!"

The machine ticked away by the hour into the night and into the dawn and through the day. The old man slept only in faint dozes, blinking awake when the machine stuttered to life, and all of space and travel and existence came to him through the mind of another:

"... *the great starred meadows of space* ..."

The machine jumped.

"Keep at it Tom, show them!" The old man waited.

The phone rang.

It was Bolton.

"We can't keep it up, Mr. Field. The continuum device will absolute out within the hour."

"Do something!"

"I can't."

The teletype chattered. In a cold fascination, in a horror, the old man watched the black lines form.

"*. . . the Martian cities, immense and unbelievable, as numerous as stones thrown from some great mountain in a rushing and incredible avalanche, resting at last in shining mounds . . .*"

"Tom!" cried the old man.

"Now," said Bolton, on the phone.

The teletype hesitated, typed a word, and fell silent.

"Tom!" screamed the old man.

He shook the teletype.

"It's no use," said the telephone voice. "He's gone. I'm shutting off the time machine."

"No! Leave it on!"

"But—"

"You heard me—leave it! We're not sure he's gone."

"He is. It's no use, we're wasting energy."

"Waste it, then!"

He slammed the phone down.

He turned to the teletype, to the unfinished sentence.

"Come on, Tom, they can't get rid of you that way, you won't let them, will you, boy, come on. Tom, show them, you're big, you're bigger than time or space or their damned machines, you're strong and you've a will like iron, Tom, show them, don't let them send you back!"

The teletype snapped one key.

The old man bleated. "Tom! You *are* there, aren't you? Can you still write? Write, Tom, keep it coming, as long as you keep it rolling, Tom, they *can't* send you back!"

"*The*," typed the machine.

"More, Tom, more!"

Odors of, clacked the machine.

"Yes?"

Mars, typed the machine, and paused. A minute's silence. The machine spaced, skipped a paragraph, and began:

The odors of Mars, the cinnamons and cold spice winds, the winds of cloudy dust and winds of powerful bone and ancient pollen—

"Tom, you're still alive!"

For answer the machine, in the next ten hours, slammed out six chapters of "Flight Before Fury" in a series of fevered explosions.

"Today makes six weeks, Bolton, six whole weeks, Tom gone, on Mars, through the Asteroids. Look here, the manuscripts. Ten thousand words a day, he's driving himself, I don't know when he sleeps, or if he eats, I don't care, he doesn't either, he only wants to get it done, because he knows the time is short."

"I can't understand it," said Bolton. "The power failed because our relays wore out. It took us three days to manufacture and replace the particular channel relays necessary to keep the Time Element steady, and yet Wolfe hung on. There's a personal factor here, Lord knows what, we didn't take into account. Wolfe lives here, in this time, when he *is* here, and can't be snapped back, after all. Time isn't as flexible as we imagined. We used the wrong simile. It's not like a rubber band. More like osmosis; the penetration of membranes by liquids, from Past to Present, but we've got to send him back, can't keep him here, there'd be a void there, a derangement. The one thing that really keeps him here now is himself, his drive, his desire, his work. After it's over he'll go back as naturally as pouring water from a glass."

"I don't care about reasons, all I know is Tom is finishing it.

He has the old fire and description, and something else, something more, a searching of values that supersede time and space. He's done a study of a woman left behind on Earth while the damn rocket heroes leap into space that's beautiful, objective, and subtle; he calls it 'Day of the Rocket,' and it is nothing more than an afternoon of a typical suburban housewife who lives as her ancestral mothers lived, in a house, raising her children, her life not much different from a cavewoman's, in the midst of the splendor of science and the trumpetings of space projectiles; a true and steady and subtle study of her wishes and frustrations. Here's another manuscript, called 'The Indians,' in which he refers to the Martians as Cherokees and Iroquois and Blackfoots, the Indian nations of space, destroyed and driven back. Have a drink, Bolton, have a drink!"

Tom Wolfe returned to Earth at the end of eight weeks.

He arrived in fire as he had left in fire, and his huge steps were burned across space, and in the library of Henry William Field's house were towers of yellow paper, with lines of black scribble and type on them, and these were to be separated out into the six sections of a masterwork that, through endurance, and a knowing that the sands were dwindling from the glass, had mushroomed day after day.

Tom Wolfe came back to Earth and stood in the library of Henry William Field's house and looked at the massive outpourings of his heart and his hand and when the old man said, "Do you want to read it, Tom?" he shook his great head and replied, putting back his thick mane of dark hair with his big pale hand, "No. I don't dare start on it. If I did, I'd want to take it home with me. And I can't do that, can I?"

"No, Tom, you can't."

"No matter *how* much I wanted to?"

"No, that's the way it is. You never wrote another novel in that year, Tom. What was written here must stay here, what was written there must stay there. There's no touching it."

"I see." Tom sank down into a chair with a great sigh. "I'm tired. I'm mightily tired. It's been hard, but it's been good. What day is it?"

"This is the fifty-sixth day."

"The *last* day?"

The old man nodded and they were both silent awhile.

"Back to 1938 in the stone cemetery," said Tom Wolfe, eyes shut. "I don't like that. I wish I didn't know about that, it's a horrible thing to know." His voice faded and he put his big hands over his face and held them tightly there.

The door opened. Bolton let himself in and stood behind Tom Wolfe's chair, a small phial in his hand.

"What's that?" asked the old man.

"An extinct virus. Pneumonia. Very ancient and very evil," said Bolton. "When Mr. Wolfe came through, I had to cure him of his illness, of course, which was immensely easy with the techniques we know today, in order to put him in working condition for his job, Mr. Field. I kept this pneumonia culture. Now that he's going back, he'll have to be reinoculated with the disease."

"Otherwise?"

Tom Wolfe looked up.

"Otherwise, he'd get well, in 1938."

Tom Wolfe arose from his chair. "You mean, get well, walk around, back there, be well, and cheat the mortician?"

"That's what I mean."

Tom Wolfe stared at the phial and one of his hands twitched. "What if I destroyed the virus and refused to let you inoculate me?"

"You can't do that!"

"But—supposing?"

"You'd ruin things."

"What things?"

"The pattern, life, the way things are and were, the things that can't be changed. You can't disrupt it. There's only one sure thing, you're to die, and I'm to see to it."

Wolfe looked at the door. "I could run off."

"We control the machine. You wouldn't get out of the house. I'd have you back here, by force, and inoculated. I anticipated some such trouble when the time came; there are five men waiting down below. One shout from me—you see, it's useless. There, that's better. Here now."

Wolfe had moved back and now had turned to look at the old man and the window and this huge house. "I'm afraid I must apologize. I don't want to die. So very much I don't want to die."

The old man came to him and took his hand. "Think of it this way: you've had two more months than anyone could expect from life, and you've turned out another book, a last book, a fine book, think of that."

"I want to thank you for this," said Thomas Wolfe, gravely. "I want to thank both of you. I'm ready." He rolled up his sleeve. "The inoculation."

And while Bolton bent to his task, with his free hand Thomas Wolfe penciled two black lines across the top of the first manuscript and went on talking:

"There's a passage from one of my old books," he said, scowling to remember it. *". . . of wandering forever and the Earth . . . Who owns the Earth? Did we want the Earth? That we should wander on it? Did we need the Earth that we were never still upon it? Whoever needs the Earth shall have the Earth; he shall be upon it, he shall rest within a little place, he shall dwell in one small room forever . . ."*

Wolfe was finished with the remembering.

"Here's my last book," he said, and on the empty yellow paper facing the manuscript he blocked out vigorous huge black letters with pressures of the pencil:

FOREVER AND THE EARTH, by Thomas Wolfe.

He picked up a ream of it and held it tightly in his hands, against his chest, for a moment. "I wish I could take it back with me. It's like parting with my son." He gave it a slap and put it aside and immediately thereafter gave his quick hand into that of his employer, and strode across the room, Bolton after him, until he reached the door where he stood framed in the late-afternoon light, huge and magnificent. "Good-bye, good-bye!" he cried.

The door slammed. Tom Wolfe was gone.

They found him wandering in the hospital corridor.

"Mr. Wolfe!"

"What?"

"Mr. Wolfe, you gave us a scare, we thought you were gone!"

"Gone?"

"Where did you go?"

"Where? Where?" He let himself be led through the midnight corridors. "Where? Oh, if I *told* you where, you'd never believe."

"Here's your bed, you shouldn't have left it."

Deep into the white death bed, which smelled of pale, clean mortality awaiting him, a mortality which had the hospital odor in it; the bed which, as he touched it, folded him into fumes and white starched coldness.

"Mars, Mars," whispered the huge man, late at night. "My best, my very best, my really fine book, yet to be written, yet to be printed, in another year, three centuries away . . ."

"You're tired."

"Do you really think so?" murmured Thomas Wolfe. "Was it a dream? Perhaps. A good dream."

His breathing faltered. Thomas Wolfe was dead.

In the passing years, flowers are found on Tom Wolfe's grave. And this is not unusual, for many people travel to linger there. But these flowers appear each night. They seem to drop from the sky. They are the color of an autumn moon, their blossoms are immense, and they burn and sparkle their cold, long petals in a blue and white fire. And when the dawn wind blows they drip away into a silver rain, a shower of white sparks on the air. Tom Wolfe has been dead many, many years, but these flowers never cease. . . .

The Better Part of Wisdom

The room was like a great warm hearth, lit by an unseen fire, gone comfortable. The fireplace itself struggled to keep a small blaze going on a few wet logs and some turf, which was no more than smoke and several lazy orange eyes of charcoal. The place was slowly filling, draining, and refilling with music. A single lemon lamp was lit in a far corner, illumining walls painted a summer color of yellow. The hardwood floor was polished so severely it glowed like a dark river upon which floated throw-rugs whose plumage resembled South American wild birds, flashing electric blues, whites, and jungle greens. White porcelain vases, brimming with fresh-cut hothouse flowers, kept their serene fires burning on four small tables about the room. Above the fireplace, a serious portrait of a young man gazed out with eyes the same color as the ceramics, a deep blue, raw with intelligence and vitality.

Entering the room quietly, one might not have noticed the two men, they were so still.

One sat reclining back upon the pure white couch, eyes closed. The second lay upon the couch so his head was pillowed in the lap of the other. His eyes were shut, too, listening. Rain touched the windows. The music ended.

Instantly there was a soft scratching at the door.

Both men blinked as if to say: people don't *scratch*, they *knock*.

The man who had been lying down leaped to the door and called: "Someone there?"

"By God, there is," said an old voice with a faint brogue.

"Grandfather!"

With the door flung wide, the young man pulled a small round old man into the warm-lit room.

"Tom, boy, ah Tom, and glad I am to see you!"

They fell together in bear-hugs, pawing. Then the old man felt the other person in the room and moved back.

Tom spun around, pointing. "Grandpa, this is Frank. Frank, this is Grandpa, I mean—oh, hell—"

The old man saved the moment by trotting forward to seize and pull Frank to his feet, where he towered high above this small intruder from the night.

"Frank, is it?" the old man yelled up the heights.

"Yes, sir," Frank called back down.

"I—" said the grandfather, "have been standing outside that door for five minutes—"

"Five minutes?" cried both young men, alarmed.

"—debating whether to knock. I heard the music, you see, and finally I said, damn, if there's a girl with him he can either shove her out the window in the rain or show the lovely likes of her to the old man. Hell, I said, and knocked, and"—he slung down his battered old valise—"there *is* no young girl here, I see—or, by God, you've *smothered* her in the closet, eh!"

"There is no young girl, Grandfather." Tom turned in a circle, his hands out to show.

"But—" The grandfather eyed the polished floor, the white throw-rugs, the bright flowers, the watchful portraits on the walls. "You've *borrowed* her place, then?"

"Borrowed?"

"I mean, by the look of the room, there's a woman's touch. It looks like them steamship posters I seen in the travel windows half my life."

"Well," said Frank. "We—"

"The fact is, Grandfather," said Tom, clearing his throat, "*we* did this place over. Redecorated."

"Redecorated?" The old man's jaw dropped. His eyes toured the four walls, stunned. "The *two* of you are responsible? Jesus!"

The old man touched a blue and white ceramic ashtray, and bent to stroke a bright cockatoo throw-rug.

"Which of you did *what?*" he asked, suddenly, squinting one eye at them.

Tom flushed and stammered, "Well, we—"

"Ah, God, no, no, stop!" cried the old man, lifting one hand. "Here I am, fresh *in* the place, and sniffing about like a crazy hound and no fox. Shut that damn door. Ask me where *I'm* going, what am *I* up to, eh, *eh?* And, while you're at it, do you have a touch of the Beast in this art gallery?"

"The Beast it is!" Tom slammed the door, hustled his grandfather out of his greatcoat, and brought forth three tumblers and a bottle of Irish whiskey, which the old man touched as if it were a newborn babe.

"Well, that's more like it. What do we drink to?"

"Why, you, Grandpa!"

"No, no." The old man gazed at Tom and then at his friend, Frank. "Christ," he sighed, "you're so damn young it breaks my bones in the ache. Come now, let's drink to fresh hearts and apple cheeks and all life up ahead and happiness somewhere for the taking. Yes?"

"Yes!" said both, and drank.

And drinking watched each other merrily or warily, half one, half the other. And the young saw in the old bright pink face, lined as it was, cuffed as it was by circumstantial life, the echo of Tom's face itself peering out through the years. In the old blue eyes, especially, was the sharp bright intelligence that sprang from the old portrait on the wall, that would be young until coins weighted them shut. And around the edges of the old mouth was the smile that blinked and went in Tom's face, and in the old hands was the quick, surprising action of Tom's, as if both old man and young had hands that lived to themselves and did sly things by impulse.

So they drank and leaned and smiled and drank again, each a mirror for the other, each delighting in the fact that an ancient man and a raw youth with the same eyes and hands and blood were met on this raining night, and the whiskey was good.

"Ah, Tom, Tom, it's a loving sight you are!" said the grandfather. "Dublin's been sore without you these four years. But, hell, I'm dying. No, don't ask me how or why. The doctor has the news, damn him, and shot me between the eyes with it. So I said instead of relatives shelling out their cash to come say good-bye to the old horse, why not make the farewell tour yourself and shake hands and drink drinks. So here I am this night and tomorrow beyond London to see Lucie and then Glasgow to see Dick. I'll stay no more than a day each place, so as not to overload anyone. Now shut that mouth, which is hanging open. I am not out collecting sympathies. I am eighty, and it's time for a damn fine wake, which I have saved money for, so not a word. I have come to see everyone and make sure they are in a fit state of half-graceful joy so I can kick up my heels and fall dead with a good heart, if that's possible. I—"

"Grandfather!" cried Tom, suddenly, and seized the old man's hands and then his shoulders.

"Why, bless you, boy, thanks," said the old man, seeing the tears in the young man's eyes. "But just what I find in your gaze is enough." He set the boy gently back. "Tell me about

London, your work, this place. You too, Frank, a friend of Tom's is as good as my son's son! Tell everything, Tom!"

"Excuse me." Frank darted toward the door. "You both have much to talk about. There's shopping I must do—"

"Wait!"

Frank stopped.

For the old man had really seen the portrait over the fireplace now and walked to it to put out his hand, to squint and read the signed name at the bottom.

"Frank Davis. Is that you, boy? *You* did this picture?"

"Yes, sir," said Frank, at the door.

"How long ago?"

"Three years ago, I think. Yes, three."

The old man nodded slowly, as if this information added to the great puzzle, a continuing bafflement.

"Tom, do you know who that *looks* like?"

"Yes, Grand-da. You. A long time ago."

"So you see it, too, eh? Christ in heaven, yes. That's me on my eighteenth birthday and all Ireland and its grasses and tender maids good for the chewing ahead and not behind me. That's me, that's me. Jesus I was handsome, and Jesus, Tom, so are you. And Jesus, Frank, you *are* uncanny. You are a *fine* artist, boy."

"You do what you can do." Frank had come back to the middle of the room, quietly. "You do what you *know*."

"And you *know* Tom, to the hair and eyelash." The old man turned and smiled. "How does it feel, Tom, to look out of that borrowed face? Do you feel great, is the world your Dublin prawn and oyster?"

Tom laughed. Grandfather laughed. Frank joined them.

"One more drink." The old man poured. "And we'll let you slip diplomatically out, Frank. But come back. I must talk with you."

"What about?" said Frank.

"Ah, the Mysteries. Of Life, of Time, of Existence. What else did *you* have in mind, Frank?"

"Those will do, Grandfather—" said Frank, and stopped, amazed at the word come out of his mouth. "I mean, Mr. Kelly—"

"Grandfather will do."

"I must run." Frank doused his drink. "Phone you later, Tom." The door shut. Frank was gone.

"You'll sleep here tonight of course, Grandpa?" Tom seized the one valise. "Frank won't be back. You'll have his bed." Tom was busy arranging the sheets on one of the two couches against the far wall. "Now, it's early. Let's drink some more, Grandfather, and talk."

But the old man, stunned, was silent, eyeing each picture in turn upon the wall. "Grand painting, that."

"Frank did them."

"That's a fine lamp there."

"Frank made it."

"The rug on the floor here now—?"

"Frank."

"Jesus," whispered the old man, "he's a maniac for work, is he not?"

Quietly, he shuffled about the room like one visiting a gallery.

"It seems," he said, "the place is absolutely blowing apart with fine artistic talent. You turned your hand to nothing like this, in Dublin."

"You learn a lot, away from home," said Tom, uneasily.

The old man shut his eyes and drank his drink.

"Is anything wrong, Grandfather?"

"It will hit me in the middle of the night," said the old man. "I will probably stand up in bed with a hell of a yell. But right now it is just a thing in the pit of my stomach and the back of my head. Let's talk, boy, let's talk."

And they talked and drank until midnight and then the old man got put to bed and Tom went to bed himself and after a long while both slept.

About two in the morning, the old man woke suddenly.

He peered around in the dark, wondering where he was, then saw the paintings, the upholstered chairs, and the lamp and rugs Frank had made, and sat up. He clenched his fists. Then, rising, he threw on his clothes, and staggered toward the door as if fearful that he might not make it before something terrible happened.

When the door slammed, Tom jerked his eyes wide.

Somewhere off in the dark there was a sound of someone calling, shouting, defying the elements, someone at the top of his lungs crying blasphemies, saying God and Jesus and Jesus and God, and finally blows struck, wild blows, as if someone were hitting a wall or a person.

After a long while, his grandfather shuffled back into the room, soaked to the skin.

Weaving, muttering, whispering, the old man peeled off his wet clothes before the fireless fire, then threw a newspaper on the coals, which blazed up briefly to show a face relaxing out of fury into numbness. The old man found and put on Tom's discarded robe. Tom kept his eyes tight as the old man held his hands out toward the dwindling blaze, streaked with blood.

"Damn, damn, damn. *There!*" He poured whiskey and gulped it down. He blinked at Tom and the paintings on the wall and looked at Tom and the flowers in the vases and then drank again. After a long while, Tom pretended to wake up.

"It's after two. You need your rest, Grand-da."

"I'll rest when I'm done drinking. And *thinking!*"

"Thinking what, Grandpa?"

"Right now," said the old man, seated in the dim room with the tumbler in his two hands, and the fire gone to ghost on the hearth, "remembering your dear grandmother in June of the year 1902. And there is the thought of your father born, which is fine, and you born after him, which is fine. And there is the thought of your father dying when you were young and the hard life of your mother and her holding you too close, maybe, in the cold beggar life of flinty Dublin. And me out in the meadows with my working life, and us together only once a month. The being born of people and the going away of people. These turn round in an old man's night. I think of you born, Tom, a happy day. Then I see you here now. That's it."

The old man grew silent and drank his drink.

"Grand-da," said Tom, at last, almost like a child crept in for penalties and forgiveness of a sin as yet unnamed, "do I *worry* you?"

"No." Then the old man added, "But what life will *do* with you, how you may be treated, good or ill—I sit up late with *that*."

The old man sat. The young man lay wide-eyed watching him and later said, as if reading thoughts:

"Grandfather, I *am* happy."

The old man leaned forward.

"*Are* you, boy?"

"I have never been so happy in my life, sir."

"Yes?" The old man looked through the dim air of the room, at the young face. "I see that. But will you *stay* happy, Tom?"

"Does anyone ever *stay* happy, Grandfather? Nothing lasts, *does* it?"

"Shut up! Your grandma and me, *that* lasted!"

"No. It wasn't *all* the same, was it? The first years were one thing, the last years another."

The old man put his hand over his own mouth and then massaged his face, closing his eyes.

"God, yes, you're right. There are two, no, three, no, four lives, for each of us. Not one of them lasts, it's sure. But the *thought* of them does. And out of the four or five or a dozen lives you live, one is special. I remember, once . . ."

The old man's voice faltered.

The young man said, "*Once*, Grandpa?"

The old man's eyes fixed somewhere to a horizon of the Past. He did not speak to the room or to Tom or to anyone. He didn't even seem to be speaking to himself.

"Oh, it was a long time ago. When I first came in this room

tonight, for no reason, strange, the memory was there. I ran back down along the shoreline of Galway to that week . . ."

"What week, when?"

"My twelfth birthday fell that week in summer, think of it! Victoria still queen and me in a turf-hut out by Galway strolling the shore for food to be picked up from the tides, and the weather so sweet you almost turned sad with the taste of it, for you knew it would soon go away.

"And in the middle of the great fair weather along the road by the shore one noon came this tinker's caravan carrying their dark gypsy people to set up camp by the sea.

"There was a mother, a father, and a girl in that caravan, and this boy who came running down by the sea alone, perhaps in need of company, for there I was with nothing to do, and in need of strangers myself.

"Here he came running. And I shall not forget my first sight of him from that day till they drop me in the earth. He—

"Ah God, I'm a failure with words! Stop everything. I must go further back.

"A circus came to Dublin. I visited the sideshows of pinheads and dwarfs and terrible small midgets and fat women and skeleton men. Seeing a crowd about one last exhibit, I thought this must be the most horrible of all. I edged over to look at this final terror! And what did I see? The crowd was drawn to nothing more nor less than: a little girl of some six years, so fair, so beautiful, so cream-white of cheek, so blue of eye, so golden of hair, so quiet in her manner that in the midst of this fleshy holocaust she called attention. By saying nothing her shout of beauty stopped the show. All *had* to come to her to get well again. For it was a sick menagerie and she the only sweet lovely Doc about to give us back life.

"Well, that girl in the sideshow was as wonderful a surprise as this boy come running down the beach like a young horse.

"He was not dark like his parents.

"His hair was all gold curls and bits of sun. He was cut out of bronze by the light, and what wasn't bronze was copper. Impossible, but it seemed that this boy of twelve, like myself, had been born on that very day, he looked that new and fresh. And in his face were these bright brown eyes, the eyes of an animal that has run a long way, pursued, along the shorelines of the world.

"He pulled up and the first thing he said to me was laughter. He was glad to be alive, and announced that by the sound he made. I must have laughed in turn, for his spirit was catching. He shoved out his brown hand. I hesitated. He gestured impatiently and grabbed my hand.

"My God, after all these years I remember what we said: 'Isn't it funny?' he said.

"I didn't ask *what* was funny. I *knew*. He said his name was Jo. I said my name was Tim. And there we were, two boys on the beach and the universe a good rare joke between us.

"He looked at me with his great round full copper eyes, and laughed out his breath and I thought: He has chewed hay! his breath smells of grass; and suddenly I was giddy. The smell stunned me. Jesus God, I thought, reeling, I'm drunk, and *why?* I've nipped Dad's booze, but God, what's *this?* Drunk by noon, hit by the sun, giddy from what? the sweet mash caught in a strange boy's teeth? No, no!

"Then Jo looked straight at me and said, 'There isn't much time.'

" 'Much time?' I asked.

" 'Why,' said Jo, 'for us to be friends. We are, *aren't* we?'

"He breathed the smell of mown fields upon me.

"Jesus God, I wanted to cry, Yes! And almost fell down, but staggered back as if he had hit me a friend's hit. And my mouth opened and shut and I said, 'Why is there so little time?'

" 'Because,' said Jo, 'we'll only be here six days, seven at the most, then on down and around Eire. I'll never see you again in my life. So we'll just have to pack a lot of things in a few days, won't we, Tim?'

" 'Six days? That's no time at all!' I protested, and wondered why I found myself suddenly destroyed, left destitute on the shore. A thing had not begun, but already I sorrowed after its death.

" 'A day here, a week there, a month somewhere else,' said Jo. 'I must live very quickly, Tim. I have no friends that last. Only what I remember. So, wherever I go, I say to my new friends, quick, do this, do that, let us make many happenings, a long list, so you will remember me when I am gone, and I you, and say: that was a friend. So, let's begin. There!'

"And Jo tagged me and ran.

"I ran after him, laughing, for wasn't it silly, me headlong after a stranger boy unknown five minutes before? We must've run a mile down that long summer beach before he let me catch him. I thought I might pummel him for making me run so far for nothing, for something, for God knew what! But when we tumbled to earth and I pinned him down, all he did was spring his breath in one gasp up at me, one breath, and I leaped back and shook my head and sat staring at him, as if I'd plunged wet hands in an open electric socket. He laughed to see me fall away, to see me scurry and sit in wonder. 'O, Tim,' he said, 'we *shall* be friends.'

"You know the dread long cold weather, most months, of Ireland? Well, this week of my twelfth birthday, it was summer each day and every day for the seven days named by Jo as the limit which would be no more days. We walked the shore, and that's all there was, the simple thing of us upon the shore, and building castles or climbing hills to fight wars among the mounds. We found on old round tower and yelled up and down from it. But mostly it was walking, our arms about each other like twins born in a tangle, never cut free by knife or lightning. I inhaled, he exhaled. Then he breathed and I was the sweet chorus. We talked, far through the nights on the sand, until our parents came seeking the lost who had found they knew not what. Lured home, I slept beside him, or him me, and talked and laughed, Jesus, laughed, till dawn. Then out again we roared until the earth swung up to hit our backs. We found ourselves laid out with sweet hilarity, eyes tight, gripped to each other's shaking, and the laugh jumped free like one silver trout following another. God, I bathed in his laughter as he bathed in mine, until we were weak as if love had put us to the slaughter and exhaustions. We panted then like pups in hot summer, empty of laughing, and sleepy with friendship. And the weather for that week was blue and gold, no clouds, no rain, and a wind that smelled of apples, but no, only that boy's wild breath.

"It crossed my mind, long after, if ever an old man could bathe again in that summer fount, the wild spout of breathing that sprang from his nostrils and gasped from his mouth, why one might peel off a score of years, one would be young, how might the flesh resist?

"But the laughter is gone and the boy gone into a man lost somewhere in the world, and here I am two lifetimes later, speaking of it for the first time. For who was there to tell? From my twelfth birthday week, and the gift of friendship, to this, who might I tell of that shore and that summer and the two of us walking all tangled in our arms and lives and life as perfect as the letter o, a damned great circle of rare weather, lovely talk, and us certain we'd live forever, never die, and be good friends.

"And at the end of the week, he left.

"He was wise for his years. He didn't say good-bye. All of a sudden, the tinker's cart was gone.

"I shouted along the shore. A long way off, I saw the caravan go over a hill. But then his wisdom spoke to me. Don't catch. Let go. Weep now, my own wisdom said. And I wept.

"I wept for three days and on the fourth grew very still. I did not go down to the shore again for many months. And in all the years that have passed, never have I known such a thing again. I have had a good life, a fine wife, good children, and you, boy, Tom, you. But as sure as I sit here, never after that was I so agonized, mad, and crazy wild. Never did drink make me as drunk. Never did I cry so hard again. Why, Tom? Why do I say this, and what was it? Back so far in innocence, back in the time when I had nobody, and knew nothing. How is it I remember him when all else slips away? When often I cannot remember your dear grandmother's face, God forgive me, why does his face come back on the shore by the sea? Why do I see us fall again and the earth reach up to take the wild young horses driven mad by too much sweet grass in a line of days that never end?"

The old man grew silent. After a moment, he added, "The better part of wisdom, they say, is what's left unsaid. I'll say no more. I don't even know why I've said all *this*."

Tom lay in the dark. "*I* know."

"Do you, lad?" asked the old man. "Well, tell me. Someday."

"Someday," said Tom. "I will."

They listened to the rain touch at the windows.

"Are you happy, Tom?"

"You asked that before, sir."

"I ask again. Are you happy?"

"Yes."

Silence.

"Is it summertime on the shore, Tom? Is it the magic seven days? Are you drunk?"

Tom did not answer for a long while, and then said nothing but, "Grand-da," and then moved his head once in a nod.

The old man lay back in the chair. He might have said, this will pass. He might have said, it will not last. He might have said many things. Instead he said, "Tom?"

"Sir?"

"Ah Jesus!" shouted the old man suddenly. "Christ, God Almighty! Damn it to hell!" Then the old man stopped and his breathing grew quiet. "There. It's a maniac night. I had to let out one last yell. I just had to, boy."

And at last they slept, with the rain falling fast.

With the first light of dawn, the old man dressed with careful quietness, picked up his valise, and bent to touch the sleeping young man's cheek with the palm of one hand.

"Tom, good-bye," he whispered.

Moving down the dim stairwell toward the steadily beating rain, he found Tom's friend waiting at the foot of the stairs.

"Frank! You haven't been down here *all night?*"

"No, no, Mr. Kelly," said Frank, quickly. "I stayed at a friend's."

The old man turned to look up the dark stairwell as if he could see the room and Tom in it warm asleep.

"Gah . . . !" Something almost a growl stirred in his throat and subsided. He shifted uneasily and looked back down at the dawn kindled on this young man's face, this one who had painted a picture that hung above the fireplace in the room above.

"The damn night is over," said the old man. So if you'll just stand aside—"

"Sir."

The old man took one step down and burst out:

"Listen! If you hurt Tom, in any way ever, why, Jesus, I'll break you across my knee! You *hear?*"

Frank held out his hand. "Don't worry."

The old man looked at the hand as if he had never seen one before. He sighed.

"Ah, damn it to hell, Frank, Tom's friend, so young you're destruction to the eyes. Get away!"

They shook hands.

"Jesus, that's a hard grip," said the old man, surprised.

Then he was gone, as if the rain had hustled him off in its own multitudinous running.

The young man shut the upstairs door and stood for a moment looking at the figure on the bed and at last went over and as if by instinct put his hand down to the exact same spot where the old man had printed his hand in farewell not five minutes before. He touched the summer cheek.

In his sleep, Tom smiled the smile of his father's father, and called the old man, deep in a dream, by name.

He called him twice.

And then he slept quietly.

Darling Adolf

They were waiting for him to come out. He was sitting inside the little Bavarian café with a view of the mountains, drinking beer, and he had been in there since noon and it was now two-thirty, a long lunch, and much beer, and they could see by the way he held his head and laughed and lifted one more stein with the suds fluffing in the spring breeze that he was in a grand humor now, and at the table with him the two other men were doing their best to keep up, but had fallen long behind.

On occasion their voices drifted on the wind, and then the small crowd waiting out in the parking lot leaned to hear. What was he saying? and now what?

"He just said the shooting was going well."

"What, where?!"

"Fool. The film, the film is shooting well."

"Is that the director sitting with him?"

"Yes. And the other unhappy one is the producer."

"He doesn't look like a producer."

"No wonder! He's had his nose changed."

"And him, doesn't he look *real?*"

"To the hair and the teeth."

And again everyone leaned to look in at the three men, at the man who didn't look like a producer, at the sheepish director who kept glancing out at the crowd and slouching down with his head between his shoulders, shutting his eyes, and the man between them, the man in the uniform with the swastika on his arm, and the fine military cap put on the table beside the almost-untouched food, for he was talking, no, making a speech.

"That's the Führer, all right!"

"God in heaven, it's as if no time had passed. I don't believe this is 1973. Suddenly it's 1934 again, when first I saw him."

"Where?"

"The Nuremberg Rally, the stadium, that was the autumn, yes, and I was thirteen and part of the Youth and one hundred thousand soldiers and young men in that big place that late afternoon before the torches were lit. So many bands, so many flags, so much heartbeat, yes, I tell you, I could hear one hundred thousand hearts banging away, we were all so in love, he had come down out of the clouds. The gods had sent him, we knew, and the time of waiting was over, from here on we could *act*, there was nothing he couldn't *help* us to do."

"I wonder how that actor in there feels, playing him?"

"Sh, he hears you. Look, he waves. Wave back."

"Shut up," said someone else. "They're talking again. I want to hear—"

The crowd shut up. The men and women leaned into the soft spring wind. The voices drifted from the café table.

Beer was being poured by a maiden waitress with flushed cheeks and eyes as bright as fire.

"More beer!" said the man with the toothbrush mustache and the hair combed forward on the left side of his brow.

"No, thanks," said the director.

"No, no," said the producer.

"More beer! It's a splendid day," said Adolf. "A toast to the film, to us, to me. Drink!"

The other two men put their hands on their glasses of beer.

"To the film," said the producer.

"To darling Adolf." The director's voice was flat.

The man in the uniform stiffened.

"I do not look upon myself—" he hesitated, "upon *him* as darling."

"He was darling, all right, and you're a doll." The director gulped his drink. "Does anyone mind if I get drunk?"

"To be drunk is not permitted," said Der Führer.

"Where does it say that in the script?"

The producer kicked the director under the table.

"How many more weeks' work do you figure we have?" asked the producer, with great politeness.

"I figure we should finish the film," said the director, taking huge swigs, "around about the death of Hindenburg, or the *Hindenburg* gasbag going down in flames at Lakehurst, New Jersey, whichever comes first."

Adolf Hitler bent to his plate and began to eat rapidly, snapping at his meat and potatoes in silence.

The producer sighed heavily. The director, nudged by this, calmed the waters. "Another three weeks should see the masterwork in the can, and us sailing home on the *Titanic*, there to collide with the Jewish critics and go down bravely singing 'Deutschland Uber Alles.'"

Suddenly all three were voracious and snapping and biting and chewing their food, and the spring breeze blew softly, and the crowd waited outside.

At last, Der Führer stopped, had another sip of beer, and lay back in his chair, touching his mustache with his little finger.

"Nothing can provoke me on a day like this. The rushes last night were so beautiful. The casting for this film, ah! I find Göring to be incredible. Goebbels? Perfection!" Sunlight dazzled out of Der Führer's face. "So. So, I was thinking just last night, here I am in Bavaria, me, a pure Aryan—"

Both men flinched slightly, and waited.

"—making a film," Hitler went on, laughing softly, "with a Jew from New York and a Jew from Hollywood. So amusing."

"I am not amused," said the director, lightly.

The producer shot him a glance which said: the film is not finished yet. Careful.

"And I was thinking, wouldn't it be fun . . ." Here Der Führer stopped to take a big drink," . . . to have another . . . ah . . . Nuremberg Rally?"

"You mean for the *film*, of course?"

The director stared at Hitler. Hitler examined the texture of the suds in his beer.

"My God," said the producer, "do you know how much it would cost to reproduce the Nuremberg Rally? How much did it cost Hitler for the original, Marc?"

He blinked at his director, who said, "A bundle. But he had a lot of free extras, of course."

"Of course! The Army, the Hitler Youth."

"Yes, yes," said Hitler. "But think of the publicity, all over the world? Let us go to Nuremberg, eh, and film my plane, eh, and me coming down out of the clouds? I heard those people out there, just now: Nuremberg and plane and torches. *They* remember. *I* remember. I held a torch in that stadium. My God, it was beautiful. And now, now I am exactly the age Hitler was when he was at his prime."

"He was never at his prime," said the director. "Unless you mean hung-meat."

Hitler put down his glass. His cheeks grew very red. Then he forced a smile to widen his lips and change the color of his face. "That is a joke, of course."

"A joke," said the producer, playing ventriloquist to his friend. "I was thinking," Hitler went on, his eyes on the clouds again, seeing it all, back in another year. "If we shot it next month, with the weather good. Think of all the tourists who would come to watch the filming!"

"Yeah. Bormann might even come back from Argentina."

The producer shot his director another glare.

Hitler cleared his throat and forced the words out: "As for expense, if you took one small ad, *one* mind you! in the Nuremberg papers one week before, why, you would have an army of people there as extras at fifty cents a day, no, a quarter, no, *free!*"

Der Führer emptied his stein, ordered another. The waitress dashed off to refill. Hitler studied his two friends.

"You know," said the director, sitting up, his own eyes taking a kind of vicious fire, his teeth showing as he leaned forward, "there is a kind of idiot grace to you, a kind of murderous wit, a sort of half-ass style. Every once in a while you come dripping up with some sensational slime that gleams and stinks in the sun, buster. Archie, *listen* to him. Der Führer just had a great bowel movement. Drag in the astrologers! Slit the pigeons and filch their guts. Read me the casting sheets."

The director leaped to his feet and began to pace.

"That *one* ad in the paper, and all the trunks in Nuremberg get flung wide! Old uniforms come out to cover fat bellies! Old armbands come out to fit flabby arms! Old military caps with skull-eagles on them fly out to fit on fat-heads!"

"I will not sit here—" cried Hitler.

He started to get up but the producer was tugging his arm and the director had a knife at his heart: his forefinger, stabbing hard.

"Sit."

The director's face hovered two inches from Hitler's nose. Hitler slowly sank back, his cheeks perspiring.

"God, you *are* a genius," said the director. "Jesus, your people *would* show up. Not the young, no, but the old. All the Hitler youth, your age now, those senile bags of tripe yelling 'Sieg Heil,' saluting, lighting torches at sunset, marching around the stadium crying themselves blind."

The director swerved to his producer.

"I tell you, Arch, this Hitler here has bilge for brains but this time he's on target! If we don't shove the Nuremberg Rally *up* this film, I quit. I mean it. I will simply walk out and let Adolf here take over and direct the damned thing himself! Speech over."

He sat down.

Both the producer and Der Führer appeared to be in a state of shock.

"Order me another goddamn beer," snapped the director.

Hitler gasped in a huge breath, tossed down his knife and fork, and shoved back his chair.

"I do not break bread with such as you!"

"Why, you bootlicking lapdog son of a bitch," said the director. "I'll hold the mug and you'll do the licking. Here." The director grabbed the beer and shoved it under Der Führer's nose. The crowd, out beyond, gasped and almost surged. Hitler's eyes rolled, for the director had seized him by the front of his tunic and was yanking him forward.

"Lick! Drink the German filth! Drink, you scum!"

"Boys, boys," said the producer.

"Boys, crud! You know what this swill-hole, this chamberpot Nazi, has been thinking, sitting here, Archibald, and drinking your beer? Today Europe, tomorrow the world!"

"No, no, Marc!"

"No, no," said Hitler, staring down at the fist which clenched the material of his uniform. "The buttons, the buttons—"

"Are loose on your tunic and inside your head, worm. Arch, look at him pour! Look at the grease roll off his forehead, look at his stinking armpits. He's a sea of sweat because I've read his mind! Tomorrow the world! Get this film set up, him cast in the lead. Bring him down out of the clouds, a month from now.

Brass bands. Torchlight. Bring back Leni Reifenstahl to show us how she shot the Rally in '34. Hitler's lady-director friend. Fifty cameras she used, fifty she used, by God, to get all the German crumbs lined up and vomiting lies, and Hitler in his creaking leather and Göring awash in his blubber, and Goebbels doing his wounded-monkey walk, the three superfags of history aswank in the stadium at dusk, make it all happen again, with this bastard up front, and do you know what's going through his little graveyard mind behind his bloater eyes at this very moment?"

"Marc, Marc," whispered the producer, eyes shut, grinding his teeth. "Sit down. Everyone sees."

"Let them see! Wake up, you! Don't you shut your eyes on me, too! I've shut my eyes on you for days, filth. Now I want some attention. Here."

He sloshed beer on Hitler's face, which caused his eyes to snap wide and his eyes to roll yet again, as apoplexy burned his cheeks.

The crowd, out beyond, hissed in their breath.

The director, hearing, leered at them.

"Boy, is this funny. They don't know whether to come in or not, don't know if you're real or not, and neither do I. Tomorrow, you bilgy bastard, you really dream of becoming Der Führer."

He bathed the man's face with more beer.

The producer had turned away in his chair now and was frantically dabbing at some imaginary breadcrumbs on his tie. "Marc, for God's sake—"

"No, no, seriously, Archibald. This guy thinks because he puts on a ten-cent uniform and plays Hitler for four weeks at good pay that if we actually put together the Rally, why Christ, History would turn back, oh turn back, Time, Time in thy flight, make me a stupid Jew-baking Nazi again for tonight. Can you see it, Arch, this lice walking up to the microphones and shouting, and the crowd shouting back, and him *really* trying to take over, as if Roosevelt still lived and Churchill wasn't six feet deep, and it was all to be lost or won again, but mainly won, because *this* time they wouldn't stop at the Channel but just cross on over, give or take a million German boys dead, and stomp England and stomp America, isn't *that* what's going on inside your little Aryan skull, Adolf? *Isn't it!*"

Hitler gagged and hissed. His tongue stuck out. At last he jerked free and exploded:

"Yes! Yes, goddamn you! Damn and bake and burn you! You dare to lay hands on Der Führer! The Rally! Yes! It must be in the film! We must make it again! The plane! The landing! The long drive through streets. The blonde girls. The lovely blond boys. The stadium. Leni Reifenstahl! And from all the trunks, in all the attics, a black plague of armbands winging on the dusk, flying to assault, battering to take the victory. Yes, yes, I, Der Führer, I will stand at that Rally and dictate terms! I—I—"

He was on his feet now.

The crowd, out beyond in the parking lot, shouted.

Hitler turned and gave them a salute.

The director took careful aim and shot a blow of his fist to the German's nose.

After that the crowd arrived, shrieking, yelling, pushing, shoving, falling.

They drove to the hospital at four the next afternoon

Slumped, the old producer sighed, his hands over his eyes. "Why, why, why are we going to the hospital? To visit that—monster?"

The director nodded.

The old man groaned. "Crazy world. Mad people. I never saw such biting, kicking, biting. That mob almost killed you."

The director licked his swollen lips and touched his half-shut left eye with a probing finger. "I'm okay. The important thing is I hit Adolf, oh, how I hit him. And now—" He stared calmly ahead. "I think I am going to the hospital to finish the job."

"Finish, *finish?*" The old man stared at him.

"Finish." The director wheeled the car slowly around a corner. "Remember the twenties, Arch, when Hitler got shot at in the street and not hit, or beaten in the streets, and nobody socked him away forever, or he left a beer hall ten minutes before a bomb went off, or was in that officers' hut in 1944 and the brief-case bomb exploded and *that* didn't get him. Always the charmed life. Always he got out from under the rock. Well, Archie, no more charms, no more escapes. I'm walking in that hospital to make sure that when that half-ass extra comes out and there's a mob of krauts to greet him, he's walking wounded, a permanent soprano. Don't try to stop me, Arch."

"Who's stopping? Belt him one for me."

They stopped in front of the hospital just in time to see one of the studio production assistants run down the steps, his hair wild, his eyes wilder, shouting.

"Christ," said the director. "Bet you forty to one, our luck's run out again. Bet you that guy running toward us says—"

"Kidnaped! Gone!" the man cried. "Adolf's been taken away!"

"Son of a bitch."

They circled the empty hospital bed; they *touched* it.

A nurse stood in one corner wringing her hands. The production assistant babbled.

"Three men it was, three men, three men."

"Shut up." The director was snowblind from simply looking at the white sheets. "Did they force him or did he go along quietly?"

"I don't know, I can't say, yes, he was making speeches, making speeches as they took him out."

"Making speeches?" cried the old producer, slapping his bald pate. "Christ, with the restaurant suing us for broken tables, and Hitler maybe suing us for—"

"Hold on." The director stepped over and fixed the production assistant with a steady gaze. "*Three* men, you say?"

"Three, yes, three, three, three, oh, three men."

A small forty-watt lightbulb flashed on in the director's head.

"Did, ah, did one man have a square face, a good jaw, bushy eyebrows?"

"Why . . . yes!"

"Was one man short and skinny like a chimpanzee?"

"Yes!"

"Was one man big, I mean, slobby fat?"

"How did you *know*?"

The producer blinked at both of them. "What goes on? What—"

"Stupid attracts stupid. Animal cunning calls to laughing jackass cunning. Come on, Arch!"

"Where?" The old man stared at the empty bed as if Adolf might materialize there any moment now.

"The back of my car, quick!"

From the back of the car, on the street, the director pulled a German cinema directory. He leafed through the character actors. "Here."

The old man looked. A forty-watt bulb went on in his head.

The director riffled more pages. "And here. And, finally, here."

They stood now in the cold wind outside the hospital and let the breeze turn the pages as they read the captions under the photographs.

"Goebbels," whispered the old man.

"An actor named Rudy Steihl."

"Göring."

"A hambone named Grofe."

"Hess."

"Fritz Dingle."

The old man shut the book and cried to the echoes.

"Son of a bitch!"

"Louder and funnier, Arch. Funnier and louder."

"You mean right now out there somewhere in the city three dumbkopf out-of-work actors have Adolf in hiding, held maybe for ransom? And do we *pay* it?"

"Do we want to finish the film, Arch?"

"God, I don't know, so much money already, time, and—"
The old man shivered and rolled his eyes. "What if—I mean—
what if they don't *want* ransom?"

The director nodded and grinned. "You mean, what if this is
the true start of the Fourth Reich?"

"All the peanut brittle in Germany might put itself in sacks
and show up if they knew that—"

"Steihl, Grofe, and Dingle, which is to say, Goebbels, Göring,
and Hess, were back in the saddle with dumbass Adolf?"

"Crazy, awful, mad! It couldn't happen!"

"Nobody was ever going to clog the Suez Canal. Nobody was
ever going to land on the Moon. Nobody."

"What do we do? This waiting is horrible. Think of something, Marc, think, think!"

"I'm thinking."

"And—"

This time a hundred-watt bulb flashed on in the director's
face. He sucked air and let out a great braying laugh.

"I'm going to help them organize and speak up, Arch! I'm a
genius. Shake my hand!"

He seized the old man's hand and pumped it, crying with
hilarity, tears running down his cheeks.

"You, Marc, on their side, helping form the Fourth Reich!?"
The old man backed away.

"Don't hit me, help me. Think, Arch, think. What was it
Darling Adolf said at lunch, and damn the expense! What,
what?"

The old man took a breath, held it, exploded it out, with a
final light blazing in his face.

"Nuremberg?" he asked.

"Nuremberg! What month is this, Arch?"

"October!"

"October! October, forty years ago, October, the big, big
Nuremberg Rally. And this coming Friday, Arch, an Anniversary

Rally. We shove an ad in the international edition of Variety:
RALLY AT NUREMBERG. TORCHES. BANDS. FLAGS. Christ, he won't
be able to stay away. He'd shoot his kidnapers to be there and
play the greatest role in his life!"

"Marc, we can't afford—"

"Five hundred and forty-eight bucks? For the ad plus the
torches plus a full military band on a phonograph record? Hell,
Arch, hand me that phone."

The old man pulled a telephone out of the front seat of his
limousine.

"Son of a bitch," he whispered.

"Yeah." The director grinned, and ticked the phone. "Son of
a bitch."

The sun was going down beyond the rim of Nuremberg
Stadium. The sky was bloodied all across the western horizon. In
another half-hour it would be completely dark and you wouldn't
be able to see the small platform down in the center of the
arena, or the few dark flags with the swastikas put up on tempo-
rary poles here or there making a path from one side of the
stadium to the other. There was a sound of a crowd gathering,
but the place was empty. There was a faint drum of band music
but there was no band.

Sitting in the front row on the eastern side of the stadium,
the director waited, his hands on the controls of a sound unit.
He had been waiting for two hours and was getting tired and
feeling foolish. He could hear the old man saying:

"Let's go home. Idiotic. He won't come."

And himself saying, "He will. He must," but not believing it.

He had the records waiting on his lap. Now and again he
tested one, quietly, on the turntable, and then the crowd noises
came from lilyhorns stuck up at both ends of the arena, murmuring, or the band played, not loudly, no, that would be later,
but very softly. Then he waited again.

The sun sank lower. Blood ran crimson in the clouds. The director tried not to notice. He hated nature's blatant ironies.

The old man stirred feebly at last and looked around.

"So this was the place. It was really *it*, back in 1934."

"This was it. Yeah."

"I remember the films. Yes, yes. Hitler stood—what? Over there?"

"That was it."

"And all the kids and men down there and the girls there, and fifty cameras."

"Fifty, count 'em, fifty. Jesus, I would have liked to have been here with the torches and flags and people and cameras."

"Marc, Marc, you don't *mean* it?"

"Yes, Arch, sure! So I could have run up to Darling Adolf and done what I did to that pig-swine half-ass actor. Hit him in the nose, then hit him in the teeth, then hit him in the *blinis!* You *got* it, Leni? Action! *Swot!* Camera! *Bam!* Here's one for Izzie. Here's one for Ike. Cameras running, Leni? Okay. *Zot!* Print!"

They stood looking down into the empty stadium where the wind prowled a few newspapers like ghosts on the vast concrete floor.

Then, suddenly, they gasped.

Far up at the very top of the stadium a small figure had appeared.

The director quickened, half rose, then forced himself to sit back down.

The small figure, against the last light of the day, seemed to be having difficulty walking. It leaned to one side, and held one arm up against its side, like a wounded bird.

The figure hesitated, waited.

"Come on," whispered the director.

The figure turned and was about to flee.

"Adolf, no!" hissed the director.

Instinctively, he snapped one of his hands to the sound-effects tape deck, his other hand to the music.

The military band began to play softly.

The "crowd" began to murmur and stir.

Adolf, far above, froze.

The music played higher. The director touched a control knob. The crowd mumbled louder.

Adolf turned back to squint down into the half-seen stadium. Now he must be seeing the flags. And now the few torches. And now the waiting platform with the microphones, two *dozen* of them! *one* of them real.

The band came up in full brass.

Adolf took one step forward.

The crowd roared.

Christ, thought the director, looking at his hands, which were now suddenly hard fists and now again just fingers leaping on the controls, all to themselves. Christ, what do I do with him when I get him down here? What, *what?*

And then, just as insanely, the thought came. Crud. You're a director. And that's *him.* And this *is* Nuremberg.

So . . . ?

Adolf took a second step down. Slowly his hand came up in a stiff salute.

The crowd went wild.

Adolf never stopped after that. He limped, he tried to march with pomp, but the fact was he limped down the hundreds of steps until he reached the floor of the stadium. There he straightened his cap, brushed his tunic, resaluted the roaring emptiness, and came gimping across two hundred yards of empty ground toward the waiting platform.

The crowd kept up its tumult. The band responded with a vast heartbeat of brass and drum.

Darling Adolf passed within twenty feet of the lower stands where the director sat fiddling with the tape-deck dials. The director crouched down. But there was no need. Summoned by the *"Sieg Heils"* and the fanfare of trumpets and brass, Der Führer was drawn inevitably toward that dais where destiny awaited him. He was walking taller now and though his uniform was rumpled and the swastika emblem torn, and his mustache moth-eaten and his hair wild, it was the old Leader all right, it was him.

The old producer sat up straight and watched. He whispered. He pointed.

Far above, at the top of the stadium, three more men had stepped into view.

My God, thought the director, that's the team. The men who grabbed Adolf.

A man with bushy eyebrows, a fat man, and a man like a wounded chimpanzee.

Jesus. The director blinked. Goebbels. Göring. Hess. Three actors at liberty. Three half-ass kidnapers staring down at . . .

Adolf Hitler climbing up on the small podium by the fake microphones and the real one under the blowing torches which bloomed and blossomed and guttered and smoked on the cold October wind under the sprig of lilyhorns which lifted in four directions.

Adolf lifted his chin. That did it. The crowd went absolutely mad. Which is to say, the director's hand, sensing the hunger, went mad, twitched the volume high so the air was riven and torn and shattered again and again and again with *"Sieg Heil, Sieg Heil, Sieg Heil!"*

Above, high on the stadium rim, the three watching figures lifted their arms in salute to their Führer.

Adolf lowered his chin. The sounds of the crowd faded. Only the torch flames whispered.

Adolf made his speech.

He must have yelled and chanted and brayed and sputtered and whispered hoarsely and wrung his hands and beat the podium with his fist and plunged his fist at the sky and shut his eyes and shrieked like a disemboweled trumpet for ten minutes, twenty minutes, half an hour as the sun vanished beyond the earth and the three other men up on the stadium rim watched and listened and the producer and the director waited and watched. He shouted things about the whole world and he yelled things about Germany and he shrieked things about himself and he damned this and blamed that and praised yet a third, until at last he began to repeat, and repeat the same words over and over as if he had reached the end of a record inside himself and the needle was fastened to a circle track which hissed and hiccuped, hiccuped and hissed, and then faded away at last into a silence where you could only hear his heavy breathing, which broke at last into a sob and he stood with his head bent while the others now could not look at him but looked only at their shoes or the sky or the way the wind blew dust across the field. The flags fluttered. The single torch bent and lifted and twisted itself again and talked under its breath.

At last, Adolf raised his head to finish his speech.

"Now I must speak of them."

He nodded up to the top of the stadium where the three men stood against the sky.

"They are nuts. I am nuts, too. But at least I know I am nuts. I told them: crazy, you are crazy. Mad, you are mad. And now, my own craziness, my own madness, well, it has run itself down. I am tired.

"So now, what? I give the world back to you. I had it for a small while here today. But now you must keep it and keep it better than I would. To each of you I give the world, but you must promise, each of you to keep your own part and work with it. So there. Take it."

He made a motion with his free hand to the empty seats, as if all the world were in his fingers and at last he were letting it go.

The crowd murmured, stirred, but said nothing loud.

The flags softly tongued the air. The flames squatted on themselves and smoked.

Adolf pressed his fingers onto his eyeballs as if suddenly seized with a blinding headache. Without looking over at the director or the producer, he said, quietly:

"Time to go?"

The director nodded.

Adolf limped off the podium and came to stand below where the old man and the younger director sat.

"Go ahead, if you want, again, hit me."

The director sat and looked at him. At last he shook his head.

"Do we finish the film?" asked Adolf.

The director looked at the producer. The old man shrugged and could find nothing to say.

"Ah, well," said the actor. "Anyway, the madness is over, the fever has dropped. I have *made* my speech at Nuremberg. God, look at those idiots up there. Idiots!" he called suddenly at the stands. Then back to the director, "Can you think? They wanted to hold me for ransom. I told them what fools they were. Now I'll go tell them again. I had to get away from them. I couldn't stand their stupid talk. I had to come here and be my own fool in my own way for the last time. Well . . ."

He limped off across the empty field, calling back quietly:

"I'll be in your car outside, waiting. If you want, I am yours for the final scenes. If not, no, and that ends it."

The director and the producer waited until Adolf had climbed to the top of the stadium. They could hear his voice drift down, cursing those other three, the man with the bushy eyebrows, the fat man, and the ugly chimpanzee, calling them many things, waving his hands. The three backed off and went away, gone.

Adolf stood alone high in the cold October air.

The director gave him a final lift of the sound volume. The crowd, obedient, banged out a last *"Sieg Heil."*

Adolf lifted his free hand, not into a salute, but some sort of old, easy, half-collapsed mid-Atlantic wave. Then he was gone, too.

The sunlight went with him. The sky was no longer blood-colored. The wind blew dust and want-ads from a German paper across the stadium floor.

"Son of a bitch," muttered the old man. "Let's get out of here."

They left the torches to burn and the flags to blow, but shut off the sound equipment.

"Wish I'd brought a record of Yankee Doodle to march us out of here," said the director.

"Who needs records. We'll whistle. Why not?"

"Why not!"

He held the old man's elbow going up the stairs in the dusk, but it was only halfway up, they had the guts to try to whistle.

And then it was suddenly so funny they couldn't finish the tune.

The Miracles of Jamie

Jamie Winters worked his first miracle in the morning. The second, third, and various other miracles came later in the day. But the first miracle was always the most important.

It was always the same: "Make Mother well. Put color in her cheeks. Don't let Mom be sick too much longer."

It was Mom's illness that had first made him think about himself and miracles. And because of her he kept on, learning how to be good at them so that he could keep her well and could make life jump through a hoop.

It was not the first day that he had worked miracles. He had done them in the past, but always hesitantly, since sometimes he did not say them right, or Ma and Pa interrupted, or the other kids in the seventh grade at school made noise. They spoiled things.

But in the past month he had felt his power flow over him like cool, certain water; he bathed in it, basked in it, had come from the shower of it beaded with glory water and with a halo of wonder about his dark-haired head.

Five days ago he'd taken down the family Bible, with real color pictures of Jesus as a boy in it, and had compared them with his own face in the bathroom mirror, gasping. He shook all over. There it *was*.

And wasn't Ma getting better every day now? Well—*there!*

Now, on Monday morning, following the first miracle at home, he worked a second one at school. He wanted to lead the Arizona State Day parade as head of his class battalion. And the principal, naturally, selected Jamie to lead. Jamie felt fine. The girls looked up to him, bumping him with their soft, thin little elbows, especially one named Ingrid, whose golden hair rustled in Jamie's face as they all hurried out of the cloakroom.

Jamie Winters held his head so high, and when he drank from the chromium fountain he bent so carefully and twisted the shining handle so exactly, so precisely—so godlike and indomitable.

Jamie knew it would be useless to tell his friends. They'd laugh. After all, Jesus was pounded nail through palm and ankle to a Calvary Hill cross because he told on himself. This time, it would be wise to wait. At least until he was sixteen and grew a beard, thus establishing once and for all the incredible proof of his identity!

Sixteen was somewhat young for a beard, but Jamie felt that he could exert the effort to force one if the time came and necessity demanded.

The children poured from the schoolhouse into the hot spring light. In the distance were the mountains, the foothills spread green with cactus, and overhead was a vast Arizona sky of very fine blue. The children donned paper hats and crepe-paper Sam

Browne belts in blue and red. Flags burst open upon the wind; everybody yelled and formed into groups, glad to escape the schoolrooms for one day.

Jamie stood at the head of the line, very calm and quiet. Someone said something, and Jamie realized that it was young Huff who was talking.

"I hope we win the parade prize," said Huff worriedly.

Jamie looked at him. "Oh, we'll win all right. I know we'll win. I'll guarantee it! Heck, yes!"

Huff was brightened by such steadfast faith. "You think so?"

"I *know* so! Leave it to me!"

"What do you mean, Jamie?"

"Nothing. Just watch and see, that's all. Just watch!"

"Now, children!" Mr. Palmborg, the principal, clapped hands; the sun shone on his glasses. Silence came quickly. "Now, children," he said, nodding, "remember what we taught you yesterday about marching. Remember how you pivot to turn a corner, and remember those special routines we practiced, will you?"

"Sure!" everybody said at once.

The principal concluded his brief address and the parade began, Jamie heading it with his hundreds of following disciples.

The feet bent up and straightened down, and the street went under them. The yellow sun warmed Jamie and he, in turn, bade it shine the whole day to make things perfect.

When the parade edged onto Main Street, and the high-school band began pulsing its brass heart and rattling its wooden bones on the drums, Jamie wished they would play "Stars and Stripes Forever."

Later, when they played "Columbia, Gem of the Ocean," Jamie thought quickly, oh, yeah, that's what he'd meant—"Columbia," not "Stars and Stripes Forever"—and was satisfied that his wish had been obeyed.

The street was lined with people, as it was on the Arizona rodeo days in February. People sweated in intent layers, five deep for over a mile; the rhythm of feet came back in reflected cadence from two-story frame fronts. There were occasional glimpses of mirrored armies marching in the tall windows of the J. C. Penney Store or of the Morble Company. Each cadence was like a whip thud on the dusty asphalt, sharp and true, and the band music shot blood through Jamie's miraculous veins.

He concentrated, scowling fiercely. Let us win, he thought. Let everyone march perfectly: chins up, shoulders back, knees high, down, high again, sun upon denimed knees rising in a blue tide, sun upon tanned girl-knees like small, round faces upping and falling. Perfect, perfect, perfect. Perfection surged confidently through Jamie, extending into an encompassing aura that held his own group intact. As he moved, so moved the na- tion. As his fingers snapped in a brisk pendulum at his sides, so did their fingers, their arms cutting an orbit. And as his shoes trod asphalt, so theirs followed in obedient imitation.

As they reached the reviewing stand, Jamie cued them; they coiled back upon their own lines like bright garlands twining to return again, marching in the original direction, without chaos.

Oh, so darn perfect! cried Jamie to himself.

It was hot. Holy sweat poured out of Jamie, and the world sagged from side to side. Presently the drums were exhausted and the children melted away. Lapping an ice-cream cone, Jamie was relieved that it was all over.

Mr. Palmborg came rushing up, all heated and sweating.

"Children, children, I have an announcement to make!" he cried.

Jamie looked at young Huff, who stood beside him, also with an ice-cream cone. The children shrilled, and Mr. Palmborg patted the noise into a ball which he made vanish like a magi- cian.

"We've won the competition! Our school marched finest of all the schools!"

In the clamor and noise and jumping up and down and hitting one another on the arm muscles in celebration, Jamie nodded quietly over his ice-cream cone, looked at young Huff, and said, "See? I told you so. Now, will you believe in me!"

Jamie continued licking his cold cone with a great, golden peace in him.

Jamie did not immediately tell his friends why they had won the marching competition. He had observed a tendency in them to be suspicious and to ridicule anyone who told them that they were not as good as they thought they were, that their talent had been derived from an outside source.

No, it was enough for Jamie to savor his minor and major victories; he enjoyed his little secret, he enjoyed the things that happened. Such things as getting high marks in arithmetic or winning a basketball game were ample reward. There was always some byproduct of his miracles to satisfy his as-yet-small hunger.

He paid attention to blonde young Ingrid with the placid gray-blue eyes. She, in turn, favored him with her attentions, and he knew then that his ability was well rooted, established.

Aside from Ingrid, there were other good things. Friendships with several boys came about in wondrous fashion. One case, though, required some little thought and care. The boy's name was Cunningham. He was big and fat and bald because some fever had necessitated shaving his skull. The kids called him Billiard; he thanked them by kicking them in the shins, knocking them down, and sitting on them while he performed quick dentistry with his knuckles.

It was upon this Billiard Cunningham that Jamie hoped to apply his greatest ecclesiastical power. Walking through the rough paths of the desert toward his home, Jamie often conjured up visions of himself picking up Billiard by his left foot and cracking him like a whip so as to shock him senseless. Dad had once done that to a rattlesnake. Of course, Billiard was too heavy for this neat trick. Besides, it might hurt him, and Jamie didn't really want him killed or anything, just dusted off a little to show him where he belonged in the world.

But when he chinned up to Billiard, Jamie got cold feet and decided to wait a day or two longer for meditation. There was no use rushing things, so he let Billiard go free. Boy, Billiard didn't know how lucky he was at such times, Jamie clucked to himself.

One Tuesday, Jamie carried Ingrid's books home. She lived in a small cottage not far from the Santa Catalina foothills. Together they walked in peaceful content, needing no words. They even held hands for a while.

Turning about a clump of prickly pears, they came face to face with Billiard Cunningham.

He stood with his big feet planted across the path, plump fists on his hips, staring at Ingrid with appreciative eyes. Everybody stood still, and Billiard said:

"I'll carry your books, Ingrid. Here."

He reached to take them from Jamie.

Jamie fell back a step. "Oh, no, you don't," he said.

"Oh, yes, I do," retorted Billiard.

"Like heck you do," said Jamie.

"Like heck I don't," exclaimed Billiard, and snatched again, knocking the books into the dust.

Ingrid yelled, then said, "Look here, you can both carry my books. Half and half. That'll settle it."

Billiard shook his head.

"All or nothing," he leered.

Jamie looked back at him.

"Nothing, then!" he shouted.

He summoned up his powers like wrathful storm clouds; lightning crackled hot in each fist. What matter if Billiard loomed four inches taller and some several broader? The fury-wrath lived in Jamie; he would knock Billiard senseless with one clean bolt—maybe two.

There was no room for stuttering fear now; Jamie was

cauterized clean of it by a great rage. He pulled away back and let Billiard have it on the chin.

"Jamie!" screamed Ingrid.

The only miracle after that was how Jamie got out of it with his life.

Dad poured Epsom salts into a dishpan of hot water, stirred it firmly, and said, "You oughta known better, darn your hide. Your mother sick an' you comin' home all banged up this way."

Dad made a leathery motion of one brown hand. His eyes were bedded in crinkles and lines, and his mustache was pepper-gray and sparse, as was his hair.

"I didn't know Ma was very sick anymore," said Jamie.

"Women don't talk much," said Dad, dryly. He soaked a towel in steaming Epsom salts and wrung it out. He held Jamie's beaten profile and swabbed it. Jamie whimpered. "Hold still," said Dad. "How you expect me to fix that cut if you don't hold still, darn it."

"What's going on out there?" Mother's voice asked from the bedroom, real tired and soft.

"Nothing," said Dad, wringing out the towel again. "Don't you fret. Jamie just fell and cut his lip, that's all."

"Oh, Jamie," said Mother.

"I'm okay, Ma," said Jamie. The warm towel helped to normalize things. He tried not to think of the fight. It made bad thinking. There were memories of flailing arms, himself pinned down, Billiard whooping with delight and beating downward while Ingrid, crying real tears, threw her books, screaming, at his back.

And then Jamie staggered home alone, sobbing bitterly.

"Oh, Dad," he said now. "It didn't work." He meant his physical miracle on Billiard. "It didn't work."

"What didn't work?" said Dad, applying liniment to bruises.

"Oh, nothing. Nothing." Jamie licked his swollen lip and

began to calm down. After all, you can't have a perfect batting average. Even the Lord made mistakes. And—Jamie grinned suddenly—yes, yes, he had *meant* to lose the fight! Yes, he had. Wouldn't Ingrid love him all the more for having fought and lost just for her?

Sure. That was the answer. It was just a reversed miracle, that was all!

"Jamie," Mother called him.

He went in to see her.

With one thing and another, including Epsom salts and a great resurgence of faith in himself because Ingrid loved him now more than ever, Jamie went through the rest of the week without much pain.

He walked Ingrid home, and Billiard didn't bother him again. Billiard played after-school baseball, which was a greater attraction than Ingrid—the sudden sport interest being induced indirectly by telepathy via Jamie, Jamie decided.

Thursday, Ma looked worse. She bleached out to a pallid trembling and a pale coughing. Dad looked scared. Jamie spent less time trying to make things come out wonderful in school and thought more and more of curing Ma.

Friday night, walking alone from Ingrid's house, Jamie watched telegraph poles swing by him very slowly. He thought, If I get to the next telegraph pole before that car behind me reaches me, Mama will be all well.

Jamie walked casually, not looking back, ears itching, legs wanting to run to make the wish come true.

The telegraph pole approached. So did the car behind.

Jamie whistled cautiously. The car was coming too fast!

Jamie jumped past the pole just in time; the car roared by. There now. Mama would be all well again.

He walked along some more.

Forget about her. Forget about wishes and things, he told

himself. But it was tempting, like a hot pie on a windowsill. He had to touch it. He couldn't leave it be, oh, no. He looked ahead on the road and behind on the road.

"I bet I can get down to Schabold's ranch gate before another car comes and do it walking easy," he declared to the sky. "And that will make Mama well all the quicker."

At this moment, in a traitorous, mechanical action, a car jumped over the low hill behind him and roared forward.

Jamie walked fast, then began to run.

I bet I can get down to Schabold's gate, I bet I can—

Feet up, feet down.

He stumbled.

He fell into the ditch, his books fluttering about like dry, white birds. When he got up, sucking his lips, the gate was only twenty yards further on.

The car motored by him in a large cloud of dust.

"I take it back, I take it back," cried Jamie. "I take it back, what I said, I didn't mean it."

With a sudden bleat of terror, he ran for home. It was all his fault, *all* his fault!

The doctor's car stood in front of the house.

Through the window, Mama looked sicker. The doctor closed up his little black bag and looked at Dad a long time with strange lights in his little black eyes.

Jamie ran out onto the desert to walk alone. He did not cry. He was paralyzed, and he walked like an iron child, hating himself, blundering into the dry riverbed, kicking at prickly pears and stumbling again and again.

Hours later, with the first stars, he came home to find Dad standing beside Mama's bed and Mama not saying much—just lying there like fallen snow, so quiet. Dad tightened his jaw, screwed up his eyes, caved in his chest, and put his head down.

Jamie took up a station at the end of the bed and stared at Mama, shouting instructions in his mind to her.

Get well, get well, Ma, get well, you'll be all right, sure you'll be fine, I command it, you'll be fine, you'll be swell, you just get up and dance around, we need you, Dad and I do, wouldn't be good without you, get well, Ma, get well, Ma. Get well!

The fierce energy lashed out from him silently, wrapping, cuddling her and beating into her sickness, tendering her heart. Jamie felt glorified in his warm power.

She *would* get well. She *must!* Why, it was silly to think any other way. Ma just wasn't the dying sort.

Dad moved suddenly. It was a stiff movement with a jerking of breath. He held Mama's wrists so hard he might have broken them. He lay against her breasts sounding the heart and Jamie screamed inside.

Ma, don't, Ma, don't, oh, Ma, please don't give up.

Dad got up, swaying.

She was dead.

Inside the walls of Jericho that was Jamie's mind, a thought went screaming about in one last drive of power: Yes, she's dead, all right, so she is dead, so what if she is dead? Bring her back to life again, yes, make her live again, Lazarus, come forth, Lazarus, Lazarus, come forth from the tomb, Lazarus, come forth.

He must have been babbling aloud, for Dad turned and glared at him in old, ancient horror and struck him bluntly across the mouth to shut him up.

Jamie sank against the bed, mouthing into the cold blankets, and the walls of Jericho crumbled and fell down about him.

Jamie returned to school a week later. He did not stride into the schoolyard with his old assurance; he did not bend imperiously at the fountain; nor did he pass his tests with anything more than a grade of seventy-five.

The children wondered what had happened to him. He was never quite the same.

They did not know that Jamie had given up his role. He could not tell them. They did not know what they had lost.

The October Game

He put the gun back into the bureau drawer and shut the drawer.

No, not that way. Louise wouldn't suffer that way. She would be dead and it would be over and she wouldn't suffer. It was very important that this thing have, above all, duration. Duration through imagination. How to prolong the suffering? How, first of all, to bring it about? Well.

The man standing before the bedroom mirror carefully fitted his cuff links together. He paused long enough to hear the children run by swiftly on the street below, outside this warm two-story house; like so many gray mice the children, like so many leaves.

By the sound of the children you knew the calendar day. By

their screams you knew what evening it was. You knew it was very late in the year. October. The last day of October, with white bone masks and cut pumpkins and the smell of dropped candle fat.

No. Things hadn't been right for some time. October didn't help any. If anything it made things worse. He adjusted his black bow-tie. If this were spring, he nodded slowly, quietly, emotionlessly, at his image in the mirror, then there might be a chance. But tonight all the world was burning down into ruin. There was no green of spring, none of the freshness, none of the promise.

There was a soft running in the hall. "That's Marion," he told himself. "My little one. All eight quiet years of her. Never a word. Just her luminous gray eyes and her wondering little mouth." His daughter had been in and out all evening, trying on various masks, asking him which was most terrifying, most horrible. They had both finally decided on the skeleton mask. It was "just awful!" It would "scare the beans" from people!

Again he caught the long look of thought and deliberation he gave himself in the mirror. He had never liked October. Ever since he first lay in the autumn leaves before his grandmother's house many years ago and heard the wind and saw the empty trees. It had made him cry, without a reason. And a little of that sadness returned each year to him. It always went away with spring.

But, it was different tonight. There was a feeling of autumn coming to last a million years.

There would be no spring.

He had been crying quietly all evening. It did not show, not a vestige of it, on his face. It was all hidden somewhere and it wouldn't stop.

A rich syrupy smell of candy filled the bustling house. Louise had laid out apples in new skins of caramel; there were vast bowls of punch fresh-mixed, stringed apples in each door, scooped, vented pumpkins peering triangularly from each cold window. There was a water tub in the center of the living room, waiting, with a sack of apples nearby, for dunking to begin. All that was needed was the catalyst, the inpouring of children, to start the apples bobbling, the stringed apples to penduluming in the crowded doors, the candy to vanish, the halls to echo with fright or delight, it was all the same.

Now, the house was silent with preparation. And just a little more than that.

Louise had managed to be in every other room save the room he was in today. It was her very fine way of intimating, Oh look, Mich, see how busy I am! So busy that when you walk into a room *I'm* in there's always something I need to do in *another* room! Just see how I dash about!

For a while he had played a little game with her, a nasty childish game. When she was in the kitchen then he came to the kitchen saying, "I need a glass of water." After a moment, he standing, drinking water, she like a crystal witch over the caramel brew bubbling like a prehistoric mudpot on the stove, she said, "Oh, I must light the pumpkins!" and she rushed to the living room to make the pumpkins smile with light. He came after her, smiling, "I must get my pipe." "Oh, the cider!" she had cried, running to the dining room. "I'll check the cider," he had said. But when he tried following she ran to the bathroom and locked the door.

He stood outside the bathroom door, laughing strangely and senselessly, his pipe gone cold in his mouth, and then, tired of the game, but stubborn, he waited another five minutes. There was not a sound from the bath. And lest she enjoy in any way knowing that he waited outside, irritated, he suddenly jerked about and walked upstairs, whistling merrily.

At the top of the stairs he had waited. Finally he had heard the bathroom door unlatch and she had come out and life belowstairs had resumed, as life in a jungle must resume once a terror has passed on away and the antelope return to their spring.

Now, as he finished his bow-tie and put on his dark coat there was a mouse-rustle in the hall. Marion appeared in the door, all skeletonous in her disguise.

"How do I look, Papa?"

"Fine!"

From under the mask, blonde hair showed. From the skull sockets small blue eyes smiled. He sighed. Marion and Louise, the two silent denouncers of his virility, his dark power. What alchemy had there been in Louise that took the dark of a dark man and bleached and bleached the dark brown eyes and black hair and washed and bleached the ingrown baby all during the period before birth until the child was born, Marion, blonde, blue-eyed, ruddy-cheeked? Sometimes he suspected that Louise had conceived the child as an idea, completely asexual, an immaculate conception of contemptuous mind and cell. As a firm rebuke to him she had produced a child in her *own* image, and, to top it, she had somehow *fixed* the doctor so he shook his head and said, "Sorry, Mr. Wilder, your wife will never have another child. This is the *last* one."

"And I wanted a boy," Mich had said, eight years ago.

He almost bent to take hold of Marion now, in her skull mask. He felt an inexplicable rush of pity for her, because she had never had a father's love, only the crushing, holding love of a loveless mother. But most of all he pitied himself, that somehow he had not made the most of a bad birth, enjoyed his daughter for herself, regardless of her not being dark and a son and like himself. Somewhere he had missed out. Other things being equal, he would have loved the child. But Louise hadn't wanted a child, anyway, in the first place. She had been frightened of the idea of birth. He had forced the child on her, and from that night, all through the year until the agony of the birth itself, Louise had lived in another part of the house. She had expected to die with the forced child. It had been very easy for Louise to hate this husband who so wanted a son that he gave his only wife over to the mortuary.

But—Louise had lived. And in triumph! Her eyes, the day

he came to the hospital, were cold. I'm alive, they said. And I have a *blonde* daughter! Just look! And when he had put out a hand to touch, the mother had turned away to conspire with her new pink daughter-child—away from that dark forcing murderer. It had all been so beautifully ironic. His selfishness deserved it.

But now it was October again. There had been other Octobers and when he thought of the long winter he had been filled with horror year after year to think of the endless months mortared into the house by an insane fall of snow, trapped with a woman and child, neither of whom loved him, for months on end. During the eight years there had been respites. In spring and summer you got out, walked, picnicked; these were desperate solutions to the desperate problem of a hated man.

But, in winter, the hikes and picnics and escapes fell away with the leaves. Life, like a tree, stood empty, the fruit picked, the sap run to earth. Yes, you invited people in, but people were hard to get in winter with blizzards and all. Once he had been clever enough to save for a Florida trip. They had gone south. He had walked in the open.

But now, the eighth winter coming, he knew things were finally at an end. He simply could not wear this one through. There was an acid walled off in him that slowly had eaten through tissue and bone over the years, and now, tonight, it would reach the wild explosive in him and all would be over!

There was a mad ringing of the bell below. In the hall, Louise went to see. Marion, without a word, ran down to greet the first arrivals. There were shouts and hilarity.

He walked to the top of the stairs.

Louise was below, taking wraps. She was tall and slender and blonde to the point of whiteness, laughing down upon the new children.

He hesitated. What was all this? The years? The boredom of living? Where had it gone wrong? Certainly not with the birth of the child alone. But it had been a symbol of all their tensions, he imagined. His jealousies and his business failures and all the rotten rest of it. Why didn't he just turn, pack a suit-case, and leave? No. Not without hurting Louise as much as she had hurt him. It was simple as that. Divorce wouldn't hurt her at all. It would simply be an end to numb indecision. If he thought divorce would give her pleasure in any way he would stay married the rest of his life to her, for damned spite. No, he must hurt her. Figure some way, perhaps, to take Marion away from her, legally. Yes. That was it. That would hurt most of all. To take Marion away.

"Hello down there!" He descended the stairs, beaming.

Louise didn't look up.

"Hi, Mr. Wilder!"

The children shouted, waved, as he came down.

By ten o'clock the doorbell had stopped ringing, the apples were bitten from stringed doors, the pink child faces were wiped dry from the apple bobbling, napkins were smeared with caramel and punch, and he, the husband, with pleasant efficiency had taken over. He took the party right out of Louise's hands. He ran about talking to the twenty children and the twelve parents who had come and were happy with the special spiked cider he had fixed them. He supervised pin the tail on the donkey, spin the bottle, musical chairs, and all the rest, amid fits of shouting laughter. Then, in the triangular-eyed pumpkin shine, all house lights out, he cried, "Hush! Follow me!" tiptoeing toward the cellar.

The parents, on the outer periphery of the costumed riot, commented to each other, nodding at the clever husband, speaking to the lucky wife. How *well* he got on with children, they said.

The children crowded after the husband, squealing.

"The cellar!" he cried. "The tomb of the witch!"

More squealing. He made a mock shiver. "Abandon hope all ye who enter here!"

The parents chuckled.

One by one the children slid down a slide which Mich had fixed up from lengths of table-section, into the dark cellar. He hissed and shouted ghastly utterances after them. A wonderful wailing filled the dark pumpkin-lighted house. Everybody talked at once. Everybody but Marion. She had gone through all the party with a minimum of sound or talk; it was all inside her, all the excitement and joy. What a little troll, he thought. With a shut mouth and shiny eyes she had watched her own party, like so many serpentines thrown before her.

Now, the parents. With laughing reluctance they slid down the short incline, uproarious, while little Marion stood by, always wanting to see it all, to be last. Louise went down without help. He moved to aid her, but she was gone even before he bent.

The upper house was empty and silent in the candle-shine.

Marion stood by the slide. "Here we go," he said, and picked her up.

They sat in a vast circle in the cellar. Warmth came from the distant bulk of the furnace. The chairs stood in a long line along each wall, twenty squealing children, twelve rustling relatives, alternately spaced, with Louise down at the far end, Mich up at this end, near the stairs. He peered but saw nothing. They had all grouped to their chairs, catch-as-you-can in the blackness. The entire program from here on was to be enacted in the dark, he as Mr. Interlocutor. There was a child scampering, a smell of damp cement, and the sound of the wind out in the October stars.

"Now!" cried the husband in the dark cellar. "Quiet!"

Everybody settled.

The room was black black. Not a light, not a shine, not a glint of an eye.

A scraping of crockery, a metal rattle.

"The witch is dead," intoned the husband.

"Eeeeeeeeeeeee," said the children.

"The witch is dead, she has been killed, and here is the knife she was killed with."

He handed over the knife. It was passed from hand to hand, down and around the circle, with chuckles and little odd cries and comments from the adults.

"The witch is dead, and this is her head," whispered the husband, and handed an item to the nearest person.

"Oh, I know how this game is played," some child cried, happily, in the dark. "He gets some old chicken innards from the icebox and hands them around and says, 'These are her innards!' And he makes a clay head and passes it for her head, and passes a soup bone for her arm. And he takes a marble and says, 'This is her eye!' And he takes some corn and says, 'This is her teeth!' And he takes a sack of plum pudding and gives that and says, 'This is her stomach!' I know how *this* is played!"

"Hush, you'll spoil everything," some girl said.

"The witch came to harm, and this is her arm," said Mich.

"Eeeee!"

The items were passed and passed, like hot potatoes, around the circle. Some children screamed, wouldn't touch them. Some ran from their chairs to stand in the center of the cellar until the grisly items had passed.

"Aw, it's only chicken insides," scoffed a boy. "Come back, Helen!"

Shot from hand to hand, with small scream after scream, the items went down, down, to be followed by another and another.

"The witch cut apart, and this is her heart," said the husband.

Six or seven items moving at once through the laughing, trembling dark.

Louise spoke up. "Marion, don't be afraid; it's only play."

Marion didn't say anything.

"Marion?" asked Louise. "Are you afraid?"

Marion didn't speak.

"She's all right," said the husband. "She's not afraid."

On and on the passing, the screams, the hilarity.

The autumn wind sighed about the house. And he, the husband, stood at the head of the dark cellar, intoning the words, handing out the items.

"Marion?" asked Louise again, from far across the cellar.

Everybody was talking.

"Marion?" called Louise.

Everybody quieted.

"Marion, answer me, are you afraid?"

Marion didn't answer.

The husband stood there, at the bottom of the cellar steps. Louise called, "Marion, are you there?"

No answer. The room was silent.

"Where's Marion?" called Louise.

"She was here," said a boy.

"Maybe she's upstairs."

"Marion!"

No answer. It was quiet.

Louise cried out, "Marion, Marion!"

"Turn on the lights," said one of the adults.

The items stopped passing. The children and adults sat with the witch's items in their hands.

"No." Louise gasped. There was a scraping of her chair, wildly, in the dark. "No. Don't turn on the lights, oh, God, God, God, don't turn them on, please, please *don't* turn on the lights, *don't!*" Louis was shrieking now. The entire cellar froze with the scream.

Nobody moved.

Everyone sat in the dark cellar, suspended in the suddenly frozen task of this October game; the wind blew outside, banging the house, the smell of pumpkins and apples filled the room with the smell of the objects in their fingers while one boy cried, "I'll go upstairs and look!" and he ran upstairs hopefully and out around the house, four times around the house, calling, "Marion, Marion, Marion!" over and over and at last coming slowly down the stairs into the waiting breathing cellar and saying to the darkness, "I can't find her."

Then . . . some idiot turned on the lights.

The Pumpernickel

Mr. and Mrs. Welles walked away from the movie theater late at night and went into the quiet little store, a combination restaurant and delicatessen. They settled in a booth, and Mrs. Welles said, "Baked ham on pumpernickel." Mr. Welles glanced toward the counter, and there lay a loaf of pumpernickel.

"Why," he murmured, "pumpernickel . . . Druce's Lake . . ."

The night, the late hour, the empty restaurant—by now the pattern was familiar. Anything could set him off on a tide of reminiscence. The scent of autumn leaves, or midnight winds blowing, could stir him from himself, and memories would pour around him. Now in the unreal hour after the theater, in this lonely store, he saw a loaf of pumpernickel bread and, as on a thousand other nights, he found himself moved into the past.

"Druce's Lake," he said again.

"What?" His wife glanced up.

"Something I'd almost forgotten," said Mr. Welles. "In 1910, when I was twenty, I nailed a loaf of pumpernickel to the top of my bureau mirror. . . ."

In the hard, shiny crust of the bread, the boys at Druce's Lake had cut their names: *Tom, Nick, Bill, Alec, Paul, Jack.* The finest picnic in history! Their faces tanned as they rattled down the dusty roads. Those were the days when roads were *really* dusty; a fine brown talcum floured up after your car. And the lake was always twice as good to reach as it would be later in life when you arrived immaculate, clean, and unrumpled.

"That was the last time the old gang got together," Mr. Welles said.

After that, college, work, and marriage separated you. Suddenly you found yourself with some other group. And you never felt as comfortable or as much at ease again in all your life.

"I wonder," said Mr. Welles. "I like to think maybe we all *knew*, somehow, that this picnic might be the last we'd have. You first get that empty feeling the day after high-school graduation. Then, when a little time passes and no one vanishes immediately, you relax. But after a year you realize the old world is changing. And you want to do some one last thing before you lose one another. While you're all still friends, home from college for the summer, this side of marriage, you've got to have something like a last ride and a swim in the cool lake."

Mr. Welles remembered that rare summer morning, he and Tom lying under his father's Ford, reaching up their hands to adjust this or that, talking about machines and women and the future. While they worked, the day got warm. At last Tom said, "Why don't we drive out to Druce's Lake?"

As simple as that.

Yet, forty years later, you remember every detail of picking up the other fellows, everyone yelling under the green trees.

"Hey!" Alec beating everyone's head with the pumpernickel and laughing. "This is for extra sandwiches, later."

Nick had made the sandwiches that were already in the hamper—the garlic kind they would eat less of as the years passed and the girls moved in.

Then, squeezing three in the front, three in the rear, with their arms across one another's shoulders, they drove through the boiling, dusty countryside, with a cake of ice in a tin washtub to cool the beer they'd buy.

What was the special quality of that day that it should focus like a stereoscopic image, fresh and clear, forty years later? Perhaps each of them had had an experience like his own. A few days before the picnic, he had found a photograph of his father twenty-five years younger, standing with a group of friends at college. The photograph had disturbed him, made him aware as he had not been before of the passing of time, the swift flow of the years away from youth. A picture taken of him as he was now would, in twenty-five years, look as strange to his own children as his father's picture did to him—unbelievably young, a stranger out of a strange, never-returning time.

Was that how the final picnic had come about—with each of them knowing that in a few short years they would be crossing streets to avoid one another, or, if they met, saying, "We've *got* to have lunch sometime!" but never doing it? Whatever the reason, Mr. Welles could still hear the splashes as they'd plunged off the pier under a yellow sun. And then the beer and sandwiches underneath the shady trees.

We never ate that pumpernickel, Mr. Welles thought. Funny, if we'd been a bit hungrier, we'd have cut it up, and I wouldn't have been reminded of it by that loaf there on the counter.

Lying under the trees in a golden peace that came from beer and sun and male companionship, they promised that in ten years they would meet at the courthouse on New Year's Day, 1920, to see what they had done with their lives. Talking their rough easy talk, they carved their names in the pumpernickel.

"Driving home," Mr. Welles said, "we sang 'Moonlight Bay.' "

He remembered motoring along in the hot, dry night with their swimsuits damp on the jolting floorboards. It was a ride of many detours taken just for the hell of it, which was the best reason in the world.

"Good night." "So long." "Good night."

Then Welles was driving alone, at midnight, home to bed.

He nailed the pumpernickel to his bureau the next day.

"I almost cried when, two years later, my mother threw it in the incinerator while I was off at college."

"What happened in 1920?" asked his wife. "On New Year's Day?"

"Oh," said Mr. Welles. "I was walking by the courthouse, by accident, at noon. It was snowing. I heard the clock strike. Lord, I thought, we were supposed to meet here today! I waited five minutes. Not right in front of the courthouse, no. I waited across the street." He paused. "Nobody showed up."

He got up from the table and paid the bill. "And I'll take that loaf of unsliced pumpernickel there," he said.

When he and his wife were walking home, he said, "I've got a crazy idea. I often wondered what happened to everyone."

"Nick's still in town with his café."

"But what about the others?" Mr. Welles's face was getting pink and he was smiling and waving his hands. "They moved away. I think Tom's in Cincinnati." He looked quickly at his wife. "Just for the heck of it, I'll send him this pumpernickel!"

"Oh, but—"

"Sure!" He laughed, walking faster, slapping the bread with the palm of his hand. "Have him carve his name on it and mail it on to the others if he knows their addresses. And finally back to me, with all their names on it!"

"But," she said, taking his arm, "it'll only make you unhappy. You've done things like this so many times before and . . ."

He wasn't listening. Why do I never get these ideas by day? he thought. Why do I always get them after the sun goes down?

In the morning, first thing, he thought, I'll mail this pumpernickel off, by God, to Tom and the others. And when it comes back I'll have the loaf just as it was when it got thrown out and burned! Why not?

"Let's see," he said, as his wife opened the screen door and let him walk into the stuffy-smelling house to be greeted by silence and warm emptiness. "Let's see. We also sang 'Row Row Row Your Boat,' didn't we?"

In the morning, he came down the hall stairs and paused a moment in the strong full sunlight, his face shaved, his teeth freshly brushed. Sunlight brightened every room. He looked in at the breakfast table.

His wife was busy there. Slowly, calmly, she was slicing the pumpernickel.

He sat down at the table in the warm sunlight, and reached for the newspaper.

She picked up a slice of the newly cut bread, and kissed him on the cheek. He patted her arm.

"One or two slices of toast, dear?" she asked gently.

"Two, I think," he replied.

Long After Midnight

The police ambulance went up into the palisades at the wrong hour. It is always the wrong hour when the police ambulance goes anywhere, but this was especially wrong, for it was long after midnight and nobody imagined it would ever be day again, because the sea coming in on the lightless shore below said as much, and the wind blowing salt cold in from the Pacific reaffirmed this, and the fog muffling the sky and putting out the stars struck the final, unfelt-but-disabling blow. The weather said it had been here forever, man was hardly here at all, and would soon be gone. Under the circumstances it was hard for the men gathered on the cliff, with several cars, the headlights on, and flashlights bobbing, to feel real, trapped as they were between a sunset they hardly remembered and a sunrise that would not be imagined.

The slender weight hanging from the tree, turning in the cold salt wind, did not diminish this feeling in any way.

The slender weight was a girl, no more than nineteen, in a light green gossamer party frock, coat and shoes lost somewhere in the cool night, who had brought a rope up to these cliffs and found a tree with a branch half out over the cliff and tied the rope in place and made a loop for her neck and let herself out on the wind to hang there swinging. The rope made a dry scraping whine on the branch, until the police came, and the ambulance, to take her down out of space and place her on the ground.

A single phone call had come in about midnight telling what they might find out here on the edge of the cliff and whoever it was hung up swiftly and did not call again, and now the hours had passed and all that could be done was done and over, the police were finished and leaving, and there was just the ambulance now and the men with the ambulance to load the quiet burden and head for the morgue.

Of the three men remaining around the sheeted form there were Carlson, who had been at this sort of thing for thirty years, and Moreno, who had been at it for ten, and Latting, who was new to the job a few weeks back. Of the three it was Latting now who stood on the edge of the cliff looking at that empty tree limb, the rope in his hand, not able to take his eyes away. Carlson came up behind him. Hearing him, Latting said, "What a place, what an awful place to die."

"Any place is awful, if you decide you want to go bad enough," said Carlson. "Come on, kid."

Latting did not move. He put out his hand to touch the tree. Carlson grunted and shook his head. "Go ahead. Try to remember it all."

"Any reason why I shouldn't?" Latting turned quickly to look at that emotionless gray face of the older man. "You got any objections?"

"No objections. I was the same way once. But after a while you learn it's best not to see. You eat better. You sleep better. After a while you learn to forget."

"I don't want to forget," said Latting. "Good God, somebody died up here just a few hours ago. She deserves—"

"She *deserved*, kid, past tense, not present. She deserved a better shake and didn't get it. Now she deserves a decent burial. That's all we can do for her. It's late and cold. You can tell us all about it on the way."

"That could be your daughter there."

"You won't get to me that way, kid. It's not my daughter, that's what counts. And it's not yours, though you make it sound like it was. It's a nineteen-year-old girl, no name, no purse, nothing. I'm sorry she's dead. There, does that help?"

"It could if you said it right."

"I'm sorry, now pick up the other end of the stretcher."

Latting picked up one end of the stretcher but did not walk with it and only looked at the figure beneath the sheet.

"It's awful being that young and deciding to just quit."

"Sometimes," said Carlson, at the other end of the stretcher, "I get tired, too."

"Sure, but you're—" Latting stopped.

"Go ahead, say it, I'm old. Somebody fifty, sixty, it's okay, who gives a damn, somebody nineteen, everybody cries. So don't come to my funeral, kid, and no flowers."

"I didn't mean . . ." said Latting.

"Nobody means, but everybody says, and luckily I got the hide of an iguana. March."

They moved with the stretcher toward the ambulance where Moreno was opening the doors wider.

"Boy," said Latting, "she's light. She doesn't weigh anything."

"That's the wild life for you, you punks, you kids." Carlson was getting into the back of the ambulance now and they were sliding the stretcher in. "I smell whiskey. You young ones think you can drink like college fullbacks and keep your weight. Hell, she don't even weigh ninety pounds, if that."

Latting put the rope in on the floor of the ambulance. "I wonder where she got this?"

"It's not like poison," said Moreno. "Anyone can buy rope and not sign. This looks like block-and-tackle rope. She was at a beach party maybe and got mad at her boyfriend and took this from his car and picked herself a spot. . . ."

They took a last look at the tree out over the cliff, the empty branch, the wind rustling in the leaves, then Carlson got out and walked around to the front seat with Moreno, and Latting got in the back and slammed the doors.

They drove away down the dim incline toward the shore where the ocean laid itself, card after white card, in thunders, upon the dark sand. They drove in silence for a while, letting their headlights, like ghosts, move on out ahead. Then Latting said, "I'm getting myself a new job."

Moreno laughed. "Boy, you didn't last long. I had bets you wouldn't last. Tell you what, you'll be back. No other job like this. All the other jobs are dull. Sure, you get sick once in a while. I do. I think: I'm going to quit. I almost do. Then I stick with it. And here I am."

"Well, you can stay," said Latting. "But I'm full up. I'm not curious anymore. I seen a lot the last few weeks, but this is the last straw. I'm sick of being sick. Or worse, I'm sick of your not caring."

"Who doesn't care?"

"Both of you!"

Moreno snorted. "Light us a couple, huh, Carlie?" Carlson lit two cigarettes and passed one to Moreno, who puffed on it, blinking his eyes, driving along by the loud strokes of the sea. "Just because we don't scream and yell and throw fits—"

"I don't want fits," said Latting, in the back, crouched by the sheeted figure. "I just want a little human talk, I just want you to look different than you would walking through a butcher's shop. If I ever get like you two, not worrying, not bothering, all thick skin and tough—"

"We're not tough," said Carlson, quietly, thinking about it, "we're acclimated."

"Acclimated, hell, when you should be *numb?*"

"Kid, don't tell us what we should be when you don't even know what we *are.* Any doctor is a lousy doctor who jumps down in the grave with every patient. All doctors did that, there'd be no one to help the live and kicking. Get out of the grave, boy, you can't see nothing from there."

There was a long silence from the back, and at last Latting started talking, mainly to himself:

"I wonder how long she was up there alone on the cliff, an hour, two? It must have been funny up there looking down at all the campfires, knowing you were going to wipe the whole business clean off. I suppose she was to a dance, or a beach party, and she and her boyfriend broke up. The boyfriend will be down at the station tomorrow to identify her. I'd hate to be him. How he'll *feel—*"

"He won't feel anything. He won't even show up," said Carlson, steadily, mashing out his cigarette in the front-seat tray. "He was probably the one found her and made the call and ran. Two bits will buy you a nickel he's not worth the polish on her little fingernail. Some slobby lout of a guy with pimples and bad breath. Christ, why don't these girls learn to wait until morning."

"Yeah," said Moreno. "Everything's better in the morning."

"Try telling that to a girl in love," said Latting.

"Now a man," said Carlson, lighting a fresh cigarette, "he just gets himself drunk, says to hell with it, no use killing yourself for no woman."

They drove in silence awhile past all the small dark beach houses with only a light here or there, it was so late.

"Maybe," said Latting, "she was going to have a baby."

"It happens."

"And then the boyfriend runs off with someone and this one just borrows his rope and walks up on the cliff," said Latting. "Answer me, now, *is* that or *isn't* it love?"

"It," said Carlson, squinting, searching the dark, "is a kind of love. I give up on what kind."

"Well, sure," said Moreno, driving. "I'll go along with you, kid. I mean, it's nice to know somebody in this world can love that hard."

They all thought for a while, as the ambulance purred between quiet palisades and now quiet sea and maybe two of them thought fleetingly of their wives and tract houses and sleeping children and all the times years ago when they had driven to the beach and broken out the beer and necked up in the rocks and lay around on the blankets with guitars, singing and feeling like life would go on just as far as the ocean went, which was very far, and maybe they didn't think that at all. Latting, looking up at the backs of the two older men's necks, hoped or perhaps only nebulously wondered if these men remembered any first kisses, the taste of salt on the lips. Had there ever been a time when they had stomped the sand like mad bulls and yelled out of sheer joy and dared the universe to put them down?

And by their silence, Latting knew that yes, with all his talking, and the night, and the wind, and the cliff and the tree and the rope, he had gotten through to them; it, the event, had gotten through to them. Right now, they had to be thinking of their wives in their warm beds, long dark miles away, unbelievable, suddenly unattainable while here they were driving along a salt-layered road at a dumb hour half between certainties, bearing with them a strange thing on a cot and a used length of rope.

"Her boyfriend," said Latting, "will be out dancing tomorrow night with somebody else. That gripes my gut."

"I wouldn't mind," said Carlson, "beating the hell out of him."

Latting moved the sheet. "They sure wear their hair crazy and short, some of them. All curls, but short. Too much make-up. Too—" He stopped.

"You were saying?" asked Moreno.

Latting moved the sheet some more. He said nothing. In the next minute there was a rustling sound of the sheet, moved now here, now there. Latting's face was pale.

"Hey," he murmured, at last. "Hey."

Instinctively, Moreno slowed the ambulance.

"Yeah, kid?"

"I just found out something," said Latting. "I had this feeling all along, she's wearing too much make-up, and the hair, and—"

"So?"

"Well, for God's sake," said Latting, his lips hardly moving, one hand up to feel his own face to see what its expression was. "You want to know something funny?"

"Make us laugh," said Carlson.

The ambulance slowed even more as Latting said, "It's not a woman. I mean, it's not a girl. I mean, well, it's not a female. *Understand?*"

The ambulance slowed to a crawl.

The wind blew in off the vague morning sea through the window as the two up front turned and stared into the back of the ambulance at the shape there on the cot.

"Somebody tell me," said Latting, so quietly they almost could not hear the words. "Do we stop feeling bad now? Or do we feel worse?"

Nobody answered.

A wave, and then another, and then another, moved in and fell upon the mindless shore.

Have I Got
a Chocolate Bar for You!

It all began with the smell of chocolate.

On a steaming late afternoon of June rain, Father Malley drowsed in his confessional, waiting for penitents.

Where in all the world were they? he wondered. Immense traffics of sin lurked beyond in the warm rains. Then why not immense traffics of confession here?

Father Malley stirred and blinked.

Today's sinners moved so fast in their cars that this old church was an ecclesiastical blur. And himself? An ancient watercolor priest, tints fading fast, trapped inside.

Let's give it another five minutes and stop, he thought, not in panic but in the kind of quiet shame and desperation that neglect shoulders on a man.

There was a rustle from beyond the confessional grate next door.

Father Malley sat up, quickly.

A smell of chocolate sifted through the grille.

Ah, God, thought the priest, it's a lad with his small basket of sins soon laid to rest and him gone. Well . . .

The old priest leaned to the grate where the candy essence lingered and where the words must come.

But, no words. No "Bless me, Father, for I have sinned . . ."

Only strange small mouse-sounds of . . . *chewing!*

The sinner in the next booth, God sew up his mouth, was actually sitting in there devouring a candy bar!

"No!" whispered the priest, to himself.

His stomach, gathering data, rumbled, reminding him that he had not eaten since breakfast. For some sin of pride which he could not now recall, he had nailed himself to a saint's diet all day, and now—*this!*

Next door, the chewing continued.

Father Malley's stomach growled. He leaned hard against the grille, shut his eyes, and cried:

"Stop that!"

The mouse-nibbling stopped.

The smell of chocolate faded.

A young man's voice said, "That's exactly why I've come, Father."

The priest opened one eye to examine the shadow behind the screen.

"*What's* exactly why you've come?"

"The chocolate, Father."

"The *what?*"

"Don't be angry, Father."

"Angry, hell, who's angry?"

"You are, Father. I'm damned and burnt before I start, by the sound of your voice."

The priest sank back in the creaking leather and mopped his face and shook his senses.

"Yes, yes. The day's hot. I'm out of temper. But then, I never had much."

"It will cool off later in the day, Father. You'll be fine."

The old priest eyed the screen. "Who's taking and who's *giving* confession here?"

"Why, you are, Father."

"Then, get *on* with it!"

The voice hastened forth the facts:

"You have smelled the chocolate, Father?"

The priest's stomach answered for him, faintly.

Both listened to the sad sound. Then:

"Well, Father, to hit it on the head, I was and still am a . . . chocolate junkie."

Old fires stirred in the priest's eyes. Curiosity became humor, then laughed itself back to curiosity again.

"And *that's* why you've come to confession this day?"

"That's it, sir, or, Father."

"You haven't come about sweating over your sister or blueprints for fornication or self-battles with the grand war of masturbation?"

"I have not, Father," said the voice in remorse.

The priest caught the tone and said, "Tut, tut, it's all right. You'll get around to it. For now, you're a grand relief. I'm full-up with wandering males and lonely females and all the junk they read in books and try in waterbeds and sink from sight with suffocating cries as the damn things spring leaks and all is lost. Get on. You have bruised my antennae alert. Say more."

"Well, Father, I have eaten, every day of my life now for ten or twelve years, one or two pounds of chocolate. I cannot leave it alone, Father. It is the end-all and be-all of my life."

"Sounds like a fearful affliction of lumps, acne, carbuncles, and pimples."

"It was. It *is.*"

"And not exactly contributing to a lean figure."

"If I leaned, Father, the confessional would fall over."

The cabinet around them creaked and groaned as the hidden figure beyond demonstrated.

"Sit still!" cried the priest.

The groaning stopped.

The priest was wide awake now and feeling splendid. Never in years had he felt so alive and aware of his happily curious and beating heart and fine blood that sought and found, sought and found the far corners of his cloth and body.

The heat of the day was gone.

He felt immensely cool. A kind of excitement pulsed his wrists and lingered in his throat. He leaned almost like a lover to the grille and prompted more spillage.

"Oh, lad, you're rare."

"And sad, Father, and twenty-two years old and put upon, and hate myself for eating, and need to do something about it."

"Have you tried chewing more and swallowing less?"

"Oh, each night I go to bed saying: Lord, put off the crunch-bars and the milk-chocolate kisses and the Hershey's. Each morning I rave out of bed and run to the liquor store not for liquor but for eight Nestle's in a row! I'm in sugar-shock by noon."

"That's not so much confession as medical fact, I can see."

"My doctor yells at me, Father."

"He should."

"I don't listen, Father."

"*You* should."

"My mother's no help, she's hog-fat and candy-wild."

"I hope you're not one of those who live at home still?"

"I loiter about, Father."

"God, there should be laws against boys loitering in the round shade of their ma's. Is your father surviving the two of you?"

"Somehow."

"And *his* weight?"

"Irving Gross, he calls himself. Which is a joke about size and weight and not his name."

"With the three of you, the sidewalk's full?"

"No bike can pass, Father."

"Christ in the wilderness," murmured the priest, "starving for forty days."

"Sounds like a terrible diet, Father."

"If I knew the proper wilderness, I'd boot you there."

"Boot away, Father. With no help from my mom and dad, a doctor and skinny friends who snort at me, I'm out of pocket from eating and out of mind from the same. I never dreamed I'd wind up with *you*. Beg pardon, Father, but it took a lot to drive me here. If my friends knew, if my mom, my dad, my crazy doctor knew I was here with *you* at this minute, oh what the hell!"

There was a fearful stampede of feet, a careening of flesh.

"Wait!"

But the weight blundered out of the next-door cubby.

With an elephant trample, the young man was gone.

The smell of chocolate alone stayed behind and told all by saying nought.

The heat of the day swarmed in to stifle and depress the old priest.

He had to climb out of the confessional because he knew if he stayed he would begin to curse under his breath and have to run off to have *his* sins forgiven at some other parish.

I suffer from Peevish, O Lord, he thought. How many Hail Marys for *that?*

Come to think of it, how many for a thousand tons, give or take a ton, of chocolate?

Come back! he cried silently at the empty church aisle.

No, he won't, not ever now, he thought, I pressed too hard.

And with that as supreme depression, he went to the parish house to tub himself cool and towel himself to distemper.

———•———

A day, two days, a week passed.

The sweltering noons dissolved the old priest back into a stupor of sweat and vinegar-gnat mean. He snoozed in his cubby, or shuffled papers in the unlined library, looked out at the untended lawn and reminded himself to caper with the mower one day soon. But most of all he found himself brambling with irritability. Fornication was the minted coin of the land, and masturbation its handmaiden. Or so it seemed from the few whispers that slid through the confessional grille during the long afternoons.

On the fifteenth day of July, he found himself staring at some boys idling by on their bicycles, mouths full of Hershey bars that they were gulping and chewing.

That night he awoke thinking Power House and Baby Ruth and Love Nest and Crunch.

He stood it as long as he could and then got up, tried to read, tossed the book down, paced the dark night church, and at last, spluttering mildly, went up to the altar and asked one of his rare favors of God.

The next afternoon, the young man who loved chocolate at last came back.

"Thank you, Lord," murmured the priest, as he felt the vast weight creak the other half of the confessional like a ship foundered with wild freight.

"What?" whispered the young voice from the far side.

"Sorry, I wasn't addressing you," said the priest.

He shut his eyes and inhaled.

The gates of the chocolate factory stood wide somewhere and its mild spice moved forth to change the land.

Then, an incredible thing happened.

Sharp words burst from Father Malley's mouth:

"You shouldn't be *coming* here!"

"What, what, Father?"

"Go somewhere else! I can't help. You need special work. No, no."

The old priest was stunned to feel his own mind jump out his tongue this way. Was it the heat, the long days and weeks kept waiting by this fiend, what, *what*? But still his mouth leaped on:

"No help here! No, no. Go for help—"

"To the shrinks, you mean?" the voice cut in, amazingly calm, considering the explosion.

"Yes, yes, Lord save us, to those people. The—the psychiatrists."

This last word was even more incredible. He had rarely heard himself say it.

"Oh, God, Father, what do *they* know?" said the young man.

What indeed, thought Father Malley, for he had long been put off by their carnival talk and to-the-rear-march chat and clamor. Good grief, why don't I turn in my collar and buy me a beard! he thought, but went on more calmly:

"What do they know, my son? Why, they claim to know everything."

"Just like the Church *used* to claim, Father?"

Silence. Then:

"There's a difference between claiming and knowing," the old priest replied, as calmly as his beating heart would allow.

"And the Church *knows*, is that it, Father?"

"And if it doesn't, *I* do!"

"Don't get mad again, Father." The young man paused and sighed. "I didn't come to dance angels on the head of a pin with you. Shall I start confession, Father?"

"It's about time!" The priest caught himself, settled back, shut his eyes sweetly, and added. "Well?"

And the voice on the other side, with the tongue and the breath of a child, tinctured with silver-foiled kisses, flavored with honeycomb, moved by recent sugars and memories or more immediate Cadbury fetes and galas, began to describe its life of getting up and living with and going to bed with Swiss delights and temptations out of Hershey, Pennsylvania, or how to chew the dark skin off the exterior of a Clark Bar and keep the caramel and textured interior for special shocks and celebrations. Of how the soul asked and the tongue demanded and the stomach accepted and the blood danced to the drive of Power House, the promise of Love Nest, the delivery of Butterfinger, but most of all the sweet African murmuring of dark chocolate between the teeth, tinting the gums, flavoring the palate so you muttered, whispered, murmured pure Congo, Zambesi, Chad in your sleep.

And the more the voice talked, as the days passed and the weeks, and the old priest listened, the lighter became the burden on the other side of the grille. Father Malley knew, without looking, that the flesh enclosing that voice was raining and falling away. The tread was less heavy. The confessional did not cry out in such huge alarms when the body entered next door.

For even with the young voice there and the young man, the smell of chocolate was truly fading and almost gone.

And it was the loveliest summer the old priest had ever known.

Once, years before, when he was a very young priest, a thing had happened that was much like this, in its strange and special way.

A girl, no more than sixteen by her voice, had come to whisper each day from the time school let out to the time autumn school renewed.

For all of that long summer he had come as close as a priest might to an alert affection for that whisper and that dear voice. He had heard her through her July attraction, her August madness, and her September disillusion, and as she went away forever in October, in tears, he wanted to cry out: Oh, stay, stay! Marry me!

But I am the groom to the brides of Christ, another voice whispered.

And he had *not* run forth, that very young priest, into the traffics of the world.

Now, nearing sixty, the young soul within him sighed, stirred, recalled, compared that old and shopworn memory with this new, somehow funny yet withal sad encounter with a lost soul whose love was not summer madness for girls in dire swimsuits, but chocolate unwrapped in secret and devoured in stealth.

"Father," said the voice, late one afternoon. "It has been a fine summer."

"Strange you would say that," said the priest. "I have thought so myself."

"Father, I have something really awful to confess to you."

"I'm beyond shocking, I think."

"Father, I am not from your diocese."

"That's all right."

"And, Father, forgive me, but, I—"

"Go on."

"I'm not even Catholic."

"You're *what!*" cried the old man.

"I'm not even Catholic, Father. Isn't that awful?"

"Awful?"

"I mean, I'm sorry, truly I am. I'll join the church, if you want, Father, to make up."

"Join the church, you idiot?" shouted the old man. "It's too late for that! Do you know what you've done? Do you know the depths of depravity you've plumbed? You've taken my time, bent my ear, driven me wild, asked advice, needed a psychiatrist, argued religion, criticized the Pope, if I remember correctly, and I *do* remember, used up three months, eighty or ninety days, and now, now, *now* you want to join the church and 'make up'?"

"If you don't mind, Father."

"Mind! Mind!" yelled the priest, and lapsed into a ten-second apoplexy.

He almost tore the door wide to run around and seize the culprit out into the light. But then:

"It was not all for nothing, Father," said the voice from beyond the grille.

The priest grew quiet.

"For you see, Father, God bless you, you have helped me."

The priest grew very quiet.

"Yes, Father, oh bless you indeed, you have helped me so very much, and I am beholden," whispered the voice. "You haven't asked, but don't you guess? I have lost weight. You wouldn't believe the weight I have lost. Eighty, eighty-five, ninety pounds. Because of you, Father. I gave it up. I gave it up. Take a deep breath. Inhale."

The priest, against his wish, did so.

"What do you smell?"

"Nothing."

"Nothing, Father, nothing! It's gone. The smell of chocolate and the chocolate with it. Gone. Gone. I'm free."

The old priest sat, knowing not what to say, and a peculiar itching came about his eyelids.

"You have done Christ's work, Father, as you yourself must know. He walked through the world and helped. You walk through the world and help. When I was falling, you put out your hand, Father, and saved me."

Then a most peculiar thing happened.

Father Malley felt tears burst from his eyes. They brimmed over. They streaked along his cheeks. They gathered at his tight lips and he untightened them and the tears fell from his chin. He could not stop them. They came, O Lord, they came like a shower of spring rain after the seven lean years and the drought over and himself alone, dancing about, thankful, in the pour.

He heard sounds from the other booth and could not be sure but somehow felt that the other one was crying, too.

So here they sat, while the sinful world rushed by on streets, here in the sweet incense gloom, two men on opposite sides of some fragile board slattings, on a late afternoon at the end of summer, weeping.

And at last they grew very quiet indeed and the voice asked, anxiously, "Are you all right, Father?"

The priest replied at last, eyes shut, "Fine. Thanks."

"Anything I can do, Father?"

"You have already done it, my son."

"About . . . my joining the church. I meant it."

"No matter."

"But it does matter. I'll join. Even though I'm Jewish."

Father Malley snorted half a laugh. "Wha-what?"

"Jewish, Father, but an Irish Jew, if that helps."

"Oh, yes!" roared the old priest. "It helps, it helps!"

"What's so funny, Father?"

"I don't know but it is, it is, funny, funny!"

And here he burst into such paroxysms of laughter as made him cry and such floodings of tears as made him laugh again until all mingled in a grand outrush and uproar. The church slammed back echoes of cleansing laughter. In the midst of it all he knew that, telling all this to Bishop Kelly, his confessor, to-morrow he would be let off easy. A church is washed well and good and fine not only by the tears of sorrow but by the clean fresh-cut meadowbrooms of that self-forgiveness and other-forgiveness which God gave only to man and called it laughter.

It took a long while for their mutual shouts to subside, for now the young man had given up weeping and taken on hilarity, too, and the church rocked with the sounds of two men who one minute had done a sad thing and now did a happy one. The sniffle was gone. Joy banged the walls like wild birds flying to be free.

At last, the sounds weakened. The two men sat, wiping their faces, unseen to each other.

Then, as if the world knew there must be a shift of mood and scene, a wind blew in the church doors far away. Leaves drifted from trees and fell into the aisles. A smell of autumn filled the dusky air. Summer was truly over.

Father Malley looked beyond to that door and the wind and the leaves moving off and gone, and suddenly, as in spring, wanted to go with them. His blood demanded a way out, but there was no way.

HAVE I GOT A CHOCOLATE BAR FOR YOU!

"I'm leaving, Father."

The old priest sat up.

"For the time being, you mean."

"No, I'm going away, Father. This is my last time with you."

You can't do that! thought the priest, and almost said it.

But instead he said, as calmly as he could:

"Where are you off to, son?"

"Oh, around the world, Father. Many places. I was always afraid, before. I never went anywhere. But now, with my weight gone, I'm heading out. A new job and so many places to be."

"How long will you be gone, lad?"

"A year, five years, ten. Will you be here ten years from now, Father.

"God willing."

"Well, somewhere along the way I'll be in Rome and buy something small but have it blessed by the Pope and when I come back I'll bring it here and look you up."

"Will you do that?"

"I will. Do you forgive me, Father?"

"For what?"

"For everything."

"We have forgiven each other, dear boy, which is the finest thing that men can do."

There was the merest stir of feet from the other side.

"I'm going now, Father. Is it true that good-bye means God Be With You?"

"That's what it means."

"Well then, oh truly, good-bye, Father."

"And good-bye in all its original meaning to you, lad."

And the booth next to his elbow was suddenly empty.

And the young man gone.

Many years later, when Father Malley was a very old man indeed and full of sleep, a final thing happened to fill out his life. Late one afternoon, dozing in the confessional, listening to rain fall out beyond the church, he smelled a strange and familiar smell and opened his eyes.

Gently, from the other side of the grille, the faintest odor of chocolate seeped through.

The confessional creaked. On the other side, someone was trying to find words.

The old priest leaned forward, his heart beating quickly, wild with amazement and surprise. "Yes?" he urged.

"Thank you," said a whisper, at last.

"Beg pardon . . . ?"

"A long time ago," said the whisper. "You helped. Been long away. In town only for today. Saw the church. Thanks. That's all. Your gift is in the poor-box. Thanks."

Feet ran swiftly.

The priest, for the first time in his life, leaped from the confessional.

"Wait!"

But the man, unseen, was gone. Short or tall, fat or thin, there was no telling. The church was empty.

At the poor-box, in the dusk, he hesitated, then reached in. There he found a large eighty-nine-cent economy-size bar of chocolate.

Someday, Father, he heard a long-gone voice whisper, *I'll bring you a gift blessed by the Pope.*

This? *This?* The old priest turned the bar in his trembling hands. But why not? What could be more perfect?

He saw it all. At Castel Gandolfo on a summer noon with five thousand tourists jammed in a sweating pack below in the dust and the Pope high up on his balcony there waving out the rare blessings, suddenly among all the tumult, in all the sea of arms and hands, one lone brave hand held high . . .

And in that hand a silver-wrapped and glorious candy bar.

The old priest nodded, not surprised.

He locked the chocolate bar in a special drawer in his study and sometimes, behind the altar, years later, when the weather smothered the windows and despair leaked in the door hinges, he would fetch the chocolate out and take the smallest nibble.

It was not the Host, no, it was not the flesh of Christ. But it was a life. And the life was his. And on those occasions, not often but often enough, when he took a bite, it tasted (O thank you, God) it tasted incredibly sweet.

Ray Bradbury has published some 500 short stories, novels, plays, and poems since his first story appeared in *Weird Tales* when he was twenty years old. His work has been published in magazines ranging from *Audubon Magazine* to *The New Yorker*, from *Nation's Business* to *The Paris Review* including *The American Mercury, Cosmopolitan, The New Republic*, and many, many others. For many years he wrote for *Alfred Hitchcock Presents* and *The Twilight Zone* and in 1953 did the screenplay for John Huston's *Moby Dick*. He has produced two of his own plays, written two musicals, two space age cantatas with Lalo Schiffrin and Jerry Goldsmith, collaborated on an animated film, *Icarus Montgolfier Wright*, which was nominated for an Academy Award in 1962, and is currently at work on a grand opera. Mr. Bradbury was Idea Consultant for the United States Pavillion at the New York World's Fair in 1963, has helped design a ride for Disney World and is doing consultant work on city engineering and rapid transit. When one of the Apollo astronaut teams landed on the moon, they named Dandelion Crater there to honor Bradbury's novel, *Dandelion Wine*. He is the author of sixteen books.

A NOTE ON THE TYPE

This book was set on the Linotype in Electra, a type face designed by W. A. Dwiggins. The Electra face is a simple and readable type suitable for printing books by present-day processes. It is not based on any historical model, and hence does not echo any particular time or fashion. Composed by Maryland Linotype Composition Co., Baltimore, Maryland. Printed and bound by The Haddon Craftsmen, Inc., Scranton, Pennsylvania. Typography and binding design by Susan Mitchell.